"Listen, Marley," Carl said reasonably. "That little scene in our office this afternoon must have triggered some—unusual— thoughts about you and that's why I'm having this weird dream. But I probably won't even remember it when I wake up."

The ghostlike version of Marley turned to face him. "Oh, you'll remember it, Carl.... It's your only hope. I'm here to tell you that before nine o'clock tonight, you'll encounter three people that you already know, who have been assigned by the powers that be—"

"The powers that be? Give me a break!"

She ignored him and continued. "—to remind you of who you were, who you are and who you're destined to be if you don't change your attitude about Christmas. And my other purpose for appearing in this dream is to tell you that what you see now..."

She pirouetted and her flowing nightie instantly changed into a set of baby dolls—pink, ruffled and sexy as hell.

"...You won't see again, not even in your wildest dreams, unless you change your ways."

Dear Reader,

My love for the classic Christmas tale of hope and redemption, *A Christmas Carol*, began the first time I picked it up at the age of thirteen, and has lasted through every annual reading of it at Christmastime till now.

Charles Dickens's story of Scrooge's escape from a life of cynicism to one of compassion is truly inspired.

In *Marley and Her Scrooge* Carl Merrick not only despises Christmas, but he has become cynical about life in general—and love in particular. Luckily the cute curmudgeon experiences his Christmas Eve miracle while he's still in his prime! And before he loses the love of his life, Marley Jacobs.

This Christmas, as you read Carl and Marley's story, I hope you'll feel the desire to "honor Christmas in your heart and keep it all the year."

Wishing you joy this holiday season.

Emily Dalton

Emily Dalton

MARLEY AND HER SCROOGE

Harlequin Books

TORONTO • NEW YORK • LONDON
AMSTERDAM • PARIS • SYDNEY • HAMBURG
STOCKHOLM • ATHENS • TOKYO • MILAN
MADRID • WARSAW • BUDAPEST • AUCKLAND

If you purchased this book without a cover you should be aware
that this book is stolen property. It was reported as "unsold and
destroyed" to the publisher, and neither the author nor the
publisher has received any payment for this "stripped book."

It just seemed fitting to dedicate this
Christmas book to a couple who really know how to
celebrate the holidays.
To Cliff and Terry Curtis...my friends.
Thanks for everything.

ISBN 0-373-16706-7

MARLEY AND HER SCROOGE

Copyright © 1997 by Danice Jo Allen.

All rights reserved. Except for use in any review, the reproduction or
utilization of this work in whole or in part in any form by any electronic,
mechanical or other means, now known or hereafter invented, including
xerography, photocopying and recording, or in any information storage
or retrieval system, is forbidden without the written permission of the
publisher, Harlequin Enterprises Limited, 225 Duncan Mill Road,
Don Mills, Ontario, Canada M3B 3K9.

All characters in this book have no existence outside the imagination of
the author and have no relation whatsoever to anyone bearing the same
name or names. They are not even distantly inspired by any individual
known or unknown to the author, and all incidents are pure invention.

This edition published by arrangement with Harlequin Books S.A.

® and TM are trademarks of the publisher. Trademarks indicated with
® are registered in the United States Patent and Trademark Office, the
Canadian Trade Marks Office and in other countries.

Printed in U.S.A.

Chapter One

Carl Merrick walked his father through the lobby to the front door of the Little Angel Christmas Card Company.

"Are you sure you won't come, son?" John Merrick asked again, turning, with one gloved hand resting on the old-fashioned cut-glass knob of the door and the other clutching a large, shiny shopping bag stuffed with presents. "There'll be a full house. People you haven't seen in ages. Every Merrick within a hundred-mile radius is coming for Christmas dinner. Everyone but *you*."

"Sorry, Dad. Too much work to do," Carl replied for at least the sixth time.

"That's just an excuse and you know it," his father scoffed.

Carl shrugged and forced an apologetic smile. "Besides, if I showed up after all these years, Uncle Ralph would choke on his fruitcake and Great-aunt Bessie would gape so hard she'd drop her teeth in the eggnog bowl."

"Everyone would be delighted to see you, Carl," his father insisted, ignoring the joke. "Everyone misses you." His silver brows lowered over his eyes in a sober expression. "The holidays just haven't been the same since you blacklisted Christmas."

"You've got it reversed, Dad," Carl remarked dryly. "It was Christmas that blacklisted *me*."

"Now, Carl, what that girl did to you had nothing to do with Christmas—"

"Never mind, Dad," Carl interrupted, clapping his father on the shoulder. "Let's not dig up an old and boring subject. Anyway, Christmas doesn't need me. It'll still steamroll its way through the month of December, leaving the usual victims in its wake...broke, exhausted and five pounds heavier."

"Carl, you've got the wrong attitude," his father argued fervently. "Christmas means much more than that. It means—"

"Isn't Mom waiting for you?" Carl again interrupted. "She's probably double-parked and frantically scanning the crowds, thinking she's somehow missed you. Although I don't know how that would be possible," he added with a raised brow, eyeing his father from head to toe.

John Merrick, president of Mount Joy, Vermont's oldest banking establishment till his retirement two years before, was a tall, distinguished-looking man with silver hair and massive eyebrows over piercing blue eyes. He was broad in the chest and shoulders and wore a charcoal gray wool coat that reached to mid-calf. A bright red scarf was draped around his neck and hung to his waist, and a large poinsettia boutonniere was pinned to his wide lapel. His cheeks were ruddy from the cold and the natural glow of vitality he always exuded, especially at Christmastime. No, he was definitely a man that would have a hard time getting lost in a crowd.

Carl's father gazed at his son with an expression of weary but affectionate resignation. "You know the invitation stands. Why don't you surprise us all tomorrow and show up? You might just surprise yourself and have a good time. What *are* your plans for Christmas, son?"

Carl sighed and gave a rueful shake of his head. "I told you the truth before, Dad. I have work to catch up on and Christmas is the perfect day to do it. I always get more done in the office when there's no one around to bug me."

John looked as if he were chomping at the bit to express his opinion of such a plan for spending Christmas Day, but he gritted his teeth and said nothing. Carl hoped his father was finally realizing how futile it was to preach and praise a holiday he no longer celebrated.

"There's Mom now," Carl said, spotting her—sure enough, double-parked—in front of the building. Inwardly he sighed with relief. He loved his dad, but he was a royal pain in the rear at Christmastime, never giving up on the deck-the-halls bit despite Carl's aversion to the whole monthlong orgy of cheerfulness.

"Goodbye, son," his father said, his breath a plume of white in the frosty air as he stepped out onto the sidewalk. "And Merry Christmas, Carl," he called over his shoulder as he sprinted to the street.

"Watch your step, Dad," Carl replied. He waited at the open door till his father was safely in the large luxury sedan his mother maneuvered like a tank through the narrow streets of town. She waved through the window, determinedly looking hopeful and happy just in case a miracle had occurred and Carl had agreed to join them for Christmas dinner. She was doomed to disappointment again, but Carl couldn't help that. For their own good, his parents ought to just give up on the sell-Carl-on-Christmas campaign.

As soon as his father got in the car—with a prompting honk from the driver behind them—they drove off. Carl closed his eyes briefly and took a deep breath, glad to have the annual standoff with his father over with for another year. But then he glanced at his watch and frowned. At five minutes to four, he had just enough time to make it to the sanctuary of his office before the mass exodus to the Christmas party began, but he'd have to hurry.

Carl strode quickly through the lobby to the elevator. Fortunately it was empty, but when he got off on the third floor, he had to walk down a long hall to get to his office. With no time, and in no mood, for chit-chat, he avoided eye contact with any employee who happened into his path.

But Carl realized he needn't worry about being detained by anybody. His employees seemed just as anxious to avoid him as he was to avoid them. When there was time, they scurried into office doorways, and when there wasn't, they fixed their gazes on each other and the walls and floor rather than meet Carl's steely gaze as he marched past them to his office. They knew his opinion of Christmas, and they knew his routine. He wouldn't be attending the Christmas party.

But everyone else would. Carl couldn't understand why the poor addled souls looked forward to it every year. At four o'clock precisely, his employees would conduct a jovial stampede to the tinsel-draped staff lounge where eggnog would be served in paper cups and cookies would be handed around on holiday-printed paper napkins. With goofy smiles on their faces and brightly wrapped packages tucked under their arms, they'd squeeze inside till it was hot enough in the room to steam fish.

It was a mystery to Carl why otherwise rational people would willingly endure all that discomfort just to eat cholesterol-laden goodies and laugh over a few white elephant gifts. "They're nuts," he muttered to himself by way of explanation, then flicked a quick, grim look over his shoulder at his partner's closed office door before entering his own.

Speaking of nuts, his childhood friend and co-owner of the Little Angel Christmas Card Company, Marley Jacobs, was one of the worst. Yeah, she was a genuine filbert, all right. He'd never seen anyone go as gaga over Christmas as she did.

Behind those closed doors, Marley was probably putting on her elf costume that very moment. It was an annual ritual that turned her from a sleek business-woman to a green-clad, pointy-toed, would-be Santa's helper. Carl had never understood her passion for making a spectacle of herself every December twenty-fourth. It was his opinion that as co-president of the company, and a mature, twenty-eight-year-old woman, she ought to conduct herself with more decorum.

Carl had barely sat down behind his huge cherry-wood desk and picked up some paperwork when Stewart Cosgrove barged in without knocking. Carl glared at the man that Marley, who took care of personnel, had hired to run their advertising department four months ago. Unlike the other employees, Stewart never seemed intimidated by Carl's sour moods. Stewart fairly oozed cheerful self-confidence and optimism, but since the guy was brilliant at his job, Carl put up with these irritating traits and kept him on.

"Hi, boss," Stewart said with the high-voltage smile that had half the women in the office swooning, or so Carl had overheard as he'd passed an open office door one day where a gossip fest was in session. But then Stewart's tall, blond good looks could have something to do with it, too.

"What is it, Cosgrove?" Carl asked him in a flat, unencouraging tone. But nothing seemed to discourage Stewart. He sat down on the edge of Carl's desk as comfortable and casual as you please, his neon smile broader than ever.

"The commercial's a big success. Little Angel Christmas cards have flown off the shelf since Thanksgiving weekend when the three-minute spot first aired, outselling every other Christmas card manufacturer this season except, of course, for Hallmark. But we're gaining on 'em!" He tossed Carl a copy of the latest sales figures. "Just off the press. I think you'll be pleased."

Carl scanned the new figures. He *was* pleased. Very pleased. But he made sure his face betrayed nothing.

"These figures are definitely up from last year," he murmured, his gaze fixed on the sheet in front of him. He paused, tapping his bottom lip with his finger, knowing that Stewart was waiting for a little praise to be thrown his way.

Carl usually gave credit where credit was due, but for some reason it went against the grain to congratulate Stewart on a job well-done. The guy might get too big for his britches or, even worse, he might start thinking of Carl as a friend. Carl made a point of never becoming too chummy with his employees; he preferred knowing as little as possible about their personal lives.

Carl finally looked up, a polite smile on his lips. "But you don't really think this huge upswing in sales can be solely attributed to the commercial, do you?"

Instead of reacting defensively, Stewart laughed. "Sure, I do! It's a *great* commercial!"

"So I hear," Carl muttered. "But we've built a reputation over the past five years and—"

"Don't tell me you still haven't seen it?" Stewart interrupted disbelievingly.

"What?"

"The commercial."

"I don't have the stomach to watch all that sentimental garbage. And, if you don't mind, I have business to—"

"Marley did a great job. She's quite an actress, you know. I'd like to use her in all the commercials."

"Well, you can discuss that with her," Carl said testily. "It's her job to take care of that end of the business."

A recorded chorus of "Jingle Bells" suddenly blared into the hallways and excited voices could be heard as the Christmas party stampede began. At the same moment, outside Carl's third-story window, the tower clock in the town square bonged four times.

"Well, gotta go," Stewart announced cheerfully. "Don't want to miss the party."

"No, of course you don't," Carl said dryly, thrilled to finally be getting rid of him.

Stewart turned at the door. "Should I make an announcement at the party about the latest sales figures, or do you plan to? Or maybe Marley would like to?"

Carl thought about this. "No, Cosgrove, I'd rather wait till our staff meeting at the first of the year." By then no one would expect the increase in sales to be reflected in an increase in their Christmas bonuses.

Stewart shrugged. "Whatever you say." Then he took himself off to be "merry."

"Another nut," Carl grumbled under his breath, trying to tune out the racket down the hall. He picked up the financial report Stewart had delivered and attempted to concentrate on the very generous profit margin it revealed, but, as usual, it was hard to block out the merrymaking sounds of yet another Christmas Eve.

With a sigh, Carl stood up and walked to the window, looking out at the throngs of Mount Joy townspeople frantically making last-minute purchases up and down Main Street, the doors and mullion windows of the quaint shops draped with old-fashioned holly garlands and bushy wreaths.

A snowfall from three days ago was growing dingy and crusted over, and it was cold. Colder than usual for Vermont, which was always pretty darn cold anyway this time of year, and an insidious fog slithered its way into every nook and cranny, chilling the blood and nipping the nose. But even the frigid temperatures weren't keeping people at home, wisely planted by a warm fire. Nope. At Christmastime everyone seemed to throw caution to the wind and play havoc with their health, their hearts and their credit ratings. Everyone but him.

"They're nuts," Carl repeated, wondering when the general population would realize that Christmas was highly overrated...as he had learned only too well seven fateful years ago that very day? It was a day he wished he could forget. But every year the distinctive sights, sounds and smells of Christmas brought it all back.

Shaking his head to clear it, Carl moved to the thermostat and turned it down several degrees, then returned to his desk. Finally losing himself in the very satisfying sales figures, soon it was nearly five o'clock. Since it was Christmas Eve, he was sure the Little Angel offices would clear out quickly. Then, with everyone gone, maybe he could really get down to work.

"Carl, have you been messing with the thermostat again? Bev is freezing!"

"Come right in," Carl drawled sardonically, looking up at his partner as she burst into the room without knocking, just as Stewart had. "You and Cosgrove go to the same charm school?"

She threw him an impatient glance and hurried over to the thermostat that regulated the temperature in his office and in the adjoining office of his secretary, Bev Cratchet.

"No wonder poor Bev is so cold. You've got it down to fifty-five!" She gave the thermostat dial a generous turn. "I swear, Carl, sometimes I think you've got ice water in your veins."

With her fists propped on her slim hips and her arms akimbo, Marley glared at Carl. Trouble was, in those green tights, a shiny red-and-white-striped vest, a hat with a bell on its long tip and with shoes to match, she was hardly intimidating. In fact, despite the absurdity of the costume she was wearing, Carl had to admit she looked rather fetching.

Her tomboyish figure was well suited for tights, her small, straight nose and large green eyes rather elfish to begin with, and her short blond hair all the rage with pixies...or so he'd concluded after seeing the movie *Peter Pan* as a child and observing the perky bob sported by the curvaceous Tinker Bell.

He wondered for the umpteenth time why Marley hadn't married yet. After all, she still believed in all that happily-ever-after propaganda and must have had plenty of offers.

But Carl betrayed no sign of reluctant admiration for his partner, or the slightest interest in her love life, as he replied, "Whenever I'm in the office alone, I always turn the thermostat down. It saves fuel, therefore it saves money. I thought that you and I were in agreement that saving money was a good thing. I didn't know Bev was still at her desk. I thought she went to the Christmas party with everyone else."

Marley tapped one foot on the carpet, the bell at the curled tip of her shoe jingling festively, although her expression was anything but festive. "First of all, there's no need to be so stingy with the heat anymore. Little Angel is no longer the struggling company it was five years ago when you and I took it over. Likewise, it's not necessary to work the long hours you do, or to slave-drive your secretary. In case you hadn't noticed, we're very much in the black these days. The financial report proved that. And, secondly, Bev isn't at the party, because she's typing some letters you told her had to be done before the twenty-sixth."

Carl waved his hand impatiently. "I just said I'd *like* them to be done by the twenty-sixth. I certainly didn't intend for her to miss the party."

"Bev is in awe of you, Carl. Your word is her command. She won't go to the party unless you reassure her that it's all right with you."

"I don't know why she didn't just go," Carl grumbled, standing up and moving from behind the desk. "Or why she didn't just knock on my door and—"

Marley gave an unladylike snort. "That's a good one. No one in their right mind knocks on your door between Thanksgiving and New Year's unless it's absolutely necessary. Not if they don't want their head snapped off."

Carl gave a humorless chuckle. "You're right about one thing. No one actually *knocks* on my door. At least, you and Cosgrove never bother. As for everyone else—"

"Everyone else is afraid of you, including Bev."

Carl furrowed his brow. "As usual, you're exaggerating."

"Give me a break!" she exclaimed. "Your aversion to Christmas is legendary. In fact, how to deal with Mr. Merrick when he's not so merry during the holidays is a documented part of the new-employee orientation."

Carl looked scornful and incredulous, then opened the connecting door between his office and Bev's and went inside to tell her to join the party…what was left of it.

Marley waited for him to return. She was used to waiting. She'd been waiting for Carl for years and years…and years. Not surprisingly, when he returned to his office, he headed straight for his desk and sat down, immediately returning his attention to the paperwork he'd been so engrossed in when Marley first came in.

Marley felt her anger flare. She'd been understanding and patient long enough. Sure, Carl's fiancée, Andrea, had left him brideless at the altar on Christmas Eve seven years ago, but did that have to sour him on

Christmas *and* women forever? And, speaking of forever, Marley suddenly decided that she wasn't about to wait that long for someone who might never change back to the wonderful man he once was.

Filled with frustration—and an eager anticipation because she was about to vent that frustration—Marley moved to the desk, placed her hands palms down on the edge of the polished surface and leaned forward, her gaze boring into Carl's dark, bent head.

He looked up and her determination wavered for a moment as she stared into the incredible eyes that had been a mainstay of all her romantic fantasies ever since first meeting Carl in her second-grade class at Lincoln Elementary School. He always had that effect on her, and not just because he grew up so handsome, with his dark hair and blue eyes and a tall, muscular body that looked fantastic in tailored suits ike the gray pin-striped one he was wearing today. It's just that, although he may have forgotten, she vividly remembered the way things used to be. The way *he* used to be.

Carl looked up, coolly observed her, then arched a brow. "What do you want, Marley? If you're waiting for me to say 'Merry Christmas' before you leave, you'd better plan on spending the holidays within the confines of these four walls. Shall we order in? What sounds good? Pizza or Chinese?"

"You're a grinch if I ever saw one," she muttered.

"At least I'm not a hypocrite."

"You don't think running a Christmas card company when you hate Christmas is being hypocritical?" she inquired dryly.

"It's business." His gaze returned to the papers on the desk. "Besides, I'd only be hypocritical if I pretended to actually enjoy the holidays. All they mean to me at this point is more green in the till.''

Marley slammed her fist on the desk, effectively regaining Carl's attention. His eyes widened with surprise and annoyance. ''Marley, what's gotten into you? Go back to the party and leave me alone, just as you've done every year before now. You know how I am. Why can't you just accept it?''

''Because I remember how you were,'' she answered him, surprising herself by the emotional tremor in her voice.

He frowned. ''You mean, how I was when you and I were kids? Hell, I don't even remember back that far.''

''That's obvious,'' she retorted. ''Your present self bears no resemblance to your past self. Heaven help us if you continue with this Dorian Gray routine. On the outside, you're still too damn handsome for your own good, but on the inside—'' She leaned over and poked his chest.

Carl looked down at her finger pressed against his shirt button, then up at her. ''What are you talking about?''

Marley leaned back and crossed her arms. ''At this rate, what will you be like in...say...seven more Christmases? A rich weirdo hermit, like Howard Hughes?''

Carl laughed, but it wasn't the heartfelt laugh Marley had grown up loving to hear and share. It was a cynical laugh. ''You're getting carried away, Marley. Just because a man doesn't get off on all this commercialized holiday crap doesn't mean he's destined for eccentricity and isolation. Although the rich part doesn't sound too bad.''

"Carl, you have no idea how much you've changed. At first it was just around Christmastime that you got moody and antisocial. But, over time, your lousy attitude has crept into every day of the year."

"Marley..."

"You work late almost every night unnecessarily. You avoid family gatherings. Your poor dad comes by every Christmas Eve day, begging you to come to Christmas dinner, and you always refuse."

"If you're so worried about my mom and dad missing a single guest at their huge dinner parties, why don't you go in my place?" Carl suggested sarcastically.

"I do," she informed him with a sniff. Responding to his look of surprise, she continued, "Yeah, that's right. I'm invited and I go every year. With my own mom and dad baking on the beach in Florida year-round, it's very nice to have a warm, welcoming place to go to on Christmas Day. Your family is so great, Carl, and you completely ignore them."

He looked down again at the papers he held, stubbornly refusing comment.

She studied his hard expression and, in a slightly softer tone, added, "I realize that the last time you attended a large family gathering it was your...well...your wedding, but—"

"You mean my *almost* wedding, don't you?" he said bitterly, never lifting his gaze from the papers in front of him. "How considerate of you to bring up such a lovely memory."

"Well, if that memory still bugs you, make *new* memories!" Marley exclaimed, exasperated.

His head reared up. "What's the matter, Marley? Afraid I'll die alone?" he joked grimly. "Afraid there won't be a grieving widow and two or three generations of posterity standing by my deathbed, weeping softly?''

"Yes, I am worried about you, Carl,'' Marley admitted, ignoring his sarcasm. "You changed after Andrea dumped you for her old boyfriend. You're so insulated and aloof. You need to—''

Carl slapped his papers on the desk. "I need to *what,* O wise one? It's easy for you to lecture me. You don't have any idea what it's like to be rejected so completely and so publicly by someone you love.''

Marley winced, hurt to the core. For a smart man he was so stupid! She debated the wisdom of, for once, being completely honest with Carl. It would give her a great deal of satisfaction to reveal her true feelings, even if afterward she wanted to die of embarrassment...especially if he claimed no reciprocal feelings.

Suddenly Marley knew she couldn't keep the truth locked inside her any longer, and, besides, she was determined to get some reaction from Carl other than hard-as-nails cynicism.

Gathering her courage, she stated, "I know exactly how it feels to be rejected by the person you love.''

Surprise and disbelief flickered in Carl's deep blue eyes. "You do? Who's rejected you, Marley? I haven't seen you seriously date a guy since college.''

Marley's face flooded with warmth as she gripped the desk and blurted, "That's because I've been stuck here with *you* ever since graduation. And when *you're* around, every other guy gets dwarfed by your shadow!''

Now Carl looked stunned.

"That's right, you idiot,'' she nearly shouted. "I'm in love with *you!* I fell in love with you the day you put that garter snake down the back of my dress during a spelling bee in the second grade. And, God help me, I've been in love with you ever since, waiting patiently as you sowed your wild oats, became engaged to Andrea, then took on the tragic martyr role when she dumped you. And if you weren't so damned self-involved and fixated on your business concerns, you'd have seen it a long time ago!''

At the end of her tirade, Marley took a deep breath, crossed her arms and took two steps back. She couldn't believe she'd bared her soul like that, but, like a sleeping volcano, she'd needed to let off steam for a long time. Trouble was, the only reaction she was getting from Carl was a look of horrified disbelief.

''By that slack-jawed, I-think-I'm-going-to-toss-my-cookies expression on your face, I guess I should have kept my feelings to myself,'' she said bitterly. ''But don't worry, Carl. I won't be mooning over you any longer. I've finally realized that you're a hopeless case...a hopeless case I'm not going to waste my time on. I deserve better.'' She smiled sadly. ''And, with that wonderful New Year's resolution still ringing in my head, I think I'll leave now.''

And, before Carl ever found his voice, that's exactly what she did. Only as the door closed behind her did Carl find the presence of mind to stand up, reach forth with one hand in a futile gesture and croak, ''Marley...?'' Realizing how belated his reaction was, however, Carl collapsed into his chair again and just sat there, staring at the door.

''I'll be damned,'' he whispered.

It had never once crossed Carl's mind that he was the reason Marley hadn't married. But how could he have worked so closely with a woman and missed the fact that she was in love with him? Was Marley right? Was he so self-involved and fixated on his business concerns that he was blind to the things that were going on around him?

For several minutes, Carl was lost in soul-searching thought. But presently he shook himself free of such an unpleasant occupation and told himself that Marley was probably just indulging in some hormonal histrionics. Women, like Christmas, could sometimes be a lot of hype and very little substance. Did Marley fit into that category? Carl was ashamed to admit he didn't know. Over the past five years, he and Marley had tended to business and neglected their friendship. Or, at least, *he* had neglected their friendship. Maybe she'd been trying to keep it going all along.

But the bottom line was, Carl didn't know what was going on with Marley and he really didn't want to know. He'd pretend the conversation between them had never happened, and after a while hopefully they'd both forget it. After all, as partners in a business, it was wise to refrain from emotional entanglements…imagined or otherwise.

Something on a visceral level told Carl this line of reasoning was a load of crap. But right now he'd rather believe anything other than the fact that Marley loved him. Since Andrea, he'd kept his relationships with women short and sweet, just long enough for both of them to have a good time. The last thing he wanted or needed was another woman in his life with the power to lift his spirits to the highest mountaintops, then plunge them headlong into the deepest quagmire…and all in one afternoon.

Besides, Marley said she considered him a hopeless case and wouldn't be "mooning" over him any longer. If she really was in love with him, at least she was trying to get over it. That was some comfort. But it was still hard for Carl to get his mind back where it belonged—on business.

At five forty-five there was a timid knock on the door connecting Carl's office with Bev's. He called, "Come in," and Bev entered the room to inquire diffidently if she could leave for the day.

"Of course you can leave," Carl said gruffly, peering sharply over his papers at her. "You didn't have to ask."

"Thank you, Mr. Merrick." Bev crossed her arms over her narrow chest, hunched deeper into her bulky cardigan and bit her bottom lip. Her large brown eyes got bigger and her chin quivered ever so slightly. He hated it when Bev acted so timid. Suddenly she looked fourteen instead of twenty-four and he felt like some stern taskmaster at a bleak boarding school.

He sighed. "What is it, Bev?"

She nervously twisted a strand of her shoulder-length brown hair. "I..I didn't quite finish those letters you wanted," she blurted. "It's just that Timmy is supposed to go to a preschool party tonight and the daycare is closing early because—"

"Never mind. Just get the letters done as soon as you arrive on the morning of the twenty-sixth."

"I will," Bev assured him. "Thank you, Mr. Merrick. Thank you! I'll lock the door on my way out."

Carl looked up. "So...everyone's gone then?"

"Yes, Mr. Merrick. Everyone but you and me."

Carl nodded curtly. "Good night."

"Good night, sir, and have a merry—"

Carl looked up again, his eyebrows lowered forbiddingly.

"—evening," Bev finished lamely.

"You, too," Carl growled.

She left. And since she had confirmed that Marley was gone, too, Carl could quit wondering if he should go to his partner's office for a heart-to-heart talk. The very idea was more than a little off-putting, but, in view of their long friendship and business connections, he realized he'd probably eventually be forced to engage in some sort of conversation to clear the air after her "confession." Until then, however, he'd try to forget the confession ever happened.

Minutes ticked by and presently the tower clock in the town square bonged six hollow notes into the chill dusk. Bev had left quickly and all was deathly quiet beyond Carl's closed door. He was completely alone now in the old building that had been erected in Mount Joy during the presidential term of Abe Lincoln. Still rich with Victorian detail, the well-preserved offices took on a different feel in the evenings when emptied of their usual human occupants. A musty nostalgia, a feeling of times past seemed to hang palpably in the air. Usually Carl could ignore this eerie phenomenon, chalk it up to the building's long history and get back to work. But tonight he seemed to be feeling the strange atmosphere more strongly than usual.

Sitting in the cramped circle of light cast by his desk lamp, Carl was surrounded by shadows and silence and second thoughts. He should have gone after Marley when she stomped out of his office in such an angry, bitter mood. But what then?

Uneasy, Carl stood up and walked to the window. The fog was so thick now, he couldn't see the street below. Only now and then a ghostly movement in the swirls of cloud suggested the existence of another human being on the planet besides himself. Only the face of the tower clock could be seen distinctly, glowing with an almost paranormal light through the fog.

Feeling uncharacteristically chilled, Carl returned to his desk and hunkered over his financial reports almost as if they could radiate a little warmth his way. But it wasn't working. And then his vision seemed to blur, the figures on the papers dancing before his eyes like performing fleas. His eyelids drooped heavily and he realized, with some surprise, that he was so sleepy he could hardly hold his head up. With a surrendering sigh, he quit trying. He folded his arms on his desk and laid his forehead against the crook of his bent elbow. Soon he was fast asleep.

Chapter Two

Startled from a deep sleep, Carl's head reared up. Bells were ringing. Somewhere in the building bells were ringing frantically, the unmelodious "clang-clang" seeming to echo from every floor. And somehow the fog had crept into the building and up three stories, the dank mist swirling knee-high and higher, shrouding and deforming every shadowy object in the room beyond the meager light of his desk lamp.

"I must be dreaming," Carl whispered hoarsely, blinking and staring and listening. "I must still be asleep."

Suddenly the bells stopped ringing and, after a deafening silence of a few seconds, the tower clock bonged six times.

Carl rubbed his eyes with the heels of his hands and frowned. "Now I *know* I'm dreaming. The tower clock struck six o'clock just before I fell asleep."

But Carl didn't feel as if he was dreaming. On the contrary, he felt very much awake. He peered around the room, finding his senses acutely alert. His dreams had never before been so vividly enhanced by every sensation. He could clearly see the fog, feel its cold dampness, even smell it. He could hear the quiet ticking of the furnace and the hum of his small refrigerator in the corner. To test the fifth and final sense, he pinched himself on the wrist. "Ouch, dammit!" he growled. If he were dreaming, wouldn't the pain wake him up?

But it *had* to be a dream. There was no other explanation for the bells and the fog and—Carl cocked his head to the side, his fingers gripping the arms of his chair, listening—*the metallic clatter of chains?* Yes, it sounded like someone was downstairs in the lobby, dragging chains across the parquet floor. Then, despite the fact that a second level of offices separated him from the lobby, he distinctly heard the ping of the elevator door opening and the muted whoosh as the doors closed.

Carl swallowed hard. Someone was in the building. But who? And why were they dragging chains? He'd heard of ghosts dragging chains, but what would a ghost want with him? He didn't believe in ghosts, but if he was dreaming he supposed anything was possible. He'd dreamed once of meeting an honest politician, and everyone knew *they* didn't exist.

Now he heard the elevator open on the third floor. The noise of clattering chains drew nearer.

Carl just sat there, staring at his office door. He wasn't exactly frightened. He supposed he was more irritated than anything. The only nightmares he'd had in the past decade or so had been about weddings, not ghosts dragging chains. He'd thought he was past dreaming about boogeymen and all the other things that go bump in the night!

Grimly awaiting this ghostly figment of his imagination, Carl resolved to eat better and get more rest. Yes, certainly he was dreaming this nonsense because he'd only slept four hours last night and had had a chocolate cupcake from the vending machine for lunch in his office instead of going down the street to Glenda's Diner for a decent salad or sandwich.

The creamy center of the cupcake had seemed a little stale and the frosting hard, but he'd been hungry and busy and he hated the holiday crowds in town at lunchtime, disturbing his usual quiet meal that he spent reading the *Wall Street Journal,* with their laughter, their chatter, their rustling paper sacks.

The chains and, presumably, the ghost who dragged them, were now just outside his office door. Despite his annoyance at such a ridiculous dream, Carl had to admit he was curious and a little alarmed. What if the ghost were gruesome looking, dressed in mummy rags and carrying its own head under its emaciated arm? What if it had sockets for eyes and its skull peeled back to reveal a bony bowl of gooey brains? What if—?

Suddenly the knob turned and the door creaked open. A pale hand fluttered through the opening, followed by a wraithlike creature in a long white gown. Slowly lifting his reluctant gaze to the phantom's face, Carl prepared himself for something truly hideous.

Carl sucked in his breath. He couldn't believe his eyes. Instead of a horrible apparition, the chain dragger was his partner in business, his childhood friend...*Marley Jacobs!* The same Marley Jacobs who had stomped out of his office just an hour ago after confessing her love for him and her determination to cease wasting her time mooning over him! A terrifying possibility occurred to Carl. What if...? But surely Marley hadn't left his office and—no, he wouldn't even entertain the idea. But *what if...?*

"Don't worry, Carl," Marley said with a faint, rueful smile. "I'm not stupid enough to do away with myself over a man. I'm not dead. Although, considering the amount of attention you pay me, I might as well be."

Carl could think of nothing to say in reply. Confused, he scanned her from head to toe. He wanted to believe her. He wanted to believe she hadn't left his office and thrown herself off a bridge, but she looked...well...she really looked like a ghost.

To begin with, she was transparent. He could see right through her to the panels of the door she stood in front of...or perhaps he should say, floated in front of, because, despite the fog, he could tell that her feet weren't touching the floor. And the outfit she wore—an intricately detailed, high-necked white nightgown, something a woman might have worn in Victorian times—fluttered in the air even though there wasn't the slightest breeze. Even her hair was stirred by a breeze Carl couldn't feel or detect in the insulated room. But, just to make sure, he turned around to see if the window behind his desk was closed. It was as tight as a coffin lid.

He turned back to look again at Marley, who simply stared back. Her face was as elfishly lovely as ever, though rather pale. Her eyes had a mischievous twinkle in them and her lips were tilted in an amused smile. The gown was demure but, with the mystical breeze causing it to caress and accentuate her curves, it was provocative at the same time. His eyes narrowed. But where were the chains?

She laughed, the sound hauntingly musical. "There never were any chains," she said, apparently having read his mind. She pulled a very real looking, very un-

Victorian miniature tape player out of a fold of her gown and flicked a tiny switch. The mournful sound of dragging chains reverberated through the room. She flicked it off. "Sound effects for atmospheric impact," she explained. "Same goes for the bells. Besides, it seemed like a good way to wake you up...kind of like an alarm clock. The bells are recorded on the other side of the tape. Want to hear?"

Carl shook his head, vowing fervently never again to eat a chocolate cupcake from a vending machine.

"It wasn't the cupcake, Carl," she informed him, stashing away the tape player into her transparent gown. When Carl still said nothing, she taunted, "Cat got your tongue?"

"Hell, Marley, what do you expect me to say?" he blurted. "Why should I say anything at all? You'll go away as soon as I open my eyes. This is just a dream. A stupid, ordinary dream."

"Ordinary?" Marley moved toward the desk. "Have you ever had a dream like this before? You know, with me...like this?"

"You mean, dressed for bed? Well...no." Carl eyed her warily. The closer she got the less transparent she appeared. By the time she reached his desk, she looked as solid as he did. And her clothes had changed. Now she was wearing a skimpy, black teddy. Carl felt his jaw drop.

"Do you like this better? It's more up-to-date."

And a hell of a lot more revealing, Carl thought, swallowing hard.

Marley smiled coyly and sat on the edge of the desk, propping one leg in an alluring pose along the length of the glossy cherry-wood surface. She leaned forward and ran her fingertips lightly, slowly, over her

leg, from ankle to bent knee to slim, sexy thigh, all
the while giving him a sultry look from under her thick
lashes.

Carl could feel the sweat beading on his forehead.
Yeah, if he'd had a dream like this one, he'd have
remembered it. He was beginning to regret he never
had.

"Yes, it is a pity, isn't it?" Marley purred, again
reading his mind. Carl was going to have to be careful
what he thought. "All the lovely dreams you might
have had. Dreams that could have come true if only
you'd emerged from your hard shell long enough to
notice me." She leaned forward on her elbow, her face
inches from his. "I'm worth noticing, Carl."

Carl could see that. But that was all the more reason
not to notice. He sat back in his chair as far as he
could go, plaiting his fingers over his chest like a smug
banker. "Listen, Marley," he began reasonably, "that
little scene in our office this afternoon must have triggered some thoughts about you I'd never entertained
before, and that's why I'm having this weird dream.
But I probably won't even remember it when I wake
up."

Marley slid off the desk, stood up and turned to face
him. Suddenly she was wearing tailored red silk
pajamas, looking as slinky and sensuous as a Siamese
cat. She propped her fists on her hips and gazed at him
with a serious expression. "Oh, you'll remember it,
Carl. I'll make sure of that. It's your only hope."

Carl laughed uneasily. "My only hope?" he
mocked. "What can you possibly mean by that?"

"To redeem yourself. To become the man you used
to be. The man who was my dearest friend. The man

I fell in love with. The man who loved Christmas as much as I do.''

Carl stood up and leaned both fists on the desk, staring into Marley's eyes with an expression as serious as her own. ''As you said yourself in my office today, Marley, I'm a hopeless case. Irredeemable. You're wasting your time trying to change me. And, what's more, I don't want to be changed. Besides, what makes you think tantalizing me with a view of you in your pj's is going to work such a miracle, anyway? Granted, you're a fetching sight, but I don't allow any woman to lead me by the nose ring anymore.''

''Oh, I don't presume to think I can change you as easily as that,'' Marley admitted. With arched brows and a thrust of her chin, she added, ''Although there are plenty of men who would eat rocks to see me in my pj's, I realize that you're a hardened case. My purpose in appearing to you in this dream is to tell you that before nine o'clock tonight you'll encounter three people that you already know—acting as emissaries, messengers, whatever—who have been assigned by The Powers That Be—

''The powers that be? Give me a break!''

She ignored him and continued. ''To remind you of who you were, who you are, and who you're destined to be if you don't change your attitude about Christmas and about women. Women meaning *moi*... if you catch my drift. And my other purpose for appearing in this dream is to tell you that what you see now—'' she pirouetted, her sleek pajamas instantly changing into a set of baby-dolls, pink, ruffled and sexy as hell ''—you won't see again, not even in your wildest dreams, unless you change your evil ways, Carl Merrick. *Capiche?''*

He capiched all right. But he didn't believe a word she'd said. It was just a lot of crazed rhetoric served up by his cupcake-poisoned brain. The pajamas bit was inspired and entertaining and stimulating enough to make him consider eating stale vending machine junk food as a regular diet, but he knew when he woke up that everything would return to normal.

''I know what you're thinking, Carl, and you're dead wrong,'' Marley warned him, backing away toward the door, growing more and more transparent and ghostlike with each step, her voice taking on the eerie echo of distance. ''You won't forget. And, even if you try, you won't be able to deny the reality of it when things start happening.''

''Things? What things?'' he asked warily.

She waggled the three middle fingers of her right hand in the air. ''Three people, Carl. Before nine o'clock tonight you'll encounter three people you already know who will remind you of who you were, who you are, and who you're destined to be.''

''Marley, wait. I don't want to be reminded of anything. I...I don't want to see three people! I don't need more interruptions. I've...I've got work to do....''

But Marley faded away into the panels of the door with an amused smile on her lips and the parting words, ''Goodbye Carl. See you in the funny papers....''

Carl woke up with a jerk, almost as if someone had banged a pair of cymbals over his head. He looked left to right and back again, scanning the room for any trace of his dream. But there was nothing and no one in the office but him. No fog. No Marley. No nothing.

"It was just a dream," he muttered, rubbing the back of his neck, trying to ease away the tension. "Just a nutty dream caused by a cupcake with an expiration date as old as this damn building."

He stared at his closed office door, remembering with a strange flutter in his stomach how ethereally lovely that figment of his imagination in the form of his partner, Marley, had looked, floating in just that spot. Then, he sneered at himself and at his silly dream. "Marley as a ghost modeling the latest creations from Victoria's Secret...humph! What a bunch of—"

Suddenly the door burst open and Carl flew back in his chair as if he'd been shot, toppling the chair and himself over and onto the floor. Stunned, lying on his back with his legs dangling and the tiny rubber wheels of the chair still spinning, Carl clutched the armrests and waited, half expecting another apparition to float over his desk and have a good laugh at his expense. Who would it be this time? Maybe Uncle Ralph in long johns?

But the wizened, disapproving face that peered over his desk at him did not belong to Uncle Ralph. He recognized those gray, unplucked eyebrows, the flared nostrils, the thin, puckered lips outlined so imprecisely with her signature Safari Red lipstick.

"Miss Hathaway?" Carl wheezed, since the fall had knocked most of the air out of his lungs.

"Yes, Carl," Miss Hathaway replied, forcing her words through the prim, corkscrew opening of her mouth, which was the way she always talked when she was royally ticked off. "It's me, your second-grade teacher. And I must say, I'm very disappointed in you."

"You gave me quite...quite a start. You're...you're not a ghost, are you?" Carl stuttered.

"Not the last time I looked," Miss Hathaway replied with a disdainful sniff. "Don't you keep up with the obituaries, young man? Or are those financial reports all you ever read?"

Carl avoided the question by struggling out of the chair, feeling just as foolish as he had in the second grade when he'd turned over his chair while rocking on the back legs, even though Miss Hathaway had just reprimanded him for such a dangerous and disrespectful habit. As he recalled, he'd been showing off for Marley.

Carl stood up, nervously smoothed down the upturned flaps of his jacket and unwrapped his tie from around his neck. Pulling back his shoulders and tucking in his stomach as if he were on military review, Carl looked down at the diminutive figure that was the unlikely source of his anxiety.

Miss Hathaway couldn't be more than four feet ten inches tall or weigh more than eighty pounds. She was wearing a short wool coat over a long wool skirt, both of them bright red. Thick black stockings plumped up her legs to the approximate girth of clarinets, her tiny ankles disappearing into a pair of stout black boots with soles like tank treads.

On her head she wore a matching red knit cap with a huge green pom-pom on the top that had been dotted with glue and sprinkled with glitter. A sprig of real holly was pinned to the cuff. The cap was pulled low over her ears, her drab gray-blond hair sticking out in uneven intervals like porcupine quills.

She still wore round wire-rim glasses that rested on the end of her small, pointed nose and she still carried an umbrella—not the usual kind that you can fold up into a compact package, but the old-fashioned style with the stout, curved handle. He suspected that the formidable-looking object doubled as a weapon in the unlikely event of an attempted mugging of an elderly female on the quiet streets of Mount Joy...unlikely particularly if the elderly female had Miss Hathaway's reputation.

In the face of such quelling disapproval, Carl tried to appear unperturbed. But even though Carl was nearly thirty years old, Miss Hathaway still made him feel like a naughty schoolboy.

"I do read the obituaries, Miss Hathaway," he assured her, as if reporting on a homework assignment. He had the ridiculous urge to inform her that he hadn't, however, read the obituaries that morning because his dog had eaten his newspaper...but managed to refrain. After all, he didn't own a dog. "And I'm very glad I haven't seen *your* picture there."

She slapped her umbrella against the file folders and financial reports on top of Carl's desk. He tried not to, but he flinched. "Enough flattery, young man," she snapped. "I won't be sidetracked by sweet talk." She glared at him.

After enduring her antagonistic appraisal for what seemed like a century, Carl ventured, "Why *are* you here, Miss Hathaway? And how—" He stopped to adjust his tie and clear his throat. "How did you get in? I thought Bev locked the door."

"I came in as Bev was leaving," Miss Hathaway explained tersely. "She directed me to your office. The poor thing looked exhausted, but relieved to get home to her little boy, I'm sure. She's got her hands full being a single mother and a full-time secretary to a demanding man like you. Her boy, Timmy, is sick, you know. Has a heart problem.''

''He does? I didn't—''

''No, you wouldn't know, would you.'' She glared at him again for several uncomfortable seconds. ''Now, as to why I'm here—''

''Excuse me, Miss Hathaway,'' Carl interrupted, pausing to smile respectfully before continuing. ''But how could Bev have let you in? She left nearly an hour ago, just before six.''

Miss Hathaway raised her beetled brows. ''An hour ago? It's going on to six o'clock now, Carl. Didn't you ever learn to properly tell time?''

Carl covered his confusion with a laugh. ''Just now six o'clock? That's impossible. The tower clock struck six times right before I fell asleep at my—''

Carl stopped mid-sentence as the tower clock began to strike. He forced that respectful smile again as he waited patiently for the clock to strike seven times, but only six loud bongs reverberated into the foggy night! Carl felt as he'd been punched in the stomach. Six o'clock? *Again?* How was that possible?

Carl turned and stared out the window at the tower clock, a source of time so reliable he'd never bothered to keep another clock in his office. Sure enough, it read six o'clock. Then, as Miss Hathaway narrowly observed him, Carl looked at his watch, shook his wrist vigorously, then looked at it again. It too read six o'clock, the crisp black numbers as plain as the smug expression on Miss Hathaway's face.

''I don't understand,'' Carl mumbled.

''It's very simple,'' Miss Hathaway informed him briskly. ''The big hand is on the twelve and the little hand—''

"No! I don't understand how it can be—oh, never mind." Carl thought it best not to try to explain the strange time warp he seemed to be in. He was probably just confused because of the dream. "You were going to tell me why you're here, Miss Hathaway," he prompted, eager to get rid of her so he could call the poison control center and inquire about the effects of stale cupcakes on brain tissue.

Miss Hathaway's narrow chest swelled and her face grew nearly as livid as her red coat. "I'm here to ask you, Carl Ebeneezer Merrick—"

Uh-oh. She'd used his full name.

"—why you aren't downstairs in the parking lot helping that nice Marley Jacobs change her flat tire! When I think of how devoted she was to you in grade school...tsk! It's freezing cold outside and the way she's struggling with that jack you'd think the poor girl couldn't see straight or...or—"

"Marley's in the parking lot with a flat tire?" Carl interrupted. "But she left a long time ago. Are you sure?"

"You seem to have your times all mixed up, Carl," Miss Hathaway observed dryly. She leaned close and sniffed. "Have you been drinking?"

"I never drink at the office, ma'am," Carl informed her, offended. "And if I'd known Marley needed my help, I'd have gone down immediately."

"Well, you know now," Miss Hathaway reminded him. "What's keeping you?"

"Nothing's keeping me," Carl said grimly, grabbing his black wool coat off the hook on the wall and shrugging into it. As he buttoned up he looked longingly at the financial reports on his desk, but he figured that changing Marley's tire shouldn't take more than a few minutes, then he could get back to doing what he most enjoyed—tending to business.

"Better put on your scarf and gloves, too," Miss Hathaway advised. "Cold outside."

Rather than argue, Carl obliged, even though he didn't think he'd need bundling up for the short amount of time he intended to be outside. He wrapped the hunter green scarf around his neck and slipped on the black leather gloves as Miss Hathaway watched with a strange little smile on her Safari Red lips, saying nothing. Carl wondered about that smile but, grateful for a reprieve from her sharp tongue, he kept silent, too.

Finally he flicked off the desk lamp and led Miss Hathaway through the building and out the front door, then around to the parking lot in the back. Sure enough, there was Marley on her knees in the cold, crusty snow, jacking up her car...or at least trying to. She was still wearing her elf costume, complete with pointed hat and belled shoes, under a blue ski parka. Seeing her for the first time since the dream, Carl got a strange feeling in his gut. Suddenly he was noticing her as a woman, not as just a platonic friend and business partner. Damn.

She turned as they approached and Carl could have sworn he detected, by the light of the overhead street lamp, damp cheeks and teary eyes. She quickly looked away, ducking behind the sleeve of her puffy jacket. When she turned around again, Carl figured he must have imagined those tears.

"I thought you were working late?" she said, flicking him a cool glance, then returning her concentration to the task at hand.

"I am, but I can take a few minutes to—"

"Heaven forbid that I should take you away from your work for even a *second*, Carl. Go away. I can do this myself. I've changed lots of tires over the years." The jack slipped and Marley gave a little grunt of frustration, then rubbed her nose, leaving a grease mark on her upper lip.

"Lots of them, eh? Could have fooled me," Carl mumbled. Louder he said, "Don't be so stubborn, Marley. You're keeping me and Miss Hathaway standing in the cold for no good reason other than your silly—"

Marley dropped the jack and turned around. "Miss Hathaway? Is that really you? I haven't seen you in ages!"

And suddenly, as Carl looked on dumbfounded, Marley threw her arms around the diminutive teacher and the two women embraced. He had no idea Marley and Miss Hathaway had so much affection for each other.

"There, there," Miss Hathaway said, thumping Marley on the back and speaking in a brusque manner as if to hide embarrassingly tender feelings. "Don't choke me like you did on the last day of school when you finished second grade. You've got a headlock like Hulk Hogan. With such a grip, I don't understand why you can't manage that jack."

"I don't know why, either. I'm not usually so inept. I'm used to taking care of myself." She slid a resentful, slightly puzzled look toward Carl. "I certainly didn't expect Carl to come to my rescue."

"I'd have come sooner if I'd known you needed me. You should have come up to the office and asked for help," he said stiffly. "But you were too mad at me to do that, I suppose."

"You're wrong, Carl," Marley replied with a jut of her chin. "Whether I was mad at you or not, I wouldn't have disturbed you. I know how important your work is to you." *More important than me*, her eyes said.

"Well, let's get this done," Carl said gruffly. "I still have paperwork to do."

While Marley and Miss Hathaway chattered about old schoolmates—names Carl only vaguely remembered—he easily got the car jacked up and the tire off. He was beginning to think the evening wouldn't be a total waste when he turned to Marley and inquired, "Will you open the trunk so I can get your spare?"

Marley's eyes widened and she bit the corner of her lip, looking as guilty as a cat with its paw in the fishbowl. "It won't do any good. My spare's flat, too. I forgot till just now, but last month I ran over a nail and had to use the spare, then I put the leaky tire in the trunk. I meant to take it in to be repaired, but with Christmas and all..."

Carl was sure his irritation showed all over his face. He just stood there and glared at Marley till Miss Hathaway poked him with her umbrella.

"Now *you're* keeping us outside in the cold for no good reason," she said. "Do the gentlemanly thing, Carl, and escort Marley home."

"Fine," Carl snapped, grudgingly resigned to postponing his paperwork for a little longer than he'd anticipated. "Or, if you want, we can take the tire to the gas station and get it repaired, then bring it back and put it on. I suppose you'll need a car to drive to my folks' house tomorrow?"

"I will, but there's no time right now to go to the gas station," Marley answered worriedly. "Sheila

Fezziwig—you remember her, don't you, Carl? She used to be Sheila Renshaw?''

Carl grunted noncommittally. *Sheila who?*

''She's having a Christmas party for her four-year-old's preschool class, and I'm supposed to show up with a bag of party favors she commissioned me to pick up from the toy store. That's why I'm still in this suit. But if I don't arrive with the loot by six o'clock, a whole lot of kids will be disappointed.''

''Well, you and the kids are flat out of luck, no pun intended,'' Carl said. ''It's past six o'clock already.''

Marley frowned. ''No, it's not. It's only five forty-five. Look at the tower clock.''

Carl did look up at the tower clock. It said five forty-five. Forcing himself to remain calm, Carl looked at his watch, too. Five forty-five. What the hell was going on?

Carl turned to Miss Hathaway. ''But when we were in the office, don't you remember the tower clock striking six times? Or am I going crazy?''

Miss Hathaway lifted her brows and shrugged. ''Crazy? Aren't we all a little crazy?''

''I wasn't asking for a rhetorical opinion, Miss Hathaway,'' Carl said caustically.

Miss Hathaway waggled her bony index finger at his nose. ''The only thing that matters right now, Carl Merrick, is that those kids aren't disappointed. You've got fifteen minutes to get to Sheila's house. What's keeping you?''

''You don't mind driving me over, do you?'' Marley asked him, moving to stand between him and Miss Hathaway and grabbing both his arms just above the wrists. Carl looked down at Marley's delicate fingers wrapped around his arms and, despite the gloves she was wearing and the thick wool coat between her skin and his, he could have sworn he felt a jolt of attraction from the contact.

He looked into her large green eyes from this proximity and noticed, for the first time, that they were a little pink. And her thick lashes seemed stuck together here and there, as if they'd been damp. Had she, as he'd originally suspected, been crying when they first saw her in the parking lot? And was she crying over the frustration of changing the tire, or was she crying over *him* and, because of her tears, couldn't see straight to change the tire?

When he didn't answer but continued to stare at her, Marley seemed to recollect herself and added soberly, "How stupid of me. Of course you mind. But, for the kids' sake, will you do it anyway?"

"Yes," he answered, feeling dazed and surprised by his own answer, his gaze lingering over the delicate features of her face and resting on the smudge of grease on her upper lip. Without thinking, he reached up and wiped the smear away with his gloved thumb.

"Th...thank you, Carl," Marley said, seeming as dazed and surprised as he was, her lips curving up in a tentative smile and her hands sliding down his arms to his hands, which she caught in a brief but warm clasp. That jolt of attraction was turning into a steady hum of electric awareness.

"I'd better come, too," Miss Hathaway announced briskly. "I've already missed my bus and my house is just a mile or so from Sheila's. Carl, you can drop me off after Marley makes her delivery."

Carl nodded mutely as he led the way to his parking space, then remembered that he hadn't driven his car that morning, but had taken the bus so he could drive home the old company truck they kept around for various errands and repairs. He planned to use it to transport some junk he'd cleaned out of the attic to the dump over the holiday. He'd decided, as he did every year, that Christmas wouldn't stand in the way of getting things done. And now that lucky decision might save him from wasting half the evening transporting Marley and Miss Hathaway to their various destinations.

He turned and forced an apologetic smile. "I just remembered I don't have my car. We'd have to squeeze into the cab of this old truck. Why don't I call a taxi for you ladies? I'll pay, of course." Escaping Marley's sudden alluring mystique was worth paying cab fare.

"There's no time to wait for a taxi or, should I say, *the* taxi? Besides, Vern probably took the evening off," Marley objected.

"But the heater in the truck doesn't work worth beans," Carl added, desperate.

"Oh, a bum heater won't matter," Miss Hathaway said, effectively pooh-poohing Carl's concerns. "We'll be so snuggled up together in the truck, we won't be cold at all!"

After Marley got her bag of party favors out of her car and they all three climbed into the cab of the truck, Carl knew that he at least wouldn't be cold...not with Marley's hip pressed against his, her perfume tickling his nose, and a vision of her in pink baby-doll pajamas dancing in his head.

No, he wouldn't be cold at all...*dammit*.

Chapter Three

As they bumped along Main Street in the old company truck, Marley held on to her bag of goodies and felt amazement wash over her. Just minutes before, she'd walked out of Carl's office resolved to get over him. She'd finally decided—and not a moment too soon—not to waste her life mooning over a man who didn't know she was alive.

Oh, sure, they made great business partners, but Marley had wanted more than that from Carl for as long as she could remember. And it was that retentive memory of hers that had kept her hopes up over the years. But enough was enough.

It had made her sad to give up. It had made her cry. But it had also given her a sense of control over her life that she hadn't felt in ages. Then, just moments ago, she'd felt herself melting again.

She'd grabbed hold of his arms and smiled at him, grateful for a simple act of kindness any decent person would have performed. But because it was Carl changing her tire and driving her to Sheila's house, she was making more out of it than it deserved. And, she reminded herself, he was only being kind because he was under duress from Miss Hathaway. It would be

foolish to get her hopes up just to have them dashed
again.

Steeling herself with these sensible thoughts, Marley tried not to notice how wonderful Carl's aftershave
smelled or how nicely his muscled thigh felt pressed
against hers.

Carl stopped at the intersection of Fifth and Main.
"Left, right, or straight ahead?"

Surprised, Marley asked, "Don't you know?"

Carl made a disgruntled noise. "Why would I
know?"

Miss Hathaway peered around Marley and said
tartly, "In a town this size, Carl, everyone knows
everyone and where they live. Everyone, that is, who
actually consorts with other human beings. That would
leave you out, I suppose."

"This isn't getting us to Sheila's house any faster,"
Carl said.

"You're right," Marley conceded. "She lives
where she used to live in elementary school."

Carl looked at her blankly.

"When she and her husband, Dave, moved back to
town last year, they bought her parents' old house."

"And that would be where, exactly?"

Marley was astonished. "You don't remember
Sheila Renshaw at all, do you, Carl?"

Carl shrugged and glanced in the rearview mirror.
"No, I don't," he admitted tersely. "Now please tell
me where the old Renshaw house is before the driver
behind us loses his patience."

"Route 12," Marley told him, still stunned by his
inability to remember the giggling, redheaded ball of
fire they went through elementary school with till she
moved away in the sixth grade.

Carl's irritation showed as he punched the gas pedal and the truck lurched forward through the intersection. "Route 12? Way the hell—"

Miss Hathaway leaned forward and glared at him.

"Heck," he corrected, "out by—"

"Reindeer Pond," Marley finished for him. She couldn't help a small reminiscent smile. "The very place where you and I first learned to ice-skate. You do remember that, don't you, Carl?"

No, Carl didn't remember that. But he was smart enough not to say so. It was obvious Marley found his lack of memory, and his lack of interest in the past, annoying. "Sure," he grunted, turning off Main onto the highway that would take them into the rural outskirts of town. Squinting into the fog and the dark, he turned his lights on high beam. These, at best, were feeble. Maybe the battery was going.

"You actually remember?" Marley sounded hopeful and skeptical at the same time.

"Sure," Carl repeated, lying through his teeth.

"Quiz him," Miss Hathaway advised. "I always found pop quizzes to be most effective."

Carl's fingers squeezed the steering wheel in frustration. He didn't have time for this nonsense.

"How old were we?" Marley asked him.

Carl sighed and made a stab at it. "Nine."

"*Bzzzzt!* Wrong!" Miss Hathaway snapped.

"We were eight, Carl," Marley informed him. "What month was it?"

"January?"

"No, December."

"Are you sure?"

"Carl, I ought to remember! It was Christmas! We both got skates that year."

"Er...right. It was a beautiful day," Carl impro-
vised.

"It was night. And it was snowing. Admit it, Carl.
You don't remember one thing about that day."

"Well, sue me for not having a memory like an
elephant's," he said sarcastically.

"You don't have to have a memory like an elephant's to remember the day when your best
friend—that used to be me—falls through the ice and
nearly drowns."

Carl was startled. She was right. How could he have
forgotten that terrifying experience? It was all coming
back to him. Marley laughing, then screaming... The
freezing water, the jagged hole in the ice with Marley's head bobbing up and down. That sick feeling in
his stomach—

"We're here," Marley said, thankfully interrupting
his thoughts. Turning on to the long gravel driveway
that led to a large white farmhouse badly in need of a
paint job, Carl looked to the right and saw through the
fog the faint glimmer of dark blue that was the frozen
expanse of Reindeer Pond and the hazy pinpoints of
white that were the electric lights that illuminated it
for skating. He shivered and speculated that maybe
he'd forgotten that particular memory on purpose.

They pulled in front of the house and parked by
three other cars Carl assumed belonged to parents of
children attending the party. He looked up at the
house, the garlands and red bows that draped the rails
of the wide porch lending a festive air to a building
that had seen better days.

The glass panes of the windows were steamy with
warmth from inside and framed with tiny white lights.
In the front bay window a tall Christmas tree covered

with multicolored bulbs, distorted by distance and the fog into the appearance of fuzzy explosions, glowed into the dark night.

Looking at this scene, with his memory jogged a bit, Carl vaguely recalled attending a couple of parties there himself many years ago. And there was another memory, too, of a red-haired, pigtailed girl with wicked brown eyes, whispering in his ear, "Marley tol' me ta give ya this note, Carl. It's a *loooove* note. Marley thinks you're dreamy, Carl, and she wants ta marry ya when she grows up and have your *baaaa-beees*—"

As Miss Hathaway and Marley scooted out on the passenger side, Carl stayed put and stared straight ahead. He hated memories.

"Aren't you going to turn off the engine and come inside, Carl?" Marley asked him.

Carl didn't budge. "No, you two go ahead. I'll just wait in the car."

"It'll probably take a few minutes. It's warm inside and freezing out here."

She made sense, but Carl would rather freeze than remember. "I've got the heater going full blast. I'll be just fine." The heater was going full blast all right, but nothing except cold air was coming out. His toes were beginning to feel like ice cubes.

"If Carl wants to stay outside, I'll keep him company," Miss Hathaway announced, hiking herself back onto the high seat.

Carl immediately turned off the engine and pushed in the knob for the lights. He turned to find a knowing smile on Miss Hathaway's primly pursed yet garishly painted lips, looking even in the dark as if some two-year-old had scribbled the color on with a red crayon.

"Changed your mind, Carl?" she inquired in an annoying singsong.

"I wouldn't dream of allowing you to freeze just to keep me company, Miss Hathaway," he said with grim politeness. "Let's go inside, shall we?" And he wouldn't dream of becoming a captive in his own company truck, a sitting duck for another tongue-lashing from the "master."

By the time they'd walked up the short sidewalk to the porch, the front door had opened and a tall, slim woman dressed in jeans and a green sweater covered with a Christmas tree print stood in a shaft of yellow light. She had auburn hair. "Marley...hi! 'Bout time you showed up! I've got some wild animals on my hands!"

Judging by the high-pitched squeals of children in the background, Carl could easily believe the statement to be true.

"Who's this?" she exclaimed, peering over Marley's shoulder as she hugged her. *"Miss Hathaway?"*

Carl stood by as the woman, who he assumed was Sheila Renshaw Fezziwig, fussed and cooed over Miss Hathaway. He was beginning to wonder if he was the only person intimidated by the pygmy-size harridan.

Uh-oh. Now Sheila was looking at him. "Carl? Carl Merrick? What are *you* doing here?"

"Well, I—"

But before Carl could offer an explanation, Sheila had thrown her arms around him and was giving him a bear hug to beat the band. As the hug went on and on, he couldn't decide what to do with his hands. He looked helplessly at Marley, who looked back at him with an amused smile. Finally he awkwardly thumped Sheila on the back a couple of times. It was apparently what she was waiting for because she finally released him.

"Carl, I thought you'd forgotten me," she exclaimed, laughing into his face. "I've seen you in town a couple of times, but you walked past me as if I were nobody. You looked pretty serious both times, so I guess you were preoccupied or something. I don't know why I thought you could forget me. Come in, you guys! Let's get out of the cold."

Out of the cold and into the chaos, Carl thought as he stepped inside the hall and had to immediately dodge a fire truck being pushed by a fast-as-lightning toddler in a firefighter's hat. The child's bowl-cut hair was nearly as red as his hat.

"Matthew, I told you, watch where you're going!" Sheila said, laughing. She turned to them and confided, "I let him open one present tonight. The other preschool kids brought presents to open, too, and they've been out of control ever since." Lending credence to her claim, three more small children zoomed past. "I'm hoping your bag of party favors will focus their attention for a few minutes...long enough to settle them down before we serve refreshments. The last thing I want is a food fight!"

Ditto, thought Carl.

Sheila escorted them into the living room and introduced them to two of the parents who had stayed to help with the party, stopping them from pursuit of pint-size partyers just long enough to exchange polite how-do-you-do's. Then a man in a rumpled shirt and jeans walked in, kissed Sheila on the cheek and handed her a redheaded baby that she propped unceremoniously on her hip. The baby's chubby face was smeared with chocolate. Miss Hathaway immediately started cooing at him and tickling his bare, chubby feet.

Sheila introduced her husband to Carl and Miss Hathaway. "His first name is plain old Dave—not Ludwig or Wolfgang—which comes as a surprise to most people since his last name is Fezziwig."

"I believe Fezziwig is an old and very noble European surname, isn't it, Dave?" Miss Hathaway said.

Dave laughed and shook first Miss Hathaway's hand then Carl's. "I've heard something like that before, but who knows? It's not a name people easily forget. Pleased to meet you both." He smiled, then immediately turned and winked at Marley. "And it's always good to see you, Marley. Lookin' good in that cute little elf outfit. Did Mrs. Santa throw you out 'cause Santa couldn't keep his mind on toy making?"

Everyone laughed except for Carl, who thought Dave's comment was juvenile. But he did take a surreptitious second glance at Marley's outfit and agreed that Santa might have trouble concentrating with a cute tush like hers in the vicinity.

"I'm goin' back upstairs with Stevie and April. We're watching *Star Wars*. Unless, of course, you need me down here?" Dave looked as though he were desperately hoping for a clean getaway, but couldn't go without at least a token offering of help.

"I'm fine," Sheila assured him, giving him an understanding and amused smile, then waving him away. "Just make sure the kids brush their teeth before they fall asleep in front of the tube."

Carl didn't bother to ask who Stevie and April were,

because it was obvious that Sheila had been busy bearing offspring since the moment she'd said "I do."

"Yes, they have four kids," Marley whispered in his ear. "And, even though they don't have every material thing they might need, they're happy. I think it's great!"

Carl recognized the defensive tone in her voice and said nothing. He personally had no opinion about family size, since he hadn't considered having his own family for...let's see...about seven years. But it was plain to see that the Fezziwigs' income didn't quite comfortably support their growing family. And here they were throwing a party! All owing to their "Christmas spirit" he supposed. Like all the rest, they were nuts.

As the women had drifted into a conversation about the littlest Fezziwig's motor skills, Carl plastered a courteous smile on his lips and sidestepped toward the tree, pretending to admire it so he could sneak away.

Eventually Carl managed to back himself against a wall, half-hidden by shadows, his arms folded over his chest and his eyes darting back and forth as he watched for incoming missiles camouflaged as children. Then the doorbell rang and he steeled himself for the onslaught of perhaps even more preschoolers.

But only one parent and one preschooler came into the room. It was his secretary, Bev, and her son, Tim. She came in apologizing for being late and gently tugging Timmy by the hand. Carl immediately recognized that Tim was smaller and paler than the other preschoolers and remembered what Miss Hathaway had said about the child having a heart problem. He watched Bev talking with Sheila and Marley, her lips upturned in a smile. At the office she never smiled. She always seemed so tense.

"She never smiles at the office because she's scared to death of you. She's afraid that one false step will cost her her job."

Miss Hathaway had crept up unawares and hissed this opinion in Carl's ear, making him jump.

"That's a bunch of bull. Bev does a good job. I wouldn't fire her over a mistake or two."

"She doesn't know that. You come across like a snarly dictator most of the time. She needs her job, because she's the only one supporting that little family. And she needs the health insurance for Timmy's sake."

Carl frowned and stared at Tim. He was a cute kid with blond hair that stuck straight up on the top in a spiky cut that a lot of the kids were wearing. The child was looking around with a tentative smile on his lips, appearing a little shy but eager to join in the fun. He looked for an especially long time, and with especially shining eyes, at Matthew's fire truck. Carl just hoped that once the kid joined the melee, he wouldn't get plowed down by some of the other boisterous, and generally larger, preschoolers.

"For some strange reason, you seem to know everything, Miss Hathaway," Carl murmured, still watching Bev and Timmy. "So tell me this, how sick *is* Timmy?"

Miss Hathaway peered at him keenly. "Why don't you ask Marley? She knows everything about Timmy's illness. Unlike you, she takes the time to really get to know the employees at your company. Here's your chance to change that, Carl."

Miss Hathaway left Carl with his thoughts, which

weren't very comfortable. He really didn't want to change anything about the way he related to his employees. He figured the less he knew about them the better. Work went smoother that way. But there was something about Timmy that seemed to just tug at his heart. Such emotions were a bad sign, a bad sign all around.

Timmy finally took off to play with the other kids—sure enough headed straight for Matthew and the fire truck—his mother gazing after him with a tender, worried expression. Carl looked away. He didn't like the way he was feeling, and he was backstepping even further into the shadows of his chosen hiding place when Marley suddenly turned and motioned to him to come over.

Bev, apparently until then unaware that Carl was present in the room, turned too, and immediately froze. She looked startled and—there was no denying it— quite anxious. Carl had no choice now but to smile politely and join them.

"H-hello, Mr. Merrick," Bev stuttered. "What are *you* doing here?"

"I'm not really sure, Bev," Carl answered with a significant look at Marley, hopefully conveying his ardent desire to leave.

Marley caught his meaning and answered him by shrugging out of her jacket and laying it on a nearby chair. Carl clenched his jaw but, despite the warmth of the room, refused to take off his own coat, or his gloves, or even his knitted scarf. He wasn't staying.

Marley ignored Carl's beleaguered expression and said, "Before I start my elf routine, Bev, tell me about Timmy's doctor's appointment at noon. Things got so crazy at work, I didn't have a chance to ask you about it earlier.''

Carl couldn't help it, he was interested. But Bev slid a nervous look his way, obviously sure her boss couldn't possibly want to know about such personal matters.

''Yes, Bev, what's the latest?'' Sheila prompted. ''Does Timmy still need the operation?''

Bev seemed to be trying to pretend that Carl didn't exist as she answered, ''I'm afraid so. His heart condition will never be totally resolved without surgery, but right now he's taking a new medication that works wonders. He's feeling a lot better these days. Trouble is, the pills are really expensive and I don't make enough—''

Bev broke off and snatched another glance at Carl, then blushed furiously.

''Don't you have insurance?'' Sheila inquired.

''Yes,'' Marley answered for her. ''But it doesn't pay for prescriptions.''

Sheila looked incredulous then laughed uncertainly. ''But, Marley, isn't that your department? Why don't you cover your employees' prescription needs? Don't you know how expensive medicine can be? Taking care of a chronically sick child would drain anyone's income.''

''I'm well aware of how expensive medicine is.'' Marley suddenly became preoccupied with a button on the sleeve of her elf costume. ''But I can't buy into an employee benefit plan without...well, without...''

An embarrassed pall fell over their little circle. Marley didn't want to say so, but Little Angel employees didn't have insurance to cover prescriptions because Carl had vetoed it. No one was verbalizing it, or even looking at him, but Carl felt as though he were being judged. But, hell, he was never sick! How did he know how much medicine cost?

"You know, you two really make a couple of good-looking co-presidents," Sheila said in a forcibly cheerful tone. Then a more natural smile curved her lips and a coy look came into her brown eyes. It was a look that brought back memories. "I just thought you'd be doing something a little more *intimate* together than running a company."

Carl was speechless. He flitted a glance toward Marley and saw that she was just as uncomfortable as he was.

"With Bev's help, I'll round up the kids," Sheila said, seemingly oblivious to the mortified expressions on their faces. "It'll take a couple minutes, so why don't you two go into the kitchen and sample my fudge? It's not as good as Mom's, but it's close."

"I don't eat fudge," Carl mumbled, desperate to avoid being scuttled off to the kitchen with Marley. They hadn't been alone together since their last conversation in his office, unless you could count the dream. And after Sheila's suggestive comment...

Sheila gave him a playful slap. "You don't eat fudge? Come on, Carl. That's a whopper if I ever heard one. I remember when you ate a whole pan of my mother's fudge and made yourself sick." She pushed them toward a door at the end of a long hall. "I'll holler when it's show time."

Carl reluctantly followed Marley down the hall and through a swinging kitchen door. He thought about retreating to his dark corner again, but he knew Miss Hathaway would turn up like a bad penny and prod him out of the shadows with the sharp end of her umbrella.

And now Marley might hit him up again about the insurance coverage for prescriptions. But was it a wise business move to take on such a big expense just to accommodate the needs of a single employee?

Carl didn't want to think about it. "What does she mean by 'show time?' You're not putting on a show, are you?"

Marley turned from the counter where she had been staring down at an oblong glass pan of uncut fudge, her eyes flashing. "What if I were? Do you honestly begrudge Timmy and his friends so little time out of your busy schedule? If—God forbid—things don't go exactly right in the next few months, this could be his last Christmas."

Carl felt his whole body go cold. "That's not why I asked. I just thought—"

"As usual, you were thinking only about yourself. About how long you were going to be stuck here, weren't you?" Marley leaned against the counter, her arms crossed over her chest. She glared at him.

She was right. He wanted to leave because he was uncomfortable and because he wanted to get back to his paperwork. He always felt most comfortable doing paperwork.

Habits are at first like cobwebs, a little voice in his head taunted him, a voice that sounded amazingly like Miss Hathaway in her best lecturing mode. *Then like chains.*

Chains. Like the kind Marley's ghost had dragged in his dream. Or, rather, like the cassette she'd played for him on her minirecorder. That gown she'd been wearing had been so...

"Cat got your tongue, Carl?" Marley asked him, jarring him out of his stupor. She was still glaring at him.

"Is that an expression you frequently use?" Carl asked her. *And do you own a black teddy? Or pink baby-doll pajamas?*

She frowned harder than ever. "I don't know. I don't think so. What a dumb question."

Carl sighed heavily and shook his head. "I'm sorry, Marley. Take as long as you want. You're right. The kids deserve a fun party and my paperwork can wait...I guess."

Now Marley was gaping. She was slack-jawed with astonishment. "Carl Ebeneezer Merrick, did you just say what I thought you said?"

"Don't get overexcited," he said irritably. "You're not witnessing a Christmas miracle or anything. I just said I didn't mind if you took a few extra minutes, that's all."

She smiled, the corners of her mouth turned up in a sweet expression that made him want to—well, he wasn't sure what he wanted to do, but he didn't like whatever it was.

"You're showing signs of being human, Carl. Now that you've seen how the lack of it affects real people, maybe this would be a good time to talk about getting our employees some insurance coverage for prescriptions." She lifted her chin in that challenging pose of hers he hadn't noticed before being so damned alluring. She had spunk. Like Lou Grant, he hated spunk, but he did find it arousing. At least on Marley.

"I guess we can talk about it," he said gruffly. "But not tonight."

"When?"

"Next week."

"Where?"

"In my office. But don't push it, Marley." Hopefully by next week, and in the businesslike atmosphere of his office, Carl would be able to be objective about the matter. In this cozy kitchen that smelled of fudge, with Marley standing so close and looking so damned cute, he didn't dare make any kind of decision.

Marley smiled, as if satisfied, and said nothing. Carl stared at her lips, suddenly realizing that what he'd been wanting to do all evening was kiss her. Not a good idea.

Marley turned, picked up a butter knife and began to cut the fudge. "I think you deserve a reward," she said.

"For saying 'maybe'?" Carl waited nervously.

"When my folks said maybe, it always meant yes." Marley turned, a square of fudge resting in the center of her open palm. Carl found the sight surprisingly arousing. But then lately he seemed to find just about everything Marley did arousing.

"I don't eat fudge...remember?"

"You used to."

"Not anymore."

"Why not?"

"It's not good for me."

"You're a grouch, and that's not good for you, either. Besides, I disagree. Fudge is full of chocolate, and chocolate is a mood elevator. Elevating your mood, Carl, is a positive thing. Especially for those of us who have to work with you."

"I don't like it." He could see she was in a playful mood. It reminded him of his dream version of Marley. The same teasing smile, the same mischievous sparkle in her eyes.

"I don't believe you," she said, lifting her hand till the fudge was just under his nose. The rich chocolaty aroma filled his nostrils. "Everyone likes fudge, Carl. Even an old grinch like you."

Carl could have stepped back, simply moved away a step or two, but he didn't. "I don't want any fudge."

"Because you ate a whole pan once and you threw up? Are you chicken to eat it again? 'Fraid you'll up-chuck the fudge, Carl?"

There was laughter in her eyes. Suddenly Carl was taken back, all the way back through the years of friendship. As a skinny tomboy with flyaway hair and big white teeth too large for her mouth—"Chiclet" teeth—Marley had often had that laughing expression in her eyes.

"I dare ya," she said, bringing back the memories full force. There had been so many dares. So much fun.

She broke off a piece of the fudge and placed it on the tip of her tongue. Like a starved puppy, Carl watched her curl her tongue and close her lips. Her eyes drifted shut.

"Oh, Carl. It's *so good*. Are you sure you don't want a taste?"

Carl swallowed hard. He wanted a taste all right, but he wouldn't mind trying it secondhand....

"Okay," he said, his voice a rasp. "I'll, er, have some." First prescription insurance, now fudge. What next?

Her face lit up. "Close your eyes."

He frowned. "Why?"

"So you'll get the full impact."

He couldn't resist. He closed his eyes.

"Now, open."

He opened his mouth and she dropped a small piece of fudge on his tongue. The taste exploded in his mouth. He hadn't eaten fudge for seven years. What had he been thinking?

He opened his eyes. "More."

She laughed. "You like it, huh?" With her free hand she reached over and caught hold of his scarf, sliding it slowly from around his neck.

Carl's heart began to beat a frantic rhythm. "What are you doing?"

She tossed the scarf on the counter. "Aren't you hot?"

Yes, but not the way you mean. "What's that got to do with fudge?"

"Nothing. I just thought you'd be more comfortable in this eighty-degree kitchen without a wool scarf wrapped around your neck. Besides, I've been wanting to check something out."

Carl's heart beat faster and faster as she began to unbutton his coat. He allowed her, feeling mesmerized.

When she had finished unbuttoning his coat down to his waist, she laid her hand, the palm flat, against his chest. Carl hoped she didn't realize how frantically his heart was beating and rightly attribute it to his attraction to her.

"Yes, I think it's growing," she said with mock seriousness.

Oh, Lord, did it show? "What's growing?" Carl asked nervously.

"Your heart," she answered with a teasing smile. "Just like the Grinch's heart grew after he gave back the Whos' Christmas. It feels two sizes bigger already!''

Carl absorbed the warmth from Marley's palm, loving it, wanting it to last forever. He looked into her eyes and saw warmth there, too. He knew if he just leaned forward a bit, he would be in the right position to kiss her—

''Show time!'' The kitchen door burst open and Sheila popped her head inside. ''Are you ready, Marley?''

Carl turned abruptly and Marley's hand slipped away from his chest. Feeling disoriented and frustrated, Carl stepped aside as Marley moved past him and through the door. He didn't immediately follow her. He needed time to compose himself, and time to think.

It didn't take him long to realize he was glad Sheila had interrupted them. What was he thinking, cozying up to Marley like that? He was only giving her false hope. He had no intention of getting serious about anyone. He and marriage didn't mix. He was better off, and much better at, short-term relationships, and Marley wanted to play for keeps.

For Marley's sake, for his sake, he needed to keep his distance. And as soon as he could get her out of this environment that made him remember his childhood and his closeness to Marley throughout those idyllic growing-up years, he'd make sure she understood that that *stuff*, that tension between them in the kitchen, hadn't meant anything.

It was hard sticking to his resolve as Carl watched Marley do her elf routine. She was a pro with the kids, sweet and funny and entertaining. But he didn't want Marley to know how impressed he was with her, so whenever she glanced at him, he made a point of glancing away and looking bored.

Later, inside the truck cab again, with Marley's empty sack folded on her lap, and Miss Hathaway holding a cellophane-wrapped plate of fudge on hers, Carl started up the engine. It sputtered and whined, but what horsepower was left in the old vehicle would hopefully be sufficient to get them home.

Carl could already feel the wall of reserve building between him and Marley. He figured she was probably having second thoughts, too, and remembering her earlier decision to write him off for good. Smart girl.

Carl looked around Marley at Miss Hathaway. "Where do you live?"

"Same place I always have," she said with a sniff. "But I guess I shouldn't expect *you* to remember."

Carl sighed. "Are you going to tell me or not, Miss Hathaway? It's not getting any warmer out here."

"Actually it is getting warmer," Miss Hathaway contradicted him. "It's going to snow."

Now she's forecasting the weather, Carl thought to himself. *She thinks she knows everything. Maybe the old gal has inhaled too much chalk dust over the years.* "Your address?" he prompted.

"I want to make one more stop before you take me home."

Carl felt like beating his head against the steering wheel. "Where would that stop be?"

"I want to go to Reindeer Pond. I want to skate."

Carl stared at her. Actually, Marley did, too.

"Are you—" Carl stopped himself.

"Crazy?" Miss Hathaway finished for him. "Aren't we all a little crazy? If we're not, we should be."

"It's too late," he argued.

"I'm barely seventy-two!"

"I mean the time!"

"But it's only six-fifteen," Miss Hathaway objected.

"It can't be," Carl said. "We were at Sheila's house for an hour or more." He flipped on the overhead light and looked at his watch. "See, it's—"

Six-fifteen. *It was only six-fifteen.*

Carl looked up and over at Miss Hathaway. She wore that impish, eerie smile she'd worn the last time they'd checked the time together. This was just too weird.

"What...what about skates?" Carl asked feebly.

"I saw several pair in the back of the truck yesterday when Harvey was unloading the staff room supplies," Marley stated, as if skates weren't at all an unusual item to carry around in the company truck. "Maybe we'll luck out and find our sizes."

Carl had no doubt that that's exactly what would happen. But luck had nothing to do with it.

Chapter Four

They pulled into the gravel parking lot at Reindeer Pond under an archway built of elk antlers. Marley had often wondered why the pond wasn't just called Elk Pond, but apparently the founding fathers had had their reasons for christening the tiny lake with a snazzier name. Besides, Christmas themes were big in Mount Joy and what could be more Christmassy than skating on Reindeer Pond?

Tonight there were fewer skaters than usual since most people were probably doing last-minute shopping or spending such a cold Christmas Eve sitting around a warm fire with their families. But the bordering lights, designed like old-fashioned street lamps, would stay on till nine o'clock as usual, along with the tiny white Christmas lights that were strung in trees and bushes along the shore.

After finding skates that exactly fitted each of them in the back of the truck—an amazing stroke of luck!—Marley sat on a bench and pulled hers on as she stared out over the frozen pond. It was beautiful with the fog drifting in patches over the glasslike surface and the Christmas lights reflecting off the ice. It was like a fairy world, just the way it was that Christmas night twenty years ago when she and Carl first learned to skate. That night had been magical...till she fell through the ice. Then Carl had come to her rescue and made everything right again.

But that was the old Carl.

Marley looked over at the bench next to her where Carl was down on one knee in front of Miss Hathaway, tying her skates while she lectured him on the best way to do it.

As she had more than once that night, Marley found herself smiling. She knew it was probably foolish to believe that the old Carl was still buried inside the gorgeous but grinchlike person he had become over the course of the past seven years. But tonight she'd seen glimpses of the old Carl. After all, he had agreed to talk about the insurance issue, and she was going to hold him to that agreement even if he tried to renege later.

That was the thing, it seemed that whenever the old Carl began to emerge, the new Carl got nervous and retreated. For instance, since the fudge episode in Sheila's kitchen, he hadn't said more than a few words to her. In turn, Marley hadn't said much to him. It was patently clear that he wasn't happy about this skating stopover en route to Miss Hathaway's...but he *had* stopped, giving in to an old lady's wishes.

Marley's smile widened. But then Miss Hathaway was a unique old lady, one you wouldn't dare say no to.

Rising to her feet, Marley clomped over on the packed snow to their bench. Now Miss Hathaway was watching and advising while Carl put on his skates. His expression was grim, as if he'd just been told he needed a root canal.

"Been awhile since you were out on the ice, Carl?" Marley inquired sweetly.

He flicked her an annoyed glance. "I don't remember the last time."

"Well, that doesn't surprise me," Miss Hathaway said tartly. "You don't remember much of anything these days."

"Do *you* remember the last time you skated, Miss Hathaway?" Carl retorted.

"Certainly. It was last Thursday. I come here every Thursday during the winter with my skating group, the SLOBs."

"The Slobs?" Carl repeated.

"Yes. Senior Ladies on Blades."

Carl was stunned and aggravated. He'd figured this particular senior lady was feeling a nostalgic yen to relive a favorite enjoyment from childhood, hence the impetuous urge to skate. He'd never suspected she did it on a regular basis, or he'd have told her she could wait till her next scheduled outing! It was Christmas Eve, for crying out loud, and he had a desk loaded with paperwork!

"Marley, wait for Carl," Miss Hathaway ordered as she sprang to her feet. "He'll need help. See you on the ice, kids!" Then, with surefooted grace, she sprinted over the snow and onto the frozen pond, gliding away like a gold medal winner at the Old Folks Olympics.

"Wow, she's good," Marley murmured.

"Why doesn't she act her age? She's going to break a hip," Carl grumbled.

"If someone breaks a bone tonight, I don't think it will be Miss Hathaway," Marley remarked, eyeing him dubiously as he struggled to his feet, then flapped his arms as he tried to gain his balance.

Carl grabbed hold of the back of the bench for support and scowled at her. "I told you it had been awhile."

Marley turned away, watching the other skaters and waving at a passing couple. "Yeah, the last time you skated was probably when a group of us went out during Christmas break our senior year of high school."

He shook his head wonderingly. "You remember the first time I skated *and* the last time. Yet it's a struggle for me to remember any of those times."

Marley turned back and met his gaze squarely. "I think that's because you've been trying to forget the bad things in your past, and in the process managed to forget all the good things, too."

"What are you, Marley, a shrink on skates?" Carl groused, breaking eye contact. "Let's get out on the ice before Miss Hathaway comes after us with her umbrella."

She sighed. "Then you'd better hold on to me for the first few minutes, otherwise you're going down."

"If I go down, you'll go down, too. I weigh considerably more than you do."

"I'm not suggesting that you use me for support, just for balance. You'll get the hang of it soon enough. It's like riding a bike, once you know how—"

"Yeah, yeah," he said gruffly. "Come over here then and let me use your shoulder for balance just till we get on the ice."

Marley scooted close enough for Carl to place his hand on her shoulder, then they walked carefully to the ice. He couldn't believe how wobbly his ankles were. He worked out regularly and jogged five times a week. He wasn't out of shape, but skating took a certain talent and technique that required practice.

"I'll be fine now," Carl told Marley as they stood at the edge of the pond. He removed his hand from Marley's shoulder and stood alone, telling himself his ankles weren't as rubbery as they felt.

"I don't know, Carl," Marley said doubtfully. "It's one thing standing, it's another thing when you actually try to move around on the ice."

"Really, I'll be fine," he insisted. "You go ahead. I'll be right behind you."

"Okay," Marley said, still sounding skeptical as she skated onto the pond, peering worriedly over her shoulder the whole time. "Just take it slow and easy," she advised him, stopping a few feet away to turn and watch. Still in her elf costume, Carl thought she looked like an escapee from the North Pole...or from the toy department of Laceys' Department Store. But cute, though. Always cute.

Carl gave her a confident smile and put one skate on the ice. His arms went up and his feet flew out from under him. Two seconds later he was sitting on the ice, looking up at Marley's suspiciously controlled face. She was trying not to laugh.

"It's not funny," Carl growled. "If I've torn these trousers, I'm sending Miss Hathaway the bill."

"Yes, it is a beautiful suit, and it would be a shame to ruin it," Marley said in a soothing voice, as if she were talking to a toddler on the verge of a tantrum. "That's why I think you should at least hold my hand till you've caught on to this skating thing again."

When Carl didn't answer right away but continued to look grim, Marley's expression changed. In a much cooler tone, she added, "Don't worry. Holding hands with you won't mislead me into thinking we're anything more than friends."

This was the closest either of them had come to alluding to "the confession." Eager to avoid a conversation remotely close to that subject, Carl immediately reached up and, with a hand from Marley, struggled to his feet.

"Now isn't this easier?" she said as they stroked forward together.

Carl had to admit it was a lot easier going duo than solo. In no time at all he had the hang of it again and would have been fine on his own, but he found himself enjoying holding hands with Marley and skirting the pond together. He'd flatly deny it if asked, but he was actually having fun, and since he could feel the cold air on his teeth, he was probably smiling and his denial wouldn't be very convincing. Anxious to hide his pleasure, which was as much a surprise to him as it would be to anyone else, he tried hard not to smile.

"You're doin' good, Carl," Marley told him. "Are you ready for some fancy stuff?"

"Fancy stuff? What do you mean? I figure I'm doing well by putting one foot in front of the other and not falling on my rear."

Marley arched a brow and smiled impishly. "Are you going to let a seventy-two-year-old woman show you up?"

As if on cue, Miss Hathaway suddenly whizzed past on one leg, the other leg and her arms lifted in a balletic pose, her umbrella held like a flag of triumph.

"But Miss Hathaway's definitely not your average senior citizen," Carl murmured, scowling at the tiny woman as she did a spin then zipped away to the other end of the pond.

"Come on, Carl, let loose a little," Marley urged, pushing forward and skating in front of him, then turning and grabbing hold of his other hand, too. "Let's do circles!"

"It appears I have no choice," Carl said, suddenly finding himself doing a spin down the middle of the pond with Marley. It was exhilarating. He couldn't help it; his traitorous lips stretched into a spontaneous smile, then he actually laughed out loud!

"That's more like it," Marley said, beaming.

Carl beamed back. Lord, she looked good, her cheeks rosy from the cold and the exercise, her eyes sparkling. Even in that dumb elf hat she was a vision.

"I'm letting go now, Carl," she informed him, abruptly releasing his hands. "I want to show you my double toe loop."

"Your double toe *what?*" Carl was balancing just fine without Marley, but he discovered he much preferred being a team. He felt bereft without Marley's hand in his, and suddenly he remembered why. For many years after Marley's fall through the ice, they'd stuck close together when they skated, frequently holding hands. It had been comforting…especially for him.

"Well, okay, it's only a *single* toe loop, but…hey…I'm no Kristi Yamaguchi. Watch me!"

And she was off, skating to the far end of the pond to build up speed for her jump. As she sped away, looking funny and cute and much younger than her twenty-eight years in her elf costume and puffy ski jacket, Carl got that sick feeling in his gut again, just like earlier when he was remembering the accident.

He watched her skate farther and farther away from him and felt an irrational fear build inside. The terror of that night twenty years ago flashed vividly through his mind.

Marley showing off. Marley's look of surprise, then horror as the ice collapsed beneath her. Carl's feeling of helplessness, then his desperate attempt to save her by lying belly-down and reaching across the brittle ice with a thin tree limb. She'd grabbed hold and hung on till her father located a rope in someone's car and lassoed her from the nearest shore.

Carl remembered her teeth chattering and her skinny arms and legs shaking like a leaf as they bundled her in blankets and rushed her into the car to take her to the hospital to be treated for hypothermia. But, most vividly of all, he remembered her parting look and smile—as much as anyone can smile when their teeth are chattering—and the words, "Th-thank you, C-Carl. Y-you saved me. Y-you're my b-best friend in the whole world."

Carl went home that night and lay in bed, staring at the ceiling for hours, contemplating what it would have been like to lose his best friend and thanking his lucky stars that he hadn't.

Now, twenty years later, Carl was contemplating the same possibility. But had he already lost Marley's friendship by freezing her out of his life for the past seven years? Or was that pure kind of friendship impossible now that they were adults and had certain needs and expectations in relationships?

Carl didn't know. All he knew for sure was that strolling down memory lane was making him think about things he was much more comfortable not thinking about. He figured the sooner he dropped off Miss

Hathaway and Marley at their respective homes and got back to the sanctuary of his office, the more comfortable he'd be...as long as he didn't fall asleep at his desk and get revisited by a sexy specter that looked just like his business partner.

Tiny chips of ice flew as Marley dug into a stop right in front of Carl, her hands clutching his shoulders to keep from falling. His arms instinctively circled her. She laughed up at him, her glowing face just inches from his.

"Did you see me? Pretty good, huh?"

Carl didn't dare tell her he hadn't seen anything because he'd been reliving the past in vivid Technicolor detail. "Yeah, you were great," he said with as much enthusiasm as he could muster.

She looked at him suspiciously, her smile fading. "What's the matter, Carl?"

He shrugged, carefully eased his arms from around her and took a step back. "I just think it's time to go."

She looked disappointed. "I thought you were having fun."

"I was, but—" Abruptly Carl asked what was uppermost on his mind. "Marley, does it ever bother you to come here?"

"What do you mean?"

"Well, you nearly drowned here once."

"That was a long time ago, Carl. It's not the only memory I have of this place. I'm certainly not going to let one admittedly horrible skating episode turn me away from skating forever. I'd just be depriving myself of something I really enjoy. Besides, you have to take risks in life or you don't really live...you know what I mean?"

Carl knew only too well what she meant, and he caught all the double meanings in her words. She was comparing nearly drowning with getting jilted at the altar, and she was giving him a broad hint to not let one catastrophe with a woman sour him on the whole sex. But he was in no mood for hokey analogies and tired platitudes.

"I see you've turned back into the shrink on skates," Carl drawled. "Now I'm positive it's time to go home."

Marley stared at him for a few seconds, a hurt look in her eyes. Then the hurt look turned hard and cynical and tired. "You're right, Carl," she said coolly. "It's time to go home." Then she turned her back on him and skated to shore, sat down on a bench and bent down to untie her skates.

"Upset her again, I see," said Miss Hathaway's voice from behind him. "You've got a real knack for hurting the people who love you, Carl Merrick."

Angry and frustrated, Carl turned to face his tiny tormentor. "How do you know who loves me and who doesn't, Miss Hathaway? And what business is it of yours anyway?"

"It's my business to show you the person you used to be, Carl," she said sternly. "It's part of the plan."

"What plan?"

"The plan to redeem you."

"From what?"

"From your current life of bitterness and cynicism."

Carl gave a huff of sheer exasperation. "I don't see you for years, Miss Hathaway, then you pop up suddenly at my office determined to redeem me? Who elected you my personal savior?"

"The Powers That Be."

Carl shook his head, incredulous. "What kind of nonsense are we talking here? I must still be dreaming!"

"This isn't a dream. This is your Christmas miracle, Carl."

"I don't believe in miracles."

"Well, it won't be a miracle anyway if you don't get with the program. You don't have all night, Carl." She vigorously tapped the face of her wristwatch with her index finger. "Just till nine o'clock!"

Carl glanced at his own watch. It read six-twenty. Even though he knew they had to have been at the pond for at least a half hour, according to his watch only five minutes had passed. But these strange time discrepancies no longer surprised Carl. He didn't even bother to ask what Miss Hathaway's watch read. He knew it would show the same time as his. What did surprise him was that the crazy dream he was having just went on and on and seemed so damned real!

"I may not have all night," Carl said dryly, "but it's going to seem that way. Time has slowed to a snail's crawl."

"It's a good thing, too," Miss Hathaway responded with a snap of her head. "Count your lucky stars, Carl, just like you did that night when you and Marley's father saved her from drowning. Believe me, a hardened case like yours needs the extra time."

Carl narrowed his eyes and peered at the little woman. "How did you know—? Oh, hell, never mind! Why am I bothering to argue with what has to be a mere figment of my imagination anyway?"

With no warning, Miss Hathaway jabbed Carl in the leg with her umbrella.

"Ouch! What the—?"

"There! Did that feel like your imagination? That's for swearing! Now, if you don't mind, this *figment* would like to be driven home. There's a Lawrence Welk rerun on at six-thirty and I like doing my aerobics to it."

Carl rubbed his sore leg and frowned at Miss Hathaway. He gestured toward the shore. "After you, ma'am."

She sniffed disdainfully. "You first, Carl. I like keepin' my eye on you."

"Oh, no, Miss Hathaway, I *insist*," Carl said with exaggerated politeness, warily keeping his eye on her umbrella. "Ladies must always go first." *Especially when they brandish dangerous accessories.*

She shrugged, then stiffened her back, lifted her chin and skated with dignity to the shore. Sighing heavily, Carl followed, wishing with all his heart that he'd wake up from this Christmas nightmare. But, as he quickly realized when he reached Marley's bench and found a man in a dove-gray overcoat on his knees helping her with her skates, the nightmare was far from over.

"Cosgrove! What are you doing here?"

"Oh, hello," Stewart said, lifting his gaze from his task long enough to smile at Carl. "I was just passing by—"

Passing by? On Route 12, the highway that leads nowhere but out of town?

"—and I decided I'd like to skate." He smiled up at Marley as he finished unraveling her laces with an efficiency that even Carl could appreciate. "I was hoping to have other plans for the evening, but I ended up on my own."

Carl noticed that Marley was blushing. "Thanks for fixing my laces, Stewart. I'd made a mess out of them. And...and I'm sorry you're on your own. Christmas Eve is a difficult time to-to—"

"Oh, it's turning out better than I thought it would," Stewart said cheerfully. "I've been shopping and caroling and I'm going to the hospital after I'm done skating."

"You're a busy guy, Cosgrove," Carl said dryly.

"I don't believe in wasting a single second, especially at this time of year." He stood up, propped his fists on his hips and took a deep breath. "I smell snow. Isn't this weather great? I love winter, and I *love* Christmas."

And I'd love to sock you in the nose, Carl thought to himself. Stewart was a Pollyanna if he'd ever seen one.

"Are you going to see Mark while you're up there, Stewart?" Miss Hathaway inquired from the adjacent bench where she was busily removing her skates.

Carl's head swiveled as he looked at Miss Hathaway and Stewart. "You two know each other?"

"We both belong to a volunteers group that routinely visits the children's ward at St. Joseph's Hospital." Stewart smiled down at Miss Hathaway. "Mark won't be there tonight. He responded so well to that last round of chemotherapy they let him go home till after the holidays."

Miss Hathaway clapped her hands. "Oh, that's wonderful!"

"Isn't it? By the way, do you need some help with those skates, Miss Hathaway?"

Miss Hathaway turned to give Carl a withering look,

then turned back to Stewart with a beaming smile. "No, Stewart, I'm fine. But *thanks for asking.*"

With a helping hand from Stewart, who seemed more than eager to assist her, Marley stood up. Her skates were off and her thick-soled elf slippers were back on.

"I thought you were in a hurry to get back to the office, Carl?" she said, looking pointedly at his skates. "You're the only one still shod for ice."

Embarrassed, Carl looked down at his skates. He'd been so involved with watching Stewart's excessively gallant behavior with the ladies, he'd forgotten to take them off. "I'll be ready in a jiff," he promised, sitting down and getting busy.

"We'll wait in the truck," Miss Hathaway informed him, and she and Marley and Stewart walked away. Carl struggled with his skates and watched them over his shoulder. Stewart had stepped between them and taken their arms in a gentlemanly gesture. Carl frowned.

So what was the deal? he wondered. Was Stewart Cosgrove putting the moves on Marley? But even if he were, what business was it of Carl's? After all, *he* didn't want a romantic relationship with her. So, why did he feel so...so...grumpy?

AFTER STEWART SAID goodbye and headed for the pond, Marley and Miss Hathaway and Carl climbed into the truck. Seeming to understand that Marley no longer wished to sit in the middle, Miss Hathaway got in first. Then, after snapping out directions to her house, she stared straight ahead, leaving Marley the luxury of hugging the passenger side door and brooding silently.

It was strange the way Stewart had showed up seemingly out of nowhere to help her. She'd been so angry and disappointed with Carl, she'd made a hopeless snarl out of her laces. Then there was Stewart, patient and cheerful and charming...everything Carl wasn't. So, why did she still want Carl?

Maybe she was masochistic. After all, she could have spent the evening with Stewart. He'd invited her to. And the two dates they'd already had were fun. Trouble was, when he'd walked her to the door and kissed her after the second date, although she'd felt something, she hadn't felt enough. She hadn't felt the way she knew she'd feel if Carl kissed her, and that was disappointing. She would have welcomed feeling something for someone who actually appreciated her as a woman, as well as a business associate.

Though the trip to Miss Hathaway's house seemed no longer than the blink of an eye, Marley still had plenty of time to chastise herself for getting her hopes up about Carl. It should be abundantly clear to her by now that he really was a hopeless case. But all he had to do was smile or laugh, showing a vestige of his former self, and she was giddy with happiness. Clenching her jaw, she promised herself that she wasn't going to let that happen again.

Even without directions, it would have been pretty hard to miss Miss Hathaway's house. Hundreds of lights covered what appeared to be an unassuming turn-of-the-century bungalow. Not a window, nor a bush in the yard, went unadorned, and, after witnessing Miss Hathaway's energy and physical strength as she skated on Reindeer Pond, Carl wouldn't have been surprised to learn she'd done all the work herself.

In addition to the lights, there was a Santa, a sled

and ten reindeer on the roof, a manger scene on the lawn, and Hanukkah candles in the window. Miss Hathaway seemed anxious to cover all the cultural bases. Carl chalked this up to her career as a teacher, and, perhaps, her broadmindedness as a person. But it seemed like a lot of unnecessary work to him. In a week it would all have to be taken down, unless Miss Hathaway was one of those irritating diehards who kept their Christmas decorations up till Valentine's Day.

"I'll walk you to your door, Miss Hathaway," he said, well aware she didn't need assistance but wanting to show at least as much courtesy to her as Stewart had.

"Yes, you will, young man," Miss Hathaway returned, "and into the house, too. I've got something to show you and Marley."

Carl knew it would be futile, as well as time-consuming, to argue. He still wanted to get some paperwork done that night, so he figured it was in his best interests to go with the flow. He attended Miss Hathaway, and a sullen Marley, up the lighted sidewalk to the front door.

As soon as they stepped inside, Carl's mouth nearly fell open at the sight of a Christmas tree that was so large it practically filled the small front parlor with its sweeping branches. And it was so tall, the angel on top came less than an inch from grazing the old-fashioned high ceiling of the house.

Despite himself, Carl was drawn to the tree and, without consciously meaning to, he stepped close to it and stared.

The amount of multicolored lights that covered the tree was dazzling, but the things that fascinated Carl the most were the ornaments. They were all delicate, filigreed stars. And somehow attached to the center of each star was a picture of a child. The tree held dozens and dozens of different wallet-size photos of smiling children.

There were little boys with buzz cuts and bowl cuts and mohawks and slicked down "Leave It to Beaver" cuts. They wore sweaters and button-down shirts and T-shirts and sweatshirts, and there were even a few wearing ties.

The girls had ponytails, pigtails, home perms and pageboys. They wore Peter Pan collars and puffed sleeves and turtlenecks and ginghams. And of course, like the boys, they wore T-shirts, too.

Carl turned to look at Marley, who seemed as awed by the tree as he was. She had come to stand beside him and was simply staring, her eyes glowing with interest and delight.

"Oh, Miss Hathaway," she whispered in a low, reverent tone. "Your tree is so beautiful."

Carl looked at Miss Hathaway, who wasn't looking at them but at the tree, her faded eyes beaming with pride and love. "These are my stars. All the children I taught for forty-five years as a second-grade teacher are on this tree. Mind you, they weren't all *stellar* students—" she twinkled at her little joke "—but there was something special about each one."

"How did you do it?" Carl asked.

"You mean how did I get all the pictures? It was simple. Whenever school pictures were taken, I asked the class to get permission from their parents to give me one to remember them by. Don't you remember giving me your picture, Carl?"

"I remember," Marley spoke up. "But I figured it

was put away in a box with a bunch of other pictures, or slotted in a scrapbook and tucked away on a shelf somewhere. I had no idea you'd do something this beautiful with it...and with all the others. Hey, look, Carl, there's Sheila!''

Carl looked. Yep. That was Sheila all right, with the carrot-red pigtails and the mischievous eyes.

''But where am I, Miss Hathaway?'' Marley asked eagerly. ''And where's Carl?''

Miss Hathaway moved to the tree and pointed. ''There you are, the two of you, up close to the angel. It's too high for me to reach without a ladder. I put you there, Marley, because you've always loved angels so much. I remember that antique angel you brought for show-and-tell at Christmastime.''

''Yes, my great-grandmother's,'' Marley murmured, a reminiscent smile on her lips.

''And, since you and Carl were inseparable in the second grade, and all through elementary school from what I could see, I naturally put him right next to you.''

Carl looked to where Miss Hathaway had pointed. Sure enough, there he was in a striped T-shirt, freckled and grinning, his hair slicked over in the front and sticking up in the back as if he'd done a hasty spit job to tidy himself for the picture taking.

Right next to his star was Marley's star, her blond hair neatly combed for a change, but her irrepressible dimples and her Chiclet teeth just the way he remembered them. Looking at that impish smile, Carl felt a sharp pang of remembrance, of longing for those simpler, happier times.

''What a wonderful way to remember your students," Marley said, turning to smile warmly at Miss Hathaway.

"I'd keep the tree up all year if I could." Miss Hathaway darted a sly look Carl's way. "But I'm not one of those 'die-hard' types who keep their decorations up till Valentine's Day."

Carl frowned. Could everyone in this crazy dream read his mind?

"The best part of Christmas is the remembering part," Miss Hathaway went on, fondly admiring her tree. "And anyone who has good things to remember is lucky. Happy memories should be cherished and celebrated every year. Every day, really."

After this little greeting-card speech, Miss Hathaway fell silent and stood looking at her tree. Marley was looking at the tree, too, her eyes shiny with emotion. It was a sentimental moment that even Carl could appreciate, because the sentiments that had been expressed were apparently genuine.

But Carl didn't want to feel sentimental. He didn't want to feel anything. He'd made it through Christmas for the past seven years by suppressing the emotions that had got him into trouble in the first place. Emotions made a person vulnerable, so damned vulnerable one could end up dressed in a monkey suit, wearing holly in a buttonhole and standing at an altar banked by rows of cheerful poinsettia plants...alone. Completely alone. And feeling like the biggest fool in the world.

"It's time to go."

Carl was startled when he realized it wasn't he who said the parting words, but Miss Hathaway. He looked at her and saw a knowing, kindly expression in her eyes, an expression, moreover, that he'd hardly ex-

pected from a woman who had been on his case all
evening and had even jabbed him with her umbrella.

"It's almost time for Lawrence Welk," Miss Hathaway announced briskly, the sympathetic expression
on her face suddenly disappearing. "I don't mean to
rush you kids, but I know you've got better things to
do on Christmas Eve than jaw the hours away with
me. Out with you! After my 'champagne music' aerobics, I've got presents to wrap for sixteen grandnieces
and nephews! Going to my sister's house tomorrow
afternoon, right after dinner at the Merricks."

"You, too?" Carl drawled.

"Yes, your mother saw me in the store the other
day and impulsively invited me. She's such a dear
woman! Too bad her only son can't be bothered to
drop by! Now ta-ta you two!"

After a flurry of talk and gentle pushes, a hasty hug
and cheerful calls of "Merry Christmas" between
Marley and Miss Hathaway, Carl suddenly found himself behind the wheel of the company truck again and
alone with Marley. He gulped. *Alone with Marley.*
Miss Hathaway had swept out of his dream as abruptly
as she'd entered it, leaving him in a situation fraught
with temptation.

Ignoring Marley—or at least trying to—wishing
again that he'd wake up at his desk, and thinking that
if he somehow managed to get there in his dream he
could get there in reality, too, Carl fitted the key in
the ignition and started the truck. Or, rather, he tried
to start the truck. The lights flickered and the motor
coughed and sputtered and whined, but that was as
good as it got.

"Oh dear," said Marley. "It sounds like the battery

has finally sparked its last engine.'' There was a pause. "And it's snowing, too.''

With fatalistic calm, Carl watched the snowflakes drift onto the windshield and slide to a building mound at the bottom. "I didn't see any jumper cables in the back of the truck when we got the skates out, did you?'' Damn, he could smell her perfume again.

"No, I didn't.''

"But then why would there be jumper cables?'' Carl muttered sarcastically, more to himself than to Marley. "Skates are a much more practical thing to carry around in your vehicle.'' Then, to Marley, he said, "Did you bring your cellular?''

"No. I gather you didn't, either.''

"I didn't think I'd be away from my desk for more than ten minutes.'' A picture of Marley in that black teddy kept creeping into his mind. Carl shook his head to clear it. The *engine* needed a jump-start, not his heart rate.

"Then we'd better—''

"I'm not asking to use Miss Hathaway's phone,'' he warned her. "There's no way I'm going to interrupt her in the middle of her champagne music aerobics.''

"Then what are we going to do?''

"Wait for Santa to come along and rescue us in his sleigh, I guess,'' Carl answered with a desperate sort of sarcasm. *Or slit my wrists. Or at least tie them together so my hands won't reach for you.* "Or, better still, why don't I walk down to the minimart on the corner of Route 12 and—''

Marley held up her hand, her expression arrested. "Wait. I hear something. It sounds like...sleigh bells.''

Carl laughed. "Yeah. Right.'' He was looking forward to that jaunt to the minimart. In lieu of a cold shower, it would have to do.

"No, really…"

"Marley, don't be silly. I don't hear anything."

Ho, ho, ho!

Uh-oh. He heard *that*. Hell…what now?

Chapter Five

Marley rolled down the window and looked around the boxy back end of the truck. "Someone's parked behind us, Carl."

"What? I didn't hear a motor. All I heard was—"

Ho, ho, ho!

In the dim light that shone through the windshield, Marley and Carl exchanged incredulous glances. "Yes, I heard it, too," she whispered. "Isn't it amazing, Carl? You make a joke about Santa rescuing us, then he suddenly shows up."

"Santa, *Shmanta*. It's probably some drunk in a rented suit. Any nut can dress up like an elf." He slid his gaze over Marley's costume and she gazed back defiantly. "And Santa, the biggest elf of them all, shows up on every street corner this time of year. But, what the heck, he might be able to jump-start us."

He opened the door and got out to determine who their jolly visitor was. As he walked around the back of the truck he discovered that their visitor had every reason to be jolly. He was driving the prettiest restored candy-apple red 1955 Chevy convertible Carl had ever seen. The fenders shone, the chrome gleamed in the light from the street lamp directly overhead, and the driver—a big man in a Santa suit, just as Carl had expected—smiled expansively, pink lips and a row of white teeth showing through a phoney white beard attached to his ears with rubber bands.

"Ho, ho, hellooo, Carl!" the man said in a deep, booming voice. He reached up and gave a yank to the string of jingle bells that hung from his rearview mirror.

Carl just stared at him. Twinkling blue eyes stared back from under bushy white eyebrows and a white wig that looked like glued-together cotton from about a hundred aspirin bottles. How did the old guy know who he was? And, more importantly, why didn't he put up his top? It was snowing, for crying out loud!

"Cat got your tongue, son?"

Carl scowled. "Why does everyone ask me that?"

"Well, I'm askin' 'cause you're just standing there staring at me when you oughta be giving me a hug or a handshake at the very least." The man spread his arms wide. "Don't you recognize me?"

There was something familiar about the man, but how could anyone tell who he was beneath all that phoney facial hair?

By now Marley had climbed out of the truck and was standing next to Carl. She took one look at Santa and her lips curved in a huge smile. "Uncle Ralph!"

"Uncle Ralph?" Carl repeated.

"Marley, honey!" Santa opened the car door and heaved himself to his booted feet. "Why, you sweet thing, come over here and give Uncle Ralph a big hug!"

Carl stood and watched, his hands stuffed in his pockets and a frown on his face, as his Uncle Ralph—used car salesman extraordinaire, renowned throughout New England for his wacky television commercials—drew Marley into his arms and lifted her off her feet in a huge hug. As big and burly as Uncle Ralph was, his substantial girth eliminating the need for padding the Santa suit, Carl just hoped he wouldn't crush Marley between those beefy arms of his. But when he finally set Marley on her feet again, she didn't look crushed, she just looked happy as ants in sugar.

"Fancy running into you in an elf suit while I'm in this," he said, beaming down at her. "A couple of weeks ago I taped a commercial for my car lot in Montpelier. You know the spiel, 'Santa'll get ya the best deal in town. Buy your sweetie a Cadillac for Christmas!'"

"Yes! I saw it."

"Well, I took a fancy to the Santa suit and decided to keep it, then thought I'd wear it when I drove up here to see the clan."

"With the top down the whole way? Weren't you freezing?"

"Santa's supposed to have rosy cheeks, ain't 'e? You should have seen the looks on the kids' faces as I drove past or had to stop beside them at a red light. It was worth every chilly breeze that whizzed down my neck! Say, I saw you in a commercial, too, Marley! You and that good-looking fella were very convincing as a pair."

"What good-looking fellow? What kind of 'pair'?" Carl asked, but they ignored him. Maybe he was going to have to view the commercial after all, no matter how sentimental it was.

"You going to wear that getup to Christmas dinner

tomorrow?'' Ralph continued. ''I'm thinking about wearin' mine.''

''No. I think I've spent enough time in this outfit for one year. Besides, I don't want Carl's folks to think I'm too off-the-wall. They might not invite me back.''

Ralph leaned forward and whispered conspiratorially, ''Well, hell, they invite *me* back every year, don't they?'' Then he bent backward and laughed so loud and hard, his midsection shook like...well...a bowl full of jelly.

''But you're family, Uncle Ralph,'' Marley said, laughing with him. ''You could never be excluded. Besides, they love you.''

''You're family, too, Marley, honey, and everyone loves you to death. I can't wait for a piece of Martha's mincemeat pie, can you?''

''It's thinking about the turkey and the mashed potatoes and gravy that makes my mouth water,'' Marley confessed.

''What about those homemade caramels...ummmm! I think Bessie gets better every year at making those yummy little goodies just melt in your—''

''Excuse me,'' Carl interrupted loudly, exasperated and feeling slightly left out. ''I hate to stop you in the middle of your bite-by-bite replay of last year's culinary delights at my folks' house, but it's freezing cold out here and snowing, your car upholstery is getting wet, and my truck won't start. Have you got jumper cables, Uncle Ralph?''

Marley curved a thumb in Carl's direction and smiled wryly at Uncle Ralph. ''Party pooper.''

Uncle Ralph laughed and grabbed hold of Carl's hand, shaking it heartily. He grinned at Carl for some time, then, as if he couldn't help it, pulled him into a manly hug and thumped him soundly on the back. "Didn't mean to ignore you, Carl. Hell, boy, it's been a coon's age since I saw you last. When I saw this truck sitting by the side of the road, with the Little Angel logo on the back, its lights flickering funny-like, I wondered if it might be you. I've missed seein' you at the family gatherings."

"Well, I've been busy," Carl said dismissively. "Now what about those jumper—"

"Like my car, do ya?" He turned and smiled proudly at the convertible.

"Yes, but the upholstery's going to be ruined if you don't put up the top."

"It's vinyl, boy. Gen-u-ine vinyl. The snow won't hurt it much, but you're right, I'd better put up the top. Soon as I wipe off the seats, you two can jump in."

"Does that mean you don't have jumper cables?" Carl asked in a beleaguered tone.

Uncle Ralph pushed aside the beard and rubbed his chin. "I've got my suitcase in the trunk and...oh, yes...a pair of ice skates, but no cables."

"Figures," Carl mumbled.

While Uncle Ralph put up the top on the convertible and wiped off the seats, Carl stood morosely alongside Marley, neither of them saying a word. He wasn't sure if he was glad Uncle Ralph had rescued them or not. Running into a relative was bound to complicate things. Uncle Ralph would probably try to talk him into going to his folks' for Christmas dinner and he'd have to stumble through his excuses with Marley as a witness.

"Get in, get in!" Uncle Ralph shouted to them

through the window. "I've got the heater on full blast! We'll be snug as bugs in a rug!"

Marley scooted to the middle of the front seat and Carl slid in beside her, staying as near the door as he could. Sitting close to Marley, particularly since he'd started remembering all the happy times they'd shared together, had become a tormenting test of willpower. He wanted to touch her, kiss her....

"You might as well forget about the truck for tonight, Carl," his uncle said, interrupting Carl's wayward thoughts. "No use bothering folks about jumper cables on Christmas Eve, and, besides, the snow's coming down real hard now. Best to get home and stay put."

Home. That was sounding better and better to Carl. He wouldn't even mind putting off his paperwork till tomorrow if he could somehow just get away from Marley and all the sentimental memories that kept springing to mind since Miss Hathaway had forced him on a trip down memory lane.

"Take Marley home first," Carl suggested.

"I will, but—I hope you kids don't mind—before I take either of you home, I'd best stop by the Putnam Road Inn."

Carl couldn't believe it—another delay! "Why?" he asked with admirable control.

"I've got a reservation for a room there tonight, but I have to check in by six-fifteen or they'll give it away to the first walk-in that comes along."

Carl had to bite his tongue to keep from swearing. "Do you really think there are going to be a lot of walk-ins on Christmas Eve? How soon will it be six-fifteen?"

"Don't you have a watch, son?"

"Apparently not one that keeps reliable time," he answered dryly.

"It's six-ten. I've got five minutes."

"Six-ten," Carl repeated, then he looked keenly at Marley for her reaction. She looked back at him questioningly, not appearing the least aware of all the time discrepancies.

Frustrated, Carl said, "Uncle Ralph, haven't you ever heard of using your credit card to hold your reservation?"

"Don't use credit cards. Only use cash."

"You could stay at Mom and Dad's house."

"They've got a full house already, Carl." Leaning forward and peering around Marley, he asked, "Why? You in a hurry to be somewhere?"

"No," Carl said resignedly. "I'm in no hurry to be anywhere."

YEAH, RIGHT, MARLEY thought to herself. Of course Carl was in a hurry. He was in a hurry to be anywhere she wasn't. She could read his body language. Without actually hanging out the window, he was as close to the car door as he could possibly be.

Marley sighed and absently watched the snow drifting against the windshield. It had been a strange day. So much had happened since she'd confronted Carl in his office, and most of it just in the past hour. One minute she was filled with hope that Carl was being influenced for the better by the memories Miss Hathaway's presence seemed to invoke, and the next minute she was wishing she'd accepted Stewart Cosgrove's invitation to spend Christmas Eve with him, even if he didn't make her feel all goose bumpy when they kissed. Maybe goose bumps were overrated.

Ironically enough, Carl didn't appear to like Stewart. He'd never said so, but he didn't have to. She wished his antipathy had something to do with Carl noticing Stewart's interest in her and being jealous, but she suspected Carl didn't like Stewart simply because the two men were so different personality-wise. Stewart was the way Carl used to be. Cheerful and charming.

"Here we are," Uncle Ralph announced with satisfaction as he pulled the car in front of the Putnam Road Inn and killed the engine. "Just in time to check in and change for dinner."

"Uncle Ralph, I thought you were going to drive us home as soon as you checked in?" Carl said, obviously irritated.

"And send you home to eat canned soup, Carl? I'll drive you home afterward."

Marley sneaked at look at Carl's profile, faintly outlined by the porch lights of the inn. His jaw was clenched, his lips thinned to a grim line. "I wasn't worried about dinner, Uncle Ralph. What I really wanted to do tonight was get back to the office and finish some paperwork."

"On Christmas Eve? Not as long as I have something to say about it. I haven't seen you for seven years and, by damn, I'm goin' to feed ya, son. Dinner's on me."

Carl voiced no further objections, although it was as plain as the frown on his face that he wasn't happy about the situation. But, judging by the grin on Uncle Ralph's face, he was oblivious to Carl's displeasure and looking forward to a pleasant meal and a catching-up conversation.

"Is this all right with you, Marley, honey?" Uncle

Ralph suddenly inquired, seemingly as an after-thought. "Or do you need to skedaddle home for something...or someone."

To Marley's surprise, Carl looked at her, too, as if he wondered the same thing and was actually inter-ested in her answer. Unable to resist such an oppor-tunity she answered offhandedly, "Well, a man from the office did ask me out for dinner and shopping, but I begged off. I'm free all evening and would be de-lighted to—"

"What man from the office?" Carl interrupted, his brows furrowed. "Not...Cosgrove?"

Marley shrugged nonchalantly. "Yes...*Cosgrove*. Stewart Cosgrove. How'd you guess?"

"Maybe it was the way he was falling all over him-self at the pond trying to impress you."

"I wouldn't go by that. He's sweet and polite to everyone, and all the time. Some people actually enjoy being pleasant, Carl."

"What a paragon," Carl snarled. "So, why'd he ask *you* out?"

Highly offended, Marley was about to reply angrily when Uncle Ralph intervened. He was laughing. "Good God, son, how can you ask such a question? He asked her out 'cause she's cute as a bug and avail-able, that's why. If I was thirty years younger and thirty pounds thinner, I'd be askin' her out, too." Then he winked at her.

Flattered and pleased by Uncle Ralph's answer, Marley smiled back at him, but she was more exas-perated than ever with Carl. Did he think that just because he didn't find her attractive, no one else did? The nerve!

"Marley, do I know this fella, Stewart Cosgrove?" Uncle Ralph asked.

"You've probably never met him, but you've seen him before," Marley answered. "He's the man in the Little Angel Christmas Card commercial with me."

"What?" Carl exclaimed. "I was aware you two worked together on the commercial...after all, that's part of your job at Little Angel...but I wasn't aware he was *in* the commercial, too."

"Well," Marley began in a haughty tone, "maybe if you'd turn on your television once in a while, or if you'd viewed the commercial with the rest of the staff, you'd know these things."

"You know I don't watch television during the holidays, and I trusted you to do a good job on the commercial without getting myself involved...even when you suddenly decided to pass on hiring a professional actress and took on the female role for yourself. But Cosgrove, too?"

"He did a great job."

"I'm sure he did," he said sarcastically. "He does everything so well. But even if I had viewed the commercial, I would have been no judge at all of the final product. You know how that sentimental Christmas stuff turns my stomach."

Marley shrugged again. "With a head-in-the-sand attitude like that, Carl, you're bound to be surprised now and then."

Carl grunted and fell silent.

After a few seconds, Ralph piped up, saying, "Well, this fella Stewart Cosgrove's misfortune is our gain, m'dear." He patted Marley's hand. "I'm glad you're here with us...and so's Carl, despite his, er, unique way of showing it. Now let's get inside before we freeze to death. I'll grab my suitcase from the trunk and meet you kids in the lobby.''

Observing Carl's deteriorated mood, which hadn't been good to begin with, Marley wasn't sure how the evening would turn out, but she was curious to see the inside of the Putnam Road Inn, which had been renovated a year and a half ago by a New York restaurateur who had fled the big city for the peace and beauty of Vermont. If nothing else, she would enjoy Uncle Ralph's company and a good meal. She was tired of letting Carl's crummy attitude depress her.

Walking up the steps of the turn-of-the century fieldstone and gray clapboard mansion, the dormer and bay windows glowing with light, Marley suddenly remembered that she was still wearing her elf costume! Forgetting her anger, she turned impetuously to Carl and blurted, ''I can't eat in this elegant inn—and on Christmas Eve, no less—wearing an elf costume!''

Carl smirked. ''Why not? You look very festive.''

''I should have known I wouldn't get any sympathy from you!''

''There's a small boutique inside, Marley,'' Uncle Ralph said as he came up behind them clutching his suitcase. ''Sells fancy little presents and a few of the nicer bits of lady's attire. Antique finery, too, I hear. Might have a dress to fit you. If it's closed, maybe I can sweet-talk the owner into loaning you something.''

''Sounds like you've been here before,'' Carl suggested, eyeing his uncle suspiciously.

''Of course I've been here before,'' Ralph breezily replied. ''Now get inside, you two.''

Opening the door, they found themselves in a wide hall papered in red toile. To their left was a Victorian settee upholstered in moss green velvet and damask where a young couple sat, totally absorbed in each other. To their right was a spindled staircase flanked by fair-haired angels constructed of crinkle paper and decorated with gilded ribbon. The banisters were festooned with pine garlands tied with red velvet ribbon. The hardwood floors were covered with Oriental rugs, and the air was filled with the aroma of delicious food.

"Ralph!"

They all turned as a sixtyish woman walked into the hall through an arched doorway, beyond which Marley caught a tantalizing glimpse of an ornate fireplace with a large marble mantel, a blazing fire, and a tall Christmas tree glittering in lights and decorations.

"Nadine! How'd you recognize me underneath this getup?"

"I'd know you anywhere, Ralph Merrick," she informed him, stepping on tiptoe to kiss him on the cheek. "I've seen your Santa commercial! Besides, how could I not recognize the best free PR man this place has ever had? So many people have come here because of your recommendations! When it started to snow, I was afraid you'd be delayed and miss dinner."

"Not on your life," Ralph declared. "When you told me on the phone you were serving your famous grilled duck breast with wild mushrooms tonight, nothing could keep me away."

Marley slid a look at Carl. It was patently clear that Uncle Ralph had been in no danger whatsoever of losing his reservation. He was obviously well-known and well-liked by the owner...which was who she assumed the woman was. But exactly how well did Uncle Ralph know her?

Carl was a bit white about the mouth and a muscle

ticked in his jaw, but he otherwise maintained a composed appearance, so Marley turned her attention back to the woman. She was tall and slim, simply but elegantly dressed in an off-white, long-sleeved blouse and a straight black skirt. Her silver hair was tucked into a sleek chignon and her makeup was impeccably and discreetly applied. The beautiful brooch at her neck and her earrings looked like antiques.

"This is Nadine Wimmer, the owner of this wonderful establishment," Uncle Ralph announced. "Nadine, this is my nephew, Carl Merrick, and Marley Jacobs is a close friend of the family. They're having dinner with me tonight."

Carl, always at least outwardly polite despite whatever swearing might be going on inside his head, smiled and shook hands. Marley did likewise, then blushed as she remembered how strange she must look to this stylish woman.

"Ralph said you had a boutique," she said. "I'd love to find something more appropriate to wear to dinner."

Nadine's warm smile dispelled Marley's embarrassment. "I think you look charming already. But I'm sure we could find something you'd feel more comfortable in."

She turned to Ralph. "You go ahead to your room, Ralph. It's the one you prefer...the green room at the top of the stairs. While you and Carl freshen up for dinner, I'll show Marley what I have in the boutique and take her to my room to change. She'll meet you in the private dining parlor at the end of the hall at six forty-five precisely."

Ralph grinned and nodded, throwing Marley another encouraging wink. Carl stared at her and said nothing, leaving her with absolutely no idea what he was thinking. But maybe that was for the best since he was probably obsessing about the paperwork he'd left on his desk and wishing he was anywhere else.

But that wasn't going to bother her, Marley decided, glancing defiantly over her shoulder at him as she walked away with Nadine. She couldn't resist; she smirked and threw him a kiss. It had its desired effect: he scowled even harder.

AT SIX FORTY-FIVE, after making use of the shower and the complimentary toiletries, Carl was seated in the private dining room with his uncle, obsessing about Marley and Stewart Cosgrove. He couldn't help it. *Stewart Cosgrove!* That guy couldn't be for real. He was too nice, too smooth, too *everything*.

"Isn't this a beautiful table and a beautiful room, Carl?"

With an effort, Carl turned his attention to his uncle. Ralph had changed out of his Santa suit and, except for less hair and a wider waistline, was looking a lot more the way Carl remembered him. He was older than his father and had a more flamboyant taste in clothing. For example, tonight, in honor of the season, he was wearing a green-and-red-plaid jacket—well made but loud—black trousers and black patent leather shoes. His silver hair was pomaded and slicked back from his receding hairline and the buttonhole on his lapel sported a huge red carnation.

"The table, Carl? The room?"

Carl gave his immediate surroundings a cursory look over. They were seated at a round table that was covered with white linen and fine china that sported a holly motif. A brace of three long white candles formed the centerpiece.

He looked around grudgingly at the room. It was big for a dining parlor, full of polished antique furniture and dressed to the hilt for Christmas. The fireplace had a carved mahogany mantel draped with pine garlands, velvet bows and strings of cranberries, and held a pair of gilt and crystal girandoles. Hanging on the wall were a couple of brass horns that had been made into wreaths with sprays of pine. In the corner, an antique rocking horse sat in front of a tall Christmas tree loaded down with old-fashioned ornaments. Carl had noticed that there were trees all over the inn…at least everywhere he'd been. It was damned oppressive.

"If you like Christmas and you like antiques, I suppose it's a nice room," Carl grumbled. He took a drink of water from a crystal tumbler and added, "That counts me out, but Marley'll love it."

"What a sweet girl she is," Uncle Ralph mused as he absently played with the intricately folded red napkin on his plate. Then he suddenly looked up at Carl, his gaze keen, a candle flame reflected in each pupil. "It's a damned shame she's got her heart set on an old humbug like you, Carl."

That last comment came out of the blue. Carl set down his water and met his uncle's gaze squarely. "What do you think you know about Marley and me?"

Uncle Ralph smiled sweetly. "I don't think—I know. I know everything."

"The hell you say—"

"And I'm here, Carl, to help you see that there's no time like the present. Every day is precious and you're wasting time, son."

Carl glared suspiciously at his uncle. "By any chance, you weren't sent here by 'The Powers That Be,' were you?"

Ralph's smile grew broader, brighter. So bright, in fact, Carl was nearly dazzled. He blinked against the brilliance of his uncle's smile. "You're finally catching on, Carl," he said at last.

Carl shook his head and gulped another swallow of water, his throat suddenly dry as a desert. "No, I don't believe you. This is just a dream. Just a stupid dream."

Ralph sighed and reached inside his jacket. "You're a tough nut to crack, Carl, but I think I've got something that will help loosen you up a bit. Marley's coming down the stairs even as we speak, and that lovely girl deserves a pleasant dinner companion. That won't happen, though, if you keep acting like a jackass." He leaned forward and tilted a clear liquid from a flask into Carl's water glass.

Carl was irate. "How do you know where Marley is 'even as we speak'? Have you got X-ray vision like Superman, Uncle Ralph? And what the hell did you put in my glass? We're having wine with dinner, so I definitely don't need my water spiked with vodka!" Besides he suddenly seemed besieged by an unquenchable thirst and he wanted nothing more than to drink another couple of glasses of pure, undoctored water.

"It's not vodka, Carl, or any other kind of alcoholic beverage. It's what I call 'the elixir of life.' It's a little potable I whip up in my bathtub twice a year. It makes you feel strange at first, but then you feel wonderful."

Carl sneered. "You don't think I'm going to drink it, do you?"

Ralph caught his gaze and held it. "I sure do."

Carl swallowed hard. His throat felt like sandpaper. He was desperate for another drink of water. "Are you trying to poison me, Uncle Ralph?" he joked grimly.

Ralph chuckled. "Heavens, no. I'm trying to redeem you, son."

Why did everyone think he needed redeeming? Carl fumed to himself. He knew he didn't need redeeming. What he really needed at the moment was rehydrating! So, since he was reasonably sure his uncle wasn't trying to poison him, and he was dreaming all this weird stuff anyway, what would be the harm of drinking this so-called elixir of life?

But as he lifted the glass, he hesitated. He looked toward the open French doors, where Marley suddenly appeared wearing some kind of frothy, full-skirted, tiny-waisted, off-the-shoulder white dress that made her look like a debutante from the forties. Or an angel.

My God, she's beautiful, Carl thought. Too beautiful. Too desirable. He lowered the glass to the table and stared at her.

"Drink it, Carl," his uncle whispered softly, compellingly. "Drink it before Marley comes to the table. Drink it now, Carl."

And for some reason beyond Carl's understanding, he obeyed, draining the glass of every drop. And when he was done, he was no longer thirsty. But, as his uncle predicted, he felt mighty strange. He was light-headed and dizzy. The room tilted. He was seeing double. Panicked, he stared at his uncle. Both of him stared back with eerie little smiles on their lips.

Oh, my God, thought Carl, *Uncle Ralph really has poisoned me.*

Chapter Six

"Don't worry, son," his uncle said, his deep, soothing voice seeming to come from a great distance to penetrate the fog of Carl's panic and confusion. "You'll feel weird for only a few seconds, then you'll feel wonderful. That's the way it works. Soon you'll be your old self again...whether you want to be or not. At least till the elixir wears off in a couple of hours, you'll be one happy camper. You might even be happier than you've ever been your entire life."

So, rather than lurch to his feet and stumble about the room gasping for help like someone in a bad dinner-theater production, Carl sat quietly and hoped his uncle was telling the truth. He reasoned that being forced to be happy for a short period of time was probably preferable to being poisoned.

By the time Marley walked into the room and was standing by the table, Carl had regained his equilibrium, and when he looked up at her, there was only one divinely beautiful angel instead of two. But instead of cursing the Fates and wishing he was sitting at his desk reassuringly surrounded by paperwork, Carl got the overwhelming urge to spring eagerly to his feet and hold out Marley's chair. And, while doing so, he felt an equally overpowering urge to...to smile. Yes! To *smile!*

Marley's mouth fell open for only a second before she sank into her seat and shifted her startled gaze away from Carl's beaming countenance. He could understand her confusion. He was confused, too. After all, he'd been a bear ever since they'd left Miss Hathaway's house, and now...well, now, for the first time in seven years, he didn't feel like being a bear or a jackass or any other kind of disagreeable animal.

Carl sat down and looked across the table at Uncle Ralph. Uncle Ralph patted his jacket pocket and nodded knowingly, a twinkle in his eye. It was an acknowledgment that the elixir was working, that Carl was, indeed, in a temporarily induced state of bliss.

Carl had forgotten what bliss felt like. The feeling had diminished to a vague memory over the years, a dangerous state of emotions he'd consciously guarded against. After all, he knew how quickly states of exquisite happiness could be altered. But as there appeared to be no ready antidote to the elixir, for the time being Carl resigned himself to being happy. Damn, but he'd forgotten how good it felt!

"That's a beautiful dress, Marley, honey," he heard Uncle Ralph saying. "It's an antique, isn't it?"

Marley sat between them, the candlelight bringing out the highlights in her fluffy cap of freshly washed hair. She smelled wonderful...like roses. She smiled shyly at Ralph, braved a peek at Carl, then immediately looked away, seemingly disconcerted by his continued good humor.

"Well, not so much antique as vintage. It's a dress from the forties. A wartime date-night dress, Nadine tells me." Her fingers fluttered self-consciously over the chiffon flounce that framed her pale, beautiful shoulders and then down the formfitting bodice, over her small rounded bosom to her cinched-in waist.

"I didn't buy it, because I don't know when I'd ever wear it again, but Nadine said she'd happily loan it to me just to see it on someone it was nicely suited for. It's made of dotted swiss chiffon, you know, which is a summer fabric. It's not very warm for this time of year, but the room is well heated."

Very well heated, thought Carl, fidgeting with his suddenly too-tight collar as his gaze followed the same trail of chiffon down the front of Marley's dress.

"The necklace and the earrings are period, too," she added, touching the pearl pendant necklace that circled her Audrey Hepburn-like neck. The earrings were pearl pendants, too, and looked feminine and fetching dangling from Marley's shell-shaped ears. "Nadine loaned these to me, too. She has so many lovely things."

"She has fabulous taste," Carl heard himself saying. "She knew exactly what would suit you. You look beautiful, Marley."

Marley turned to Carl with a shocked expression.

He laughed. "What? Can't I pay a friend a compliment?"

"It's just that you haven't in so long, Carl, I don't even remember the last time," Marley explained, still looking stunned.

"It's not that I haven't thought them," he confessed, surprised at his own honesty. Honesty, like happiness, felt good for a change, but he did feel a little nervous about what he might say next. Even Marley looked nervous. She probably didn't have a clue what to make of him.

MARLEY DIDN'T HAVE A CLUE what to make of Carl. While she'd been showering and changing, he'd apparently undergone a startling personality change. He was behaving like the old Carl. He was smiling and being pleasant. He was actually having fun. He'd even complimented her, making her feel as shy and nervous as a schoolgirl. What, she wondered, could have happened?

While Marley pondered this mystery, Nadine came in and introduced their server, a pretty brunette in an old-fashioned red dress and a white ruffled apron. She recited the evening's menu and asked for preferences in wine, bread and salad dressing. She left, returning immediately with the wine. Uncle Ralph did the honors, pouring a glass for Nadine, as well, then stood and lifted his filled glass in the air to propose a toast. Everyone else stood up, too.

"To good friends." He smiled warmly at Nadine. They all touched glasses and drank.

"To Christmas," Marley proposed next, watching Carl for his reaction. He stunned her again by joining in without a single grumble.

"To love," Nadine continued, flitting a sly smile around the circle.

When it was Carl's turn, Ralph prompted him, saying, "What'll it be, son?" There was a wait while Carl appeared to sink into a state of deep thought. He frowned and chewed on the inside of his lip, looking so serious Marley was sure he was going to say he could think of nothing worth toasting, or that he didn't have time for such frivolity and needed to get back to the office. But finally his brow cleared and he lifted his glass.

"To beauty," he said, looking straight at Marley. "Both outward beauty and the kind that's soul deep."

While Uncle Ralph and Nadine laughed and exclaimed, applauding Carl's poetic speech, Marley stood stock-still, blushing to her roots and wondering if Carl's body had been taken over by an alien. A nice alien. A charming alien.

"I think I need to sit down," Marley announced shakily, reaching behind her to feel for her chair.

"Too much wine, Marley?" Carl teased, setting down his own glass and catching hold of her hand to guide her into her seat. The feel of his fingers over hers sent a thrill of awareness to every nerve ending in Marley's body. And the warm look in his eyes gave her goose bumps...like the kind she wished Stewart gave her.

This just isn't fair! Marley fumed to herself. Every time she gave up on Carl, something happened to make her wonder if there was still hope for them. The day had had so many ups and downs, she felt as though she were on a nonstop roller coaster ride. What could possibly happen next?

"At seven-thirty a few of the other guests are meeting in the parlor to socialize and dance," Nadine said as the server brought in their salad and bread. "I've got some great big-band music from the forties on CDs. You're welcome to join the party. Marley, you're even dressed for the part." She smiled at Ralph. "And I'm counting on you for the fox-trot. You do it so well."

"Well, that depends...." Ralph stalled, looking to Carl for his reaction.

Carl's sudden transformation notwithstanding, Marley expected him to beg off, to remind Ralph that he'd promised to drive them home right after dinner, that he had scads of paperwork to do and needed to get back to the office. But, unless she wasn't hearing right, he said, "If you want to wait to take us home a little later, Ralph, I don't mind. You can't disappoint Nadine." He turned and smiled at Marley, adding, "Besides, it sounds like fun. Marley and I haven't danced together since high school."

Marley was beyond surprise. She thought she returned Carl's smile, but she couldn't be sure. She felt numb. And, while the food looked and smelled delicious, she couldn't eat more than a bite or two of each course. Carl's turnabout was too much to take in all at once. She needed time to get used to it. On the other hand, she was afraid to get used to it, because it might vanish as quickly as it had appeared.

It was fortunate that Uncle Ralph was eating dinner with them, because he kept Carl busy "catching up," allowing Marley the time she needed to recover from and adjust to Carl's dramatic change in attitude. She listened avidly as they discussed every Merrick in the book, both of them remembering and laughing over old times. And when Ralph talked about things that had happened in the seven years that his nephew had been absent from the family get-togethers, Carl showed a strong interest in every amusing or touching story. He even appeared wistful. Imagine that...Carl *wistful!*

When dinner was over and Nadine motioned to them from the door to join her and the other guests in the parlor, Marley hung back and grabbed hold of Ralph's arm. "What's going on, Uncle Ralph?" she whispered. "What's the matter with Carl? Is he sick or something?"

Ralph waited till Nadine had ushered Carl out of the room, the two of them laughing over some shared joke, then he smiled down at Marley. "Why, he's just happy, honey. That's all."

"But that's just my point," she persisted. "Carl's never that happy. Something's happened. What did you do? Did you slip him something...like a bottle or two of Prozac?"

Ralph laughed and shrugged his big shoulders. "Heavens, no. I gave him a little swig of some mountain spring water I get up Montpelier way, but that's all. It's perfectly harmless and doesn't *make* a person happy. But why look a gift horse in the mouth, Marley? Why not just enjoy Carl's good mood?" He leaned close to her ear and whispered, "Hell, honey, why not take advantage of it?"

Marley was suddenly overcome with embarrassment. Did Ralph know how she felt about Carl? Was she that transparent?

"What I mean, Marley, is why don't you take advantage of the chance to dance with a pro? From what I remember, Carl really knows how to cut a rug."

Marley relaxed a little and smiled. "Yes, I remember that, too. It would be fun, wouldn't it?"

"And good for the boy, too. While he's in this admittedly strange but happy mood, honey, you'd be doing him a favor to make sure he has a really good time."

When it was put to her that way, Marley had to agree. Yes, it made sense. Once Carl got the hang of it again, maybe he'd find it easier to let loose and enjoy himself on occasion. She'd actually be doing him a good deed.

As for herself, she'd try not to invest her own feelings. She'd try not to allow herself to hope that one short evening of fun could lead to something more permanent.

With all this worked out in her mind, Marley smiled at Uncle Ralph and slipped her arm in his, then they strolled down the hall together to the parlor.

CARL HAD MADE THE ROUNDS of the guests with Nadine, shaking hands with total strangers and exchanging pleasantries, before Marley and Uncle Ralph finally made it to the parlor. He was already enjoying himself, but Marley's presence made his happiness complete. The fire was warmer, the tree more glowing and beautiful, the company more stimulating and friendly just because Marley was in the room.

During dinner, he'd struggled to keep his hands to himself and had encouraged Ralph to talk endlessly about the "Family Merrick." Surprisingly enough, he'd enjoyed hearing about all his relatives, but he'd had an ulterior motive; he wanted to get Ralph all talked out so he'd leave him and Marley alone once they removed to the parlor.

Carl shook his head in wonderment. Normally he'd be tense and uncomfortable in a roomful of smiling strangers. He'd find the glittering tree and cheerful decorations oppressive, the steady fall of snow outside the large bay window worrisome. But tonight, because of the elixir, he was enjoying the company, the festive atmosphere and the Christmas-like weather that made being inside so cozy.

Once the elixir wore off, of course, he'd be back to his normal self. His enchanted view of the world would disappear and the real world would come back with the force of a marine invasion. He'd see Christmas for what it really was...a crass commercial enterprise that fooled people into a false sense of contentment for a few harried weeks each year. Then January and the harsh reality of biting winter and big bills to pay would come crashing down on them.

In Carl's realist view, it was foolish to set yourself up for such a letdown. And under normal circumstances he'd never dream of doing so. But tonight—because of the elixir—he just couldn't help himself. He was as gaga over Christmas as the rest of the assorted nuts at the Putnam Road Inn.

As for Marley...well, he didn't know how he'd feel about her once the elixir wore off. But right now, this minute, he thought she was the most beautiful woman in the world and his best, most cherished friend.

Maybe he wasn't the marrying kind, but for the present, for this moment stolen out of a dream—or out of a flask of euphoria-inducing liquid his uncle had mixed up in his bathtub—Carl had the overwhelming urge to forget all his reservations about romantic involvements. To forget that seven years ago that very night he'd set himself up for a huge letdown by having expectations about women as unrealistic as believing in Santa Claus and the rest of the Christmas myth. To give women—meaning Marley Jacobs—a chance to make his grinch's heart grow two sizes bigger.

WHEN MARLEY STEPPED into the parlor, she could actually feel Carl watching her. A self-conscious and utterly delicious warmth enveloped her from head to toe. She looked up and met Carl's gaze across the crowded room. *Across the crowded room,* she repeated to herself with a sigh. When she got up that morning, she'd have never guessed she'd be having such a romantic interlude…especially with Carl.

While she politely endured introductions to the other guests, she continued to feel his gaze following her. Finally she'd said her last how-do-you-do and found herself standing alone by the eggnog bowl. But not for long.

"So, dollface…come here often?" Carl had sidled up to her and stretched his mouth into a teasing leer. He had taken a quarter from his pocket and was tossing it and catching it like some slickster from a black-and-white forties movie. Marley's heart slammed against her ribs. She used to love it when he teased her. She was surprised he still remembered how.

"Only when my husband's fleet is somewhere in the South Pacific," she teased back, propping her fist on her hip and wiggling her bare shoulders. In the background, recorded dance music had begun and couples were moving into each other's arms.

"A gorgeous dame like you—" Carl's eyes glinted provocatively as his gaze flickered over her "—I'm surprised he doesn't tie you up till he gets back."

She arched a brow. "I was a Campfire girl. I can undo every kind of knot there is."

"Glad t' hear it." He gestured nonchalantly toward the other dancers. "Wanna trip the light fantastic…whatever the hell that means?"

"But I don't even know your name," she said coyly.

"Carl," he growled. "Carl Merrick."

She held out her hand. "Charmed, I'm sure."

"And you are?"

She batted her lashes, Betty Boop–style. "Marley. Marley Jacobs."

Carl laughed, pocketing the quarter and reverting to his normal persona. "Well, Marley Jacobs, do you want to take a chance with me on the dance floor?"

"Do you dance better than you skate?"

"So I'm told. But, be warned, I'm a little out of practice at this, too."

Marley moved into Carl's arms. She hadn't been this close to him in far too long. "That's okay. Me, too. Well, except for last Saturday night when..." Marley's voice trailed off. It abruptly occurred to her that mentioning Stewart Cosgrove might throw a wrench in Carl's good mood.

Carl raised a brow. "Last Saturday?"

With his warm, strong hand at her waist, guiding her expertly through the dance steps, and his other hand clasping hers, Marley dreaded the possible repercussions of a truthful answer. She wanted to stay exactly where she was, in Carl's arms. "Oh, I just went dancing at the Grange," she said offhandedly, then quickly added, "Isn't this a Tommy Dorsey number?"

CARL KNEW WHY MARLEY WAS avoiding a more complete answer to his question. Obviously she'd gone to the Grange with Stewart Cosgrove. But even as he drew Marley close, bending his head to inhale the scent of her hair and spreading his hand in a caress over the small of her back, Carl felt a twisting sensation in his stomach. She'd apparently not only been asked out by Stewart Cosgrove, she'd accepted the invitation once or twice...or more.

His first thought was, *Damn that Stewart Cosgrove.* And his second thought was, *The elixir must be wearing off, or else why would I suddenly not feel as happy?*

But when Marley responded to his possessive move by snuggling against his chest, the elixir's effects seemed to kick into gear again. He was happy...very happy. And he was definitely getting aroused.

For such a slender female, Marley was curvy. And those curves were driving him crazy at the moment, making him wish he really was a sailor on shore leave, picking up a beautiful woman for a wildly romantic weekend, instead of Marley's friend and the co-president of a company they ran together. Responsibly speaking, he had no right to dally with Marley's feelings by kissing her...et cetera. But kissing her...et cetera...was exactly what he wanted to do. But with no strings attached. Damn, there was the rub.

But under the influence of the elixir, was he really responsible for what he might do? And if this was really just a dream, why should he worry about consequences? Hmm, now there was something to think about.

Marley pulled back a couple of inches and looked up at him. At such proximity, she was lovelier than ever, her green eyes soft and luminous, her skin like porcelain. "Miss Hathaway's tree was beautiful, wasn't it?"

They hadn't talked about the tree since leaving Miss Hathaway's, probably because he'd been in such a foul mood and she didn't dare. But now he suspected she was trying to divert the conversation away from any topic that might lead to Stewart Cosgrove.

"It was amazing," he answered. "But I thought it was ironic that as devilish as I was in elementary school I still ended up close to the angel on her tree."

He smiled down at her. "I suppose I owe that distinction to you."

She laughed. "If you recall, I got in trouble nearly as often as you did."

"It was the company you kept," he murmured dryly.

"She really only put us where she did because of my fascination with angels."

"I didn't realize you liked them so much."

She looked amused. "Why else would I have a cabinet full of angels I've collected over the years and from all over the country if I weren't crazy about them?"

He had a feeling he was about to stick his foot in his mouth, but he had to ask, "Why haven't I ever seen your collection?"

"You see it every day at the office. The cabinet I keep it in is behind my desk at work, every winged cherub on display through sliding glass doors."

He shook his head ruefully. "I guess I am sometimes a little too focused on work."

"I'll say."

"What about your great-grandmother's angel? Is that on display, too?"

Marley's smile faltered. "When my folks moved to Florida, they took a lot of stuff to the Goodwill and we think the angel was somehow given away with a lot of other Christmas ornaments my mother wanted to get rid of."

"I'm sorry."

"Since it was my great-grandmother's, I'll never be able to replace it, of course. But someday I want to find another one just like it. It was a Nuremberg angel."

"A what?"

"The first one of its type was made in the mid 1800s in Nuremberg, Germany, where a family began creating them in memory of their daughter. It was about nine inches tall with a beautiful wax face and a golden robe and halo. It was very Old World and I just loved it."

"You can't find one anywhere?"

"Not so far. Not around here, anyway."

"Well, you'll just have to keep—"

"Carl! Hey, Carl!"

Carl turned to see his uncle close by with Nadine in his arms. They were both grinning.

"What?" Carl asked with a chuckle. Their grins were full of mischief, a clear indication that something was afoot.

"Don't ya see where you're standin', son?" Ralph raised his bushy brows and pointed with his nose toward the ceiling.

Carl looked up and saw that they were standing directly under a bunch of mistletoe that hung from a red velvet ribbon suspended from an old-fashioned crystal chandelier. Marley looked up, too, then they both looked at each other.

Carl couldn't believe his luck. He'd been wanting to kiss Marley ever since that crazy dream. But could a person have dreams *inside* other dreams? he wondered. Surely it was possible, because he was still dreaming, wasn't he?

"What are ya waitin' for, Carl?" his uncle prompted. "Kiss 'er!"

Carl hesitated. He wanted to kiss her, and she looked willing enough, although possibly a little stunned and nervous—just like him. And with all the other people in the room there seemed to be little chance he'd get carried away and turn a simple kiss into some kind of torrid love scene. And that was important, because suddenly he realized that he didn't want to hurt Marley by giving her false hope.

He didn't want to set himself up for hurt, either, which was exactly what would happen if he became disillusioned again by a member of the female sex he held in high esteem.

He stared at her soft, slightly parted lips. On the other hand, if this really was just a dream, what were the actual risks of either of them getting hurt at all? Nil, that's what.

"Is it okay with you, Marley?" he finally asked, shifting the decision-making responsibility to her.

"Only if you really want to," she answered, shifting the responsibility back to him.

"Oh, I want to, all right."

Her cheeks glowed, her eyes grew shiny. "Then what's stoppin' ya?"

Carl couldn't resist. He reached down to cup Marley's chin, lowered his head, then tentatively kissed her. Her lips were as sweet as he'd imagined, as soft and inviting as he'd feared. He'd thought that having other people in the room would curtail passion, but Carl discovered that he'd been dead wrong about that. Desire raced through him like a rampant fever.

Driven by an uncontrollable urge, his arms encircled her, pulling her close. Her lips parted on a sigh and he deepened the kiss, probing the honeyed warmth of her mouth with his tongue. She responded eagerly. She even trembled in his arms.

The sound of clapping recalled Carl's scattered wits. He pulled away and looked around him, dazed. People were smiling, laughing, congratulating him on a fine performance. Suddenly Carl was reminded of a wedding and of the general oohs and aahs and applause that followed the kissing done by the newly married husband and wife. The similarities were too close for comfort.

Carl knew the congratulations of the crowd were offered in fun, but suddenly he resented the intrusion of so many people into his private affairs. He felt his old antipathies and prejudices coming to the surface again. The tree, the fire, the snow, the mistletoe...everything seemed superficial and dripping with rigged sentimentality.

He looked down at Marley, her dazed expression probably a mirror of his own, but he could only see her as part of the whole phoney picture. Then he realized why. The elixir had worn off prematurely and now he was seeing things the way they really were!

Not wanting to embarrass Marley, Carl managed to plaster a suitably sheepish smile on his face just long enough to escort her out of the room and into the hall. The knowing smiles on the roomful of romantic well-wishers clearly showed what they were thinking, that Carl was taking his girl to a more private spot for further smooching. But while that would be nice—very nice—it was the last thing on Carl's agenda.

"Marley, would you mind waiting here while I talk to Uncle Ralph for a minute?" he asked her, leading her to the Victorian settee that had been occupied by a pair of absorbed lovers when they'd first arrived at the inn.

"S-sure," she stuttered, looking perplexed and a little anxious.

He left her, got Ralph's attention by gesturing from

the doorway of the parlor, then took his uncle into a nearby vestibule for a little man-to-man talk.

"Uncle Ralph, I don't want you to give me that elixir ever again, do you hear me?"

Uncle Ralph peered at him keenly. "Why not, son? It looked like you were having an awfully good time."

"That's just the problem," Carl said agitatedly. "I was having *too* much fun. I was behaving irresponsibly! It isn't fair to Marley, or to me. That damned 'elixir of life' made me do things I'd never normally do. I don't like Christmas and I don't want to get serious about a woman, least of all Marley. And that elixir made me think I liked the tree and the decorations and all those smiling people! It even made me think I care for Marley in a way that I really—"

"Carl," his uncle interrupted in a serious tone. "I didn't give you any 'elixir of life.' I made that up. All I put in your water glass was more water. Every feeling you had tonight was yours, son, and as gen-u-ine as the vinyl in my '55 Chev."

Chapter Seven

"What do you mean you made up the elixir of life?"

"Just what I said, Carl. The clear liquid I poured in your water glass before dinner was just some mountain spring water I bought in Montpelier yesterday."

"But why?"

"Well, because I like the taste of it better than tap water and it—"

"No, Uncle Ralph, why did you tell me it was some special potion you mixed up in your bathtub? And if it wasn't a special potion, why did it make me feel so strange?"

Ralph shrugged and looked a little sheepish. "I admit I stretched the truth a bit."

Carl dragged a hand through his hair. "A bit?"

"But all for a good cause. I wanted to give you an out, Carl. A way of allowing you to behave like you really wanted to, then blaming it on me and the elixir."

"The way I *wanted* to behave? That's nuts! Besides, how do you explain the dizziness, the double vision?"

"Power of suggestion, Carl. I told you you'd feel strange, so you felt strange." Ralph smiled. "I'm pretty good at the power of suggestion. How do you think I outsell every other used car salesman in Vermont?''

Carl shook his head, unable to take it all in. "I don't believe you. I haven't enjoyed Christmas in years, and I don't want a serious relationship with a woman, so why would I act like I have for the past hour unless I was under the influence of some potent drug or herbal potion or something?''

Ralph's eyes twinkled. "That's a good question, Carl. Maybe enough time has passed and you've finally realized that Christmas and Marley have taken the brunt of your bitterness long enough. And maybe the spirit and magic of the season, with a hearty dose of love thrown in, has finally plucked that thorn from your paw.''

Carl shook his head again and waved his hands in front of him, backing away from his uncle as if he had a contagious disease. "No. Oh, no. I'm not buying that bogus bag of goods. There's no thorn in my paw, whatever that means. There's nothing spiritual or magical about Christmas, and I'm not in love with anyone...least of all, Marley.''

Carl turned around and nearly walked straight into the person he had just vehemently denied being in love with. The expression on her face told all. She'd heard, if not everything, enough of their conversation to be hurt.

He placed his hands on her shoulders. "Marley, I was just coming back to—''

She shrugged out of his grasp. "No need to explain, Carl," she said coolly. "I came around the corner just in time to hear your impassioned speech. But that's okay, 'cause nothing you said was late-breaking news, was it? You hate Christmas and you aren't in love with me. Ho-hum. No one will stop the presses for that information.''

''Marley, please don't—''

Her eyes sparked with anger. ''Don't what? Don't believe what you do, only what you say? It's a little contrary to what I was taught as a child, but it's sage advice in this case. Don't worry, I'll be much more careful from now on. Only do me a favor, will you?''

Carl hung his head and pinched the bridge of his nose, sighing heavily. ''Of course, Marley. What is it?''

''Don't jerk me around, okay? You know how I feel about you, because I was stupid enough to tell you. For the sake of our friendship and our partnership, don't ever touch me again...don't ever kiss me like you did in there under the mistletoe...unless you mean it.''

She lifted her chin and glared into his eyes, her own eyes shiny with emotion. ''Not that I'll give you the opportunity. I've said it before, but this time I really mean it. I give up on you, Carl Merrick. If you want to be unhappy and bitter the rest of your life, I'm not going to be dragged down that sorry path with you.''

A horrible silence followed this speech, which was even more impassioned than Carl's. And he could tell by the pain and the flinty determination in her eyes that Marley meant every word. Carl got a hollow feeling in his stomach, as if he'd just seen her head bob out of sight forever beneath the icy water of Reindeer Pond.

Marley's gaze shifted to a point over Carl's shoulder. ''Uncle Ralph, do you think you could take me home now?''

"Sure, honey. But you'll want to change again, I expect."

Marley nodded and smiled wanly. "Maybe Nadine has some jeans and a sweater she could loan me. I don't really feel like putting on that elf costume again."

Ralph came over and slid his arm around Marley's delicate shoulders. "I'm sure she does. That woman has the resources of the Red Cross and Bergdorf's all rolled into one. Let's go see if we can lure her from her guests."

As they walked away, Ralph looked over his shoulder at Carl with an expression that had more pity in it than reproof, although there were hefty portions of each. Carl clenched his jaw and lifted his chin. *Don't pity me, Uncle Ralph,* he said to himself. *I'd rather be alone than be a fool.* Then he followed them, lagging a few steps behind as they rounded the corner to the center hall.

As they passed the front door, it suddenly opened, sending a blast of cold air across the hardwood floors so strong that it lifted the edges of the Oriental carpets and blew out several candles that were part of an arrangement that rested on an antique chest by the stairs. The windows rattled, the fireplace belched smoke, the lights flickered, and the room went dark. A half minute later, the lights came on again and standing in the middle of the hall was Stewart Cosgrove.

"What ill wind blew you in?" Carl asked him. "Or were you...just passing by?"

Stewart gave an ingenuous smile in reply to these caustic inquiries, then Marley descended on him like an infatuated teenager.

"Stewart! What are you doing here?" she exclaimed, but unlike Bev when she'd asked Carl the same question at Sheila's house, she didn't sound disappointed. Then, without waiting for an answer, she drew Ralph near and said, "I'd like to you to meet Carl's uncle, Ralph Merrick."

"Please t' meet ya, Stewart!" Ralph bellowed. "Seen your commercial. Liked it. Seen mine?"

Stewart smiled. "Thanks. And, yes, I've seen yours, too. They're...er...hypnotizing." He sobered. "I'm afraid I've come with some bad news."

"Bad news for whom?" Carl asked warily.

"For you and Marley. Bev Cratchet and her son, Tim, were in a car accident and—"

Marley grabbed his arm. "No! Are they all right?"

Stewart squeezed Marley's hand reassuringly. "Tim is fine—just a few scratches—but Bev received a concussion. She's conscious, but they want to keep her overnight. She asked me to find you two and see if you'd come up to the hospital."

"Are you sure she wanted both of us?" Carl asked doubtfully. Why would Bev ask for him? She'd worked for him for three years, but he didn't know her at all personally. He was certainly relieved that both she and Tim were going to be fine, but he could see how easy it would be to get caught up in Bev's problems. Was that wise?

"Yes, she asked specifically for both of you," Stewart answered firmly.

"Well, I'm happy to go," Marley said briskly. "I'll do whatever she needs. I'm just so glad they're going to be okay!"

"It's a helluva thing to happen on Christmas Eve," Ralph commented.

Carl chuckled bitterly to himself. He was used to

bad things happening on Christmas Eve. "How did the accident happen? Road conditions?"

Stewart shook his head. "No, actually, I think she fell asleep at the wheel."

"How do you know all this, Cosgrove?" Carl asked suspiciously. "And how did you know how to find us?"

"Remember, I told you when I saw you at Reindeer Pond that I was going up to the hospital to visit the children's ward? Well, I was leaving through the emergency room entrance when I saw them bringing Bev in. I stuck around till they let me see her, and then she asked me to find you guys. When neither of you answered your phones, I called Miss Hathaway. She told me exactly where I could find you."

Carl frowned. "But Miss Hathaway didn't know we were headed—"

"What does it matter how he found us?" Marley interrupted, flashing him an irritated look. "I'm just glad he did." She turned to Ralph. "Let's find Nadine, Uncle Ralph. I want to get changed right away."

"I'd better be on my way, too," Stewart said.

"What? You're not coming with us?" Carl inquired with mock surprise. He was sure Stewart would take every opportunity to hang around Marley.

Stewart smiled benignly. "I have some shopping I need to finish before the stores close."

"Of course you do," Carl drawled.

"Be careful out there, son," Ralph called over his shoulder as he steered Marley toward the parlor.

"Don't worry," Stewart replied, his gaze fixed on Carl and a cryptic smile curving his lips. "Nothing bad ever happens to *me*."

NOTHING BAD EVER HAPPENS to him because it happens to me first, Carl groused to himself as he made the long drive to the hospital. The distance wasn't far, but the going was slow due to packed roads and a steady fall of snow. At least he didn't have to endure the torment of sitting next to Marley again since she'd decided on her own to get in the back "where she'd have more room." But the tension in the air was thick enough to cut with a knife.

Carl sensed Ralph's disapproval and disappointment in him, and he knew only too well where he stood in Marley's book. And he didn't blame either of them. He just wished he could skulk off to his office and return to the company of his financial reports where absolutely nothing was expected of him. It was more comfortable that way, although admittedly a bit lonely.

But he repeated to himself the phrase that he was beginning to think would serve well as his own personal creed: he'd rather be alone than be a fool.

At the hospital, they found it easy to locate a parking space near the main door since every patient who could possibly be released had been sent home to "enjoy" the holidays with his or her family. And hardly anyone scheduled surgeries or other elective procedures this time of year although Carl thought it would be the perfect time. It would mean fewer patients in the hospital, more privacy, and better individual care.

And what would they be missing on the outside? Just the chaos and the costliness of Christmas. He made a mental note: if he ever got sick, he'd remember to plan his hospital stay for over Christmas.

After they parked, Carl got out and pushed the front seat forward so Marley could climb out of the back. He offered his hand, but she ignored it as she squeezed around the vinyl seat and stood up. Nadine had loaned her a sweater and a pair of her granddaughter's jeans, a stout pair of snow boots and a blue knit cap with a white pom-pom on the top. With her ski parka on over all this, she looked toasty warm. But her gaze as she walked around him to Ralph's side of the car was cold as ice.

"What have you got there, Uncle Ralph?" Marley asked as Ralph opened the trunk and pulled out a garment bag.

"It's my Santa suit. I got to thinking that some of those kids at the hospital might enjoy a visit from Saint Nick just before they go to sleep tonight. Then they'd be guaranteed a few sugarplum dreams, wouldn't they?"

Marley smiled and slid her hand around his arm. "Ralph Merrick, you're a man after my own heart. You really know how to make the holidays a happy event for everyone you come in contact with. A person would have to be a miserable old grinch not to catch *your* Christmas spirit." She flicked a scathing look at Carl, then walked, arm in arm, with Ralph up the hospital steps.

Knowing full well that he was the miserable old grinch Marley referred to, Carl sighed resignedly and followed them into the red brick building that had been erected a few years prior to World War II.

His father routinely donated to the hospital for improvements, but no matter how much money benefactors sank into the place to spiff it up, it was just too small for the patient load, the rooms were cramped, and the ICU layout hardly conducive for utilizing the latest medical technology, or so his father said. But, since Carl was never sick, he never thought about the hospital and what might be done to improve it.

From the lady at the volunteer station, they quickly learned that Bev was in Room 305 and they took the small elevator up to that floor. Marley carefully avoided Carl's eyes and made friendly chitchat with Ralph. Carl told himself that she wouldn't be able to keep up the cold shoulder treatment forever—after all, they did have to work together—and tried not to let it bother him. But it did.

And he couldn't quit thinking about that kiss under the mistletoe.

Entering Bev's room, the first thing Carl noticed was Timmy. He sat in a chair next to his mother's bed, looking small and forlorn. He had a scratch on his forehead; other than that appeared unharmed. But the red balloon tied to the chair arm and the teddy bear tucked in next to him could not, apparently, cheer him up.

Carl fought it, but sympathy welled inside him. Suddenly he remembered what it was like to be a kid on Christmas Eve. All the giddy excitement and expectation. All the wonder and magic. It had to be a real bummer to find yourself at the hospital for the night with your mother bedridden and her forehead covered with tape and bandages. Scary, too.

"Oh, you're here!" Bev said as they filed into the room. "I was afraid Stewart wouldn't be able to locate you, but I shouldn't have worried. He's incredible."

Glad you think so, Carl mumbled to himself, then walked around to the other side of Bev's bed and stood, feeling awkward, his hands stuffed deep in his coat pockets, as Marley introduced Ralph.

While brief pleasantries were exchanged, Timmy

turned his solemn eyes to Carl and stared. Carl squirmed under the child's relentless scrutiny. He'd unbuttoned his coat in the elevator, so he looked down to make sure his fly was closed. It was. So what did the kid find so fascinating about him?

"I'll leave you and Carl to visit with Bev," Ralph said, backing toward the door. He winked at Marley. "I just thought of something I need to do."

"Oh, okay, Ralph," Marley said, winking back.

"See you later in the lobby," he finished up, then also winked at Timmy on his way out.

Timmy saw the wink, but he quickly returned his steadfast gaze to Carl.

"I was so relieved to hear you and Timmy were okay," Marley said as she bent and kissed Bev on the cheek, then grabbed one of her hands and started rubbing it. "Although I'm sure your head must be killing you."

Carl fidgeted, worried that Bev might expect him to hold her other hand. And rubbing it was totally out of the question. He stuffed his fists further inside his coat pockets.

"My head does hurt, but I'm relieved, too, because the accident could have been so much worse." Bev's eyes suddenly brimmed with tears. Carl looked away. "Timmy could have been hurt. I can't believe—" Her voice cracked. "I can't believe I fell asleep at the wheel."

"Don't blame yourself. It happens. Have you been staying up late?" Marley flitted a glance at Timmy. "You know...preparing things for Christmas?"

"There wasn't much to prepare this year," she whispered ruefully, then abruptly changed the subject. "Thank you for coming." She turned toward Carl and he was forced to look at her. She had either fought back, or wiped away, the impending tears. "Both of you." Suddenly she reached up and grabbed his hand, then clung to it. "I need to talk to you, Mr. Merrick."

"Er, okay," he said uneasily. "But if it's about taking a few sick days off, that's fine, Bev. I can get Marley's secretary to help me out till you're well enough to return." He tried to gently pull his hand away, but she held fast.

"Well, thank you, I'll return as soon as I possibly can. I might need the sick days later...for something else." He supposed she meant Timmy's surgery. She lifted her chin and looked him straight in the eye, which was quite unusual for Bev. "I have a confession to make."

Lord, no. Not another confession!

"I...I just thought you should know that I've...I've been moonlighting."

Carl blinked. "Moonlighting?" She'd looked so serious, he'd half expected her to say she'd been embezzling. But how could she possibly moonlight? She spent ten hours a day at the office!

She started talking very fast. "I know how you feel about giving your all to your job, and I've tried very hard to be the best secretary I can be, Mr. Merrick, and I know I haven't been up to your usual high standards lately."

"You haven't?"

"Well, those letters you wanted out by the 26th...."

"Oh, those. Don't worry about—"

"I just don't want you to be angry about my second job."

"Bev," Marley interrupted, "what is your second job?"

Bev turned her wide, scared eyes toward Marley. "I do telemarketing from the house. Every night after Timmy's in bed, I call the West Coast, Alaska and Hawaii until three a.m."

"No wonder you're exhausted!" Marley exclaimed. Carl was horrified, too. Telemarketing was bad enough, but till three in the morning? "Heavens, Bev, don't we pay you enough? I frequently check our salaries against the national scale, and I'm pretty sure you're on the high end for executive secretaries."

"My salary is great," Bev assured her. "And I love my job. I need my job." Her voice lowered. "It's just that the medicine for Timmy...well, you know." She looked anxious. She either didn't want to bring up the subject in front of Timmy, or she didn't want it to seem as if she were complaining to her bosses because the company insurance didn't cover prescriptions.

"I didn't bring this up so I could discuss money. I really just wanted you to know about my second job, Mr. Merrick, before someone else told you. I feel I need to explain why I fell asleep at the wheel. I don't want people thinking I'm a bad mother."

"No one who sees you with Timmy could ever think that," Marley assured her.

Bev smiled tentatively, then turned back to Carl. Now she grasped both his hands. "But what about my job, Mr. Merrick? Is it secure?"

Carl couldn't believe she was even asking him this question. He also couldn't believe she was holding both of his hands! Bev was quiet and timid at the office, but he'd never guessed she felt so insecure about her job. But then he'd also totally missed the fact that his business partner was in love with him, so he obviously wasn't paying much attention to the human things going on around him.

But now that he thought about it, he didn't suppose he'd ever done or said anything to reassure Bev that he valued her skills and wouldn't fire her no matter how many jobs she had outside the office. He frankly admired her for being able to hold down one job— and that job very demanding—and be a single mother of a sick child, too.

He glanced over at Timmy, who was still watching him for some reason, and felt an overpowering urge to tell this kid's mother what a great secretary she was and how much he appreciated her. It was the least he could do. It would feel damned awkward, but he knew he could do it if he really put his mind to it.

As Bev watched nervously, Carl pulled free of her tenacious grasp, dragged a chair close to the bed and sat down. This time he was the one to reach for *her* hand.

Dumbfounded, Marley watched as a smile curved Carl's usually stern mouth. She stared, flabbergasted, as he held Bev's hand and said, "I should have told you this a long time ago. You're a fantastic secretary. I wouldn't trade you for a million bucks. You're worth twice that and I only wish I could pay you what you're worth. Don't worry about the second job, because you're not going to need it, anyway. We're going to call our insurance company as soon as the holidays are over and get that coverage for Tim's medicine. Right, Marley?"

Carl said all this very fast and in a very businesslike tone. Then, as if realizing that he was being gawked at by every occupant of the room, his cheekbones pinkened slightly and he abruptly let go of Bev's hand

and stood up. He almost looked as if he wished he could take back everything he'd said. And judging by his on-again, off-again behavior of late, Marley was afraid he just might!

"Right, Carl," Marley hurriedly agreed.

"Thank you, Mr. Merrick!" Bev gushed. She turned to Marley and pulled her into a fierce hug. "Thank you both...so much!"

"Don't thank us, just get better," Carl said gruffly, and Marley noticed that he stepped back gingerly till he was too far away to be grabbed and hugged. "Lots of work to do at the office."

"We'd better go, Bev, so you can get some rest," Marley said, pulling out of Bev's embrace. She was eager to get Carl out of there before he slipped back into grinch mode.

"Wait, there's one more thing." Bev sat up straighter against her stacked pillows.

"Yes?" *Talk fast, Bev.*

"Marley, I...I was wondering if you could take care of Tim tonight?"

Surprised, Marley snatched a glance at Tim, who sat as still and silent as a sphinx. "Oh! I never even thought...that is, I assumed he'd stay here with you."

"The nurses offered to set up a cot for him, but the hospital is a lousy place for a kid to spend Christmas Eve. And, frankly, I'm afraid that once I go to sleep, I'll be so out of it I won't wake up if he needs me. I'd rather he slept in his own bed."

"His own bed?"

"Yes, that's why I asked you, Marley, instead of Sheila. I think it would be less upsetting for Tim if he could stay at our house, then came up here in the morning to open his presents with me. Sheila has that big family to take care of, and I didn't dare ask her to stay at my house overnight. My mom's my closest relative and she's flying in tomorrow afternoon from Kentucky, renting a car, then picking me up here at the hospital. But until she gets here I have to depend on friends.'' She bit her lip, her eyes full of a mother's anxious concern for her child. ''But then maybe you...you have other plans?''

The only plans Marley had were going home to Nat King Cole Christmas CD's, a Duraflame log, and instant cocoa. Suddenly the idea of having a child to spend the evening with was appealing. That is, if she could get the child in question to smile. ''I'm at your service, Bev.''

Bev smiled her relief. ''Thanks, Marley. You don't know how much I appreciate this. Now, I'd better write down a few things for you...like where his medicine is and how much and when he needs to take it. Although Timmy could probably tell you all this himself.'' She smiled encouragingly at Timmy, but Timmy did not smile back.

''Is he always so quiet?'' Marley whispered.

''Around people he doesn't know very well,'' Bev whispered back. ''But when he gets to know you and grows to like you, he warms up.''

''What if he doesn't grow to like me?''

''He will. What's not to like?'' Then, louder, ''Tim, this is the nice lady I told you about. You've met her before. You remember. Her name is Marley Jacobs. She was at the party at Matt's house, and she says she'll be happy to stay with you at our house just to make sure Santa doesn't get mixed up about where you—''

"I'm not going, Mommy. I'm not leavin' you here by yourself."

So the kid speaks, Carl thought, watching this new development with interest. He was glad the attention had shifted away from him to Marley and the boy. He was feeling damned foolish being "the hero" over that insurance stuff, but now Marley was center stage. He was sure glad Bev hadn't asked him to take the kid. He had to draw the line between employer and employee somewhere. Besides, he knew more about the Australian emu than he knew about children.

Bev pushed up on her elbows and scooted higher on the pillows, trying to hide the pain it was causing. Then she patted a spot next to her on the bed. "Sit here, Tim. I want to talk to you."

Timmy climbed up obediently and sat down by his mother, staring with unblinking solemnity into her face.

Bev stroked his spiky hair. "Mommy's not going to be alone. The nurses will take care of me. There's really no reason for you to stay here, Timmy. It'll be much more comfortable and much more Christmassy for you if you go home. After all, if you don't go home, who'll turn on our Christmas lights? Who'll water the tree? Who'll feed Felix?"

"Felix?" Carl repeated. "Let me guess...the cat, right?"

Bev smiled. "Right."

"She's making a lot of sense, Tim," Carl advised him. The idea of Marley taking care of Tim for the night seemed like an excellent idea to Carl. Having a kid around would discourage male visitors. Not that he really cared whether or not Stewart showed up at Marley's and put the moves on her.

Well, okay, he did care, but only because he didn't trust Stewart. He wanted Marley to find someone someday—if that's what she really wanted; not that he could recommend shackling yourself to someone for life—but not Stewart Cosgrove.

Carl realized that Tim was giving his advice a lot of thought. He stared at Carl for a long moment, his fine blond brows drawn together in a frown. Such a serious expression on such a little boy was almost comical.

"Okay, mister."

Bev looked delighted. "Then you'll go with Marley?"

Tim nodded his head slowly. "Yes, Mommy, I'll go. I'll go with Marley and sleep at my house—" he lifted his arm and pointed a short, stubby finger at Carl "—as long as he sleeps there, too."

Chapter Eight

After a stunned silence, Bev finally said in a voice just above a whisper, "What did you say, honey?"

"I want him t' stay at our house with Marley and me," he repeated, pointing again to Carl.

"That's what I was afraid you said." Bev darted an embarrassed look at Carl, then at Marley. Carl was still too surprised to react, and Marley seemed just as immobilized. All they were apparently capable of doing was staring across the hospital bed at each other. The very idea of spending the night in the same house together, with only a small boy as chaperon, was preposterous, scandalous, out of the question and...very exciting.

"I'm sorry, Mr. Merrick," Bev said, interrupting his thoughts, which seemed headed inevitably toward contemplation of Marley in various styles of lingerie. *Damn that dream.* "Tim just doesn't understand."

"Of course he doesn't," Marley spoke up, trying to come across nonchalant despite the way her cheeks bloomed with color. "I'll just explain to him that it wouldn't work out." She leaned near Tim and smiled into his face. "Mr. Merrick has to go home to his own house tonight, Timmy. He'd like to stay with you, but he has so many things to do to get ready for Christmas.''

Yeah, like recharge the truck battery so I can take that attic junk to the dump, just the way I've planned. Timmy looked at Carl and Carl did his damnedest to look apologetic.

"You understand, don't you, sweetheart?" Bev prompted him.

Instead of answering his mother, Timmy turned to Carl again. "Do you have kids, mister?"

"Er...no."

"Do ya have a Chris'mas tree?"

"No."

"Do ya gotta a cat?"

"Well, no. You see I work a lot of hours and I—"

"Gosh, it sounds like you don't have nothin' at your house. You'd better come home with me and Marley, 'cause I've got all those things at my house." He poked his chest, a smile finally breaking over his small, solemn face. He obviously felt very blessed and wanted to share.

Carl felt like a rat. He didn't want to disappoint the kid, but what he was asking him to do went way beyond the call of duty for any boss, much less one like him who hardly knew his employees in the first place. And Marley being part of the equation made it all that much worse. Hell, it made it impossible.

"Timmy, I'd like to see all those things," Marley said, still smiling determinedly. Carl couldn't figure out why the kid wasn't responding to her. She'd always been great with kids and they always took to her like frogs to a lily pond. "I love Christmas trees, and I love cats, and I'd *love* to see your dinosaur collection."

Timmy's eyes showed a spark of interest. "You know I got a dinosaur collection?"

"Yes, your mommy told me. I think it's great. I really like Tyrannosaurus rex. What's your favorite?"

"The brontosaurus. He's got a *biiiig* tail."

"I'd love to see it."

Timmy seemed about to take the bait and Carl was breathing a sigh of relief, when the spark went out of his eyes again and the sad expression returned. "I think I'll just stay here with my mommy."

"Timmy," his mother exclaimed, embarrassed and exasperated, "Marley's going to think you don't like her. And I know you do. Why won't you go home with her?"

"I like her," Timmy admitted, his head bent and his chubby fingers toying with a strand of his mother's hair. "She's nice an' she's pretty and I liked it when she was an elf and came to Matt's party an' gave out presents. But she's a girl. I wish I could show Mr. Merrick my dinosaur collection. He's a guy, and I just want a guy aroun' for a change. A guy like..." Timmy's words trailed off and his bottom lip stuck out like a window awning.

Bev's eyes got shiny again and she pulled Timmy against her chest in a hug. "Oh, honey."

Carl looked at Marley, his brows furrowed in puzzlement. Something seemed to have happened and he'd completely missed the point. Looking grave, she motioned to Carl to join her in the hall.

"We'll be right back," she whispered, and Bev nodded, a tiny smile trembling on her lips.

In the hall, Carl asked, "What was that all about?"

"He misses his dad," Marley stated bluntly.

"Why doesn't Bev just get hold of him on the

phone and Tim can talk to him? Does he live around here?''

"His father's dead, Carl," Marley said angrily. "Didn't you know that?"

Carl was shocked. "I thought Bev was divorced."

"Her husband was in the service and was killed in a helicopter crash just before she started at Little Angel. I know we discussed this when she first started. I can't believe you don't remember!"

Carl couldn't believe it, either. Feeling defensive, he grumbled, "Then how could Tim miss him? He couldn't have been more than a year old when his father died."

"Bev has always kept Rick's memory alive for Tim with pictures and stories. But I think what Timmy's really missing right now is a man's influence in his life. And, heaven knows why, but he's taken a shine to you and seems determined to show you his tree and his cat and his dinosaur collection."

Carl released a hiss of frustration. "But I can't stay the night, Marley. You know that. And I know you don't want me to."

"You're right, Carl." Marley glared at him through narrowed eyes. "I don't want you around spoiling my Christmas Eve. And I know you'd rather go back to your cheerless house without a single Christmas decoration to offend you, where you can turn down the thermostat to a frugal fifty-five and contemplate the folly of the human race and feel smug all by your lonesome."

She put her hands on her hips and thrust her face to within inches of his. "But once, just once," she whispered fiercely, "it might be a kick to try putting someone else's wishes and well-being ahead of yours.

I'm willing to make the sacrifice for Timmy's sake. Are you?''

Carl couldn't believe his ears. ''You mean, you want me to spend the night with you at Bev's house?''

''Not the whole night. Just till Timmy's in bed. After that, he won't know and he won't care where you are.''

Carl grimaced. ''But won't he want to do Christmas things?''

''I'm sure he will. And, since he doesn't realize what a grinch you are, he'll probably want you doing all those Christmas things with him. Think you can handle it, Carl?''

He wouldn't like it, but Carl figured he could handle it for one night for Tim and Bev's sake. Besides, how late could a four-year-old stay up? It was probably already past his bedtime.

Carl stretched his arm and looked at his watch. It was only five minutes after seven! How the hell had he got himself into this endless purgatory of a Christmas Eve?

Marley tapped her toe on the linoleum floor. ''So what are you going to do, Carl?''

Carl contemplated the options. He could just say no and go home, knowing he'd disappointed Bev and Tim and Marley and essentially spoiled their Christmas Eve. Or he could say yes and spoil *his* Christmas Eve. Not that there was much to spoil, since Christmas didn't mean anything to him, anyway. Looking at it that way, he supposed it would be just a night like any other night getting sucked down the drain.

The other thing bothering him, which was perhaps the real reason he was so nervous about going to Bev's house, was having to fight his attraction to Marley while cohabitating in close quarters. It was just for an evening, but the way this evening was crawling by it was going to feel like a year. Marley's renewed determination to shut him out of her heart, however, ought to work well as a safeguard against passion.

"Okay, I'll do it."

"You will?" Marley seemed genuinely surprised.

"Did I really have any choice?"

"Yes, but since you don't think you did, it means there's a tiny heart in there somewhere," Marley muttered.

Carl must have looked as though he already regretted improving her opinion of him, because she quickly added, "But don't worry. Your showing a little heart—a very little, I might add, 'cause I know you're doing this grudgingly—won't change my mind about you, Carl. I have no intention of ever again hanging my hopes of happiness on a man who teeter-totters between total grinch and not-so-total grinch. I deserve better. Now, let's go inside and tell Bev and Tim the good news."

What good news? Carl groused to himself. Spending Christmas Eve with a kid who saw him as a sub for his dad, and a hands-off female who looked sexy even bundled up in a puffy ski parka, was not his idea of something to shout about.

"Wait," Carl said, grabbing Marley's arm, then abruptly letting go when he felt the shock of awareness that happened now whenever they touched.

He could tell that Marley felt the electricity, too, but she crossed her arms and tried to look unfazed. "What, Carl?"

"I assume that Uncle Ralph will take us to Bev's house, but how will I get home after Timmy's in bed?

Maybe Ralph should take me by my house first, then—''

He stopped talking when he noticed her shaking her head and smiling ruefully. ''What?''

''You don't even know that Bev lives exactly three blocks away from your house, do you? I think you could easily walk that distance, Carl.''

Feeling chagrined, Carl simply nodded and they walked back to Bev's room without another word. When they entered, Bev looked up with an anxious, hopeful expression. Tim looked as solemn as ever, as if too worldly-wise to get his hopes up.

''Looks like you've convinced Mr. Merrick that Christmas Eve won't be complete without meeting your cat and seeing your dinosaur collection,'' Marley said cheerfully. ''He's coming home with us, Tim.''

Carl braced himself for an embarrassing melee of glee, with him as the stiff recipient of a four-year-old's grateful hugs. But Tim surprised him by doing none of those things. Although Carl did detect a gleam in his eye, the kid didn't even smile. He simply gave his mother a sedate kiss on the cheek, scooted off the bed till his sneakered feet touched the floor, then walked over and slid his fingers around Carl's gloved hand. He looked way up, and Carl looked way down.

''Let's go, mister,'' he said. ''Felix is prob'ly real hungry by now.''

Against his judgment, against his very will, Carl was charmed, he was flattered, he was touched. He was actually looking forward to meeting Felix and seeing the dinosaur collection.

He smiled. ''Okay, Tim. Let's go.''

Five minutes later, after listening to Bev's instructions and directions, receiving a key to the house and a written schedule of Tim's medicine dosages, Marley and Carl and Tim headed for the door. A small delay was occasioned by Tim's touching last-minute sprint to his mother's bed for a final hug goodbye, but they were soon on their way down the hall to the elevator.

"See you in the morning!" Bev called after them, waving a cheerful goodbye, but Marley knew Bev must be very disappointed not to be able to spend Christmas Eve with her son.

Having Carl along would make things more difficult, but Marley would do everything in her power to make sure Bev never regretted placing her trust in them. Tim was going to have a happy Christmas Eve despite the accident and the absence of his mother. And despite Carl.

If she had to, Marley would force Carl to fake some Christmas spirit...but maybe she wouldn't have to. Judging by his behavior in the past few minutes, at least, maybe he did have enough heart left in him to put aside his own hang-ups for the night and be the kind of "guy" Tim wanted him to be. So far Timmy seemed very pleased with the arrangement and, by the time they got to the lobby he was clinging tightly to both their hands. But as soon as he saw who was waiting for them there, he stopped in his tracks and stared.

"Santa?"

"Hi there, young man!" Ralph shouted as he turned from the window where he'd apparently been contemplating the unrelenting snowfall. He swaggered over, his thumbs hooked in his shiny black belt, his smile peeking out between a cotton mustache and whiskers.

Marley hadn't expected this, and by the resigned look on Carl's face, he hadn't, either. She just hoped Timmy believed what he was seeing and wasn't wondering where the large man named Ralph was that had just been introduced to him in his mother's hospital room.

"What are you doing here, Santa?" Tim asked him, point-blank. "Aren't you s'posed to be delivering toys?"

Ralph held his stomach and let loose with a hearty "Ho, ho, ho" that sounded genuine enough to convince any small boy that he was, indeed, the real Santa Claus. Marley was half convinced herself.

Ralph bent at the waist and talked to Tim at his level. "That's exactly what I've been doing, Tim. Did you know that in Australia it's now Christmas Day and many children have already opened their presents?"

Tim's eyes grew wide.

"So, you see, I've been busy for several hours. But I couldn't pass by St. Joseph's without stopping in to see all my little friends in the children's ward."

"But how do you get ever'thing done in one night, Santa?"

Marley slid a glance at Carl and caught him smiling. He was actually getting a kick out of Tim. She felt a pang of remorse that Carl didn't normally allow himself the luxury of enjoying these sorts of human contacts. And while Tim seemed to be having a softening effect on him, Marley knew only too well that Carl's mood could change at the drop of a hat, or a kiss.

She remembered that kiss under the mistletoe with a mix of longing and bittersweet regret. In a way she wished it had never happened, because now she knew how good it could be if only Carl would cooperate and fall in love with her!

"I can see you're a thinking man, Tim," Ralph was

saying as he eased into a well-cushioned chair and invited Tim to sit on his knee by patting that spot with his white-gloved hand. Tim hesitated for a moment, then let go of Carl and Marley's hands and climbed into Ralph's lap.

"You see, Tim, time is a relative thing. It goes by fast sometimes, and slow sometimes. On Christmas Eve, when Santa has so much to do, time goes by very slowly. It doesn't seem slow to most people, but it allows Santa plenty of time to visit every home where there's a child who believes."

"Believes what?"

"Believes in me, Tim." He lifted his gaze and grinned at Carl over Tim's head. Then he winked. "And believes in miracles."

Carl glowered at his uncle. Ralph was spouting double-talk, sending none-too-subtle messages through his conversation with Tim. In Santa's case, the slowing of time was getting toys delivered to every believing child in the world, and in Carl's case it was his redemption from a bitter life. Pretty heavy stuff. And all of it a bunch of baloney! Carl still believed he was having a bad dream. It was the only possible explanation for everything that had happened that night.

"There are a lot more chimneys for Santa to slide down tonight," Ralph said, lifting Tim and setting him on his feet, then standing up himself. "But I've saved just enough time to give you and Carl and Marley a ride home."

"We're all goin' t' my house," Tim happily informed him. "We're havin' a sleepover."

Ralph's brows lifted and his eyes glinted with speculation and amusement as he gave Carl and Marley a lingering appraisal. "*Well*...is that so? Sounds like a lot of fun."

"Bev asked Marley to stay at her house with Tim, and Tim wanted me to come along," Carl explained stiffly. He longed to add that he wasn't staying, but he couldn't do that in Tim's presence.

Ralph nodded soberly, but his eyes danced with merriment. "Okay, then, is everyone ready to go?"

"Are you taking us in your sleigh?" Tim wanted to know.

Ralph laughed again: "Ho, ho, ho! No, Tim. Wish I could, but with all the presents piled high in there, there's just not enough room for all three of us. I've got the rig parked on the hospital roof for now."

"Is that snazzy red car out front yours, Santa?" Marley asked, playing along. "It looks just like something a jolly old elf would drive."

Ralph's eyes twinkled as he smiled appreciatively at Marley. "Sure is. Why don't we hop in? I know Tim wants to get home so he can feed Felix, water the Christmas tree, and show off his dinosaur collection."

While Carl lagged behind and wondered how Ralph knew all the activities Tim had planned for the evening, the others headed for the door. Just before going out, Tim remembered his new friend and turned, saying, "Come on, mister. You can sit by me."

But Ralph had other ideas for the seating arrangement.

"There are just the two seat belts in front, so for safety's sake, Tim had better sit in front with me and you two can crawl in the back," Ralph announced as they reached the car.

"Can't one of us sit in the front with you and Tim?" Marley suggested as she slid a nervous look toward Carl. "I don't mind sitting in the front without a seat belt."

"Well, I mind," Ralph answered. "Without seat belts, you're safer in back." He smiled smugly at Carl. "That's okay with you, isn't it?"

No, it wasn't okay but he was not going to argue with Santa Claus in front of Tim. And there really was no question that Tim would get the only passenger seat belt, not to mention the honor of sitting next to Santa Claus.

The thing that really confused and aggravated Carl was that he distinctly remembered there being *three* seat belts in the front when they'd driven over from the Putnam Road Inn. But when would Ralph have had the time and opportunity to remove the extra seat belt? It was a small miracle that he'd even had time to change into his Santa suit and entertain the patients in the children's ward in the short time they'd spent with Bev.

But then Santa had help on Christmas Eve to get everything done, didn't he? Time was on his side.

Carl frowned. What was he thinking? Ralph was not Santa Claus! And not only that, there was no Santa Claus!

"What are you waiting for, Carl?" Marley muttered in his ear. "Don't stand there like a dunce. I don't like the idea of squeezing into that tiny space with you any more than you do, but we have no choice. Get in!"

Ducking his head and contorting his tall frame, Carl did as he was told. He got in. And once in, he realized that the area they were supposed to occupy was smaller than he expected because Ralph had jammed a box back there, taking up half the seating space.

"Ra—"

Marley's hand flew inside the car and clamped over Carl's mouth. After the shock, Carl was grateful for her intervention. He'd nearly let the cat out of the bag by calling Santa by his real name. Tim was already ensconced in the front seat, his spiky blond hair just visible above the top of the seat, and he and Ralph were having a conversation about the wonders of vinyl. Carl would just have to take Ralph to task later for what appeared to him to be deliberate matchmaking tactics. It looked like Marley was going to have to—*gulp*—sit on his lap!

Marley removed her hand from Carl's mouth, then stuck her head and one leg in the car. "Can't you move over a little, Carl?" she said irritably. "*Now*, please. I'm getting snowed on out here!"

Carl made a grimacing smile. "Believe me, I'd move over if I could. As it is, I can't budge another inch without causing permanent scars from the sharp edges of a certain cardboard container."

Then it dawned on Marley, as it had on Carl. "You mean I'm going to have to—?"

"I promise not to bite," he joked weakly.

"I don't trust you. Have you had your shots?"

"Very funny. Get in. We'll just have to make the best of this."

With an expression that would perfectly suit someone about to dive into a tub of cow manure, Marley climbed into the car and gingerly perched herself on Carl's lap. She braced herself with one hand against the window on her right, and the other hand clutching the back of the front seat near Timmy's head. She didn't lean back, but sat awkwardly forward, obviously trying to avoid putting her entire weight against Carl at any point their bodies made contact.

Carl couldn't help it, he laughed. "Marley, you're not going to be very comfortable riding that way. Relax!"

"I'm very relaxed and very comfortable," Marley insisted in a haughty tone.

Ralph looked back at them. His eyes twinkled mischievously. "You two comfy?"

"Didn't I just say so?" Marley snapped, then changed her tone and forced a strained smile as Timmy looked back at them, too. "We're fine, Santa. Just fine. But better hurry home 'cause Timmy's cat is hungry."

"Can't go too fast," Ralph answered complacently. "The roads are packed with snow. Might have to just mosey along. Now where did you say you lived, Tim?"

Ralph started the car and eased out of the parking lot and onto the highway. Once up to his "mosey" speed, he turned the radio on to a station playing non-stop Christmas carols and got Timmy singing them with him. During the commercials, he told Timmy jokes and kept up an engrossing one-on-one conversation that effectively discouraged participation from the back. This left Marley and Carl to their own devices, and in their own dark, cozy little world.

Marley was beside herself. She didn't know how long she would be able to remain seated in such an awkward position. Her arms and back ached and quivered from the strain of leaning forward, and her knees were pressed painfully against the back of the front seat. But the alternative was to lean against Carl's chest, and that would play havoc with her only recently hardened heart. It was difficult enough trying to ignore the arousing sensation of his strong thighs beneath her and the musky-clean smell of him.

So far he hadn't touched her, hadn't even spoken to her since Ralph started the engine. But as they turned a corner, despite her attempts to brace against it, she began to slide off Carl's lap and against the box. That's when his hands came up and caught her waist, the firm fingers making themselves known even through the down lining of her ski parka.

Marley swallowed hard, her skin erupting in delicious little shivers.

"I'm fine now," she whispered, turning her head slightly so only Carl could hear her. "You can let go."

"There'll be other turns in the road. Like I said, the sharp edge of that box could leave permanent scars. Maybe I should hang on just in case." His voice was low timbred, the words softly whispered.

"That won't be necessary, Carl." She tried to sound stern, but her voice seemed to have risen an octave.

He laughed, the sound coming from deep in his throat. "I wouldn't even have to hold on to you if you'd just lean back. You're very precariously perched, you know."

When she did not reply, he added, "You're being silly. I told you I wouldn't bite."

Maybe I want you to. Maybe that's the problem. "I'm not worried about…about that." *Liar, Liar.*

"Then lean back. It's got to be tiring holding yourself so stiffly."

He was right. It was tiring and she was being silly. Certainly she had enough control over herself to tolerate being close to Carl without tossing to the wind her resolve to remain emotionally distant. She'd learned her lesson. She knew he was past the pale, out of reach, not worth the pain.

Muscle by muscle, in tiny increments of movement and time, she relaxed her position. Her fingers unclenched, her shoulders came down, her back curved. She leaned back ever so slowly till her knees were no longer pressed against the seat. By now she could feel the friction of Carl's coat against hers. Then the warmth of his chest, the solid maleness of it, as she sank against him. With a tiny sigh she hoped he hadn't heard, she rested her head against his shoulder.

"Now isn't that better?"

It would have been better if he'd not said a word. But now she knew exactly how close his mouth was to her ear. He must have turned his head and was looking down at her. She could feel his warm breath slightly stirring the bangs that had escaped her knit hat.

When she didn't reply, he didn't press for an answer. After a moment, she relaxed even more and closed her eyes. A sigh of contentment—quite audible this time—escaped her lips before she knew what she was doing. And when his arms came up and crossed under her breasts, pulling her even more securely against him, she snuggled close, riding the swell of his chest with each breath he took. She was in heaven.

Carl was in hell. Marley was one delectable lapful and it felt wonderful to have his arms around her, but his reaction to her was more than physical. *This is Marley,* his heart said. *Your friend, your childhood companion, your loyal and incredibly talented business partner.* To add to this long list of credentials, she was a gorgeous, sexy female that he wouldn't mind taking to bed.

At this point, Carl was having trouble explaining to himself why he'd repulsed Marley's overtures of romance, but he closed his eyes and concentrated hard. *Oh, yeah.* She wanted commitment. She wanted marriage and babies and happily-ever-after. That would require a wedding, and his last wedding had been a fiasco. No use playing a losing card twice.

Carl felt as though he had a pint-size devil sitting on one shoulder and an angel sitting on the other giving him differing advice. The angel had spoken, urging him not to toy with Marley's feelings by being physically affectionate. The devil was telling him that the entire night was a dream anyway, so why not experiment?

How was it that the little devil always knew what you really wanted to do, then told you to do it? Carl wondered.

Taking the devilish advice, Carl reached up and carefully pushed aside the standing collar of Marley's coat, then he bent his head and nuzzled her neck. Mm...it was so fragrant, so smooth, so warm. And since she didn't pull away or hiss a warning in his ear, Carl continued, trailing his lips from her ear almost to her collarbone.

He heard her gasp, then she turned ever so slightly in his lap till their lips were kissing-close, till her sweet breath mingled with his.

"Carl?" Her voice was soft and breathy.

"Yes, Marley?" He was dying to kiss her, and expecting an invitation to do just that. He was already puckering up....

Chapter Nine

"Keep your lips to yourself," Marley snapped, shocking him with the sudden change in her tone of voice, "or you can expect permanent scars, all right, but not from that cardboard box."

Carl's ardor was effectively cooled. He gave an uncertain chuckle. "Jeez, Marley, you don't have to threaten me."

"I asked you not to jerk me around, Carl," she reminded him, a slight tremor in her voice revealing that she was as much hurt as angry. "I was only kidding about the scars, but I just don't know how to get through to you. In case you're not clear on what I mean, I mean don't kiss me, don't touch me, don't even nuzzle me, because while it may not mean anything to you, it does to me." She squirmed forward, trying to put distance between them.

"You don't have to do that," Carl urged her. "I'll behave myself, I promise. I just thought—"

"You thought I'd melt in your arms. Well, I won't. Not anymore. And, thank God, we're finally here."

Carl looked out the window. Yes, they'd arrived. Or, at least, he assumed the small bungalow they'd just pulled to a stop in front of was Bev's house. And he did recognize the neighborhood as being quite close to his own address.

"Ho, ho, ho! We're here!" Ralph announced as he clicked off the radio and the blare of Christmas music suddenly stopped. Marley sat forward, obviously eager for Tim to get out so she could get out, too. But Tim didn't appear to be in much of a hurry.

"Can you come in and see my dinosaur collection, too, Santa?" Tim asked eagerly.

"I'd like that a lot, Tim, but I'm running late. Besides, I've seen quite a few of your dinosaurs already. Remember, I gave you several last year for Christmas?"

"Oh, yeah," Tim replied with a sort of embarrassed laugh. "I remember. Thanks for the ride, Santa."

"You're welcome. Now you have a good Christmas and don't worry about your mom. She's going to be just fine."

Tim nodded, suddenly sober again. "I'll see her tomorrow and that's when we'll open presents."

"Sounds like a wonderful plan. Tell her I said hi."

Timmy nodded again and finally undid his seat belt and scooted to the door. Ralph leaned over and helped him with the door handle and Timmy scrambled out. In five seconds flat, Marley had pushed up the car seat and climbed out behind him.

"Bye, Santa," Marley called, walking carefully up the snow-covered sidewalk with Tim. "See you tomor—I mean, see you soon."

As Ralph waved to Marley, Carl started to lever himself out of the back seat, but Ralph pushed the seat back into place. "Not so fast, Carl. You and I need to have a little talk."

Carl crossed his arms and heaved an irritated sigh.

After Marley snapping at him, he was in no mood for more of his uncle's maudlin speeches. "What now, Uncle Ralph? What miracle are you going to try to sell me on now?"

Looking deadly serious, with no trace of his jovial Santa persona in evidence, Ralph said, "Your facetious attitude is a mistake, Carl. The things that are happening to you tonight are not figments of your imagination."

Carl opened his mouth.

"No, it's not a dream, either. It's really happening and if you don't start taking it seriously, you're not only going to miss out on lots of wonderful Christmases, you're going to lose the one woman on this earth who can make you truly happy."

Ralph's words made Carl uneasy, but he refused to give credence to so many unbelievable events. "You're right, Uncle Ralph. This isn't a dream, it's a nightmare."

"If you think this is a nightmare, you wait and see what's in store for you in the future if you don't start listening to your heart and start living the present the way it's supposed to be lived."

Carl felt as sulky as a schoolboy. He'd never liked being lectured—particularly by a guy in a fake white beard. "I'll live my life the way I choose."

"And suffer the consequences. Because, yes, Carl, there will be consequences for being so stubborn and cold and joyless. And you won't like them."

"What consequences, Uncle Ralph?" He became sarcastic. "Oh, that's right, you can't tell me! I'm supposed to get three visitors, and you're just number two. It was Miss Hathaway's job to show me what a great kid I was and what a great childhood I had, and it's your job to show me what a jackass I've become. Then someone else is supposed to pop up and show me what an incredibly worse jackass I'm destined to be if I don't shape up. Do I have it right?''

"Pretty much.''

Carl shook his head. "And you expect me to believe this is really happening?''

"It's your miracle, Carl. You can believe it or not. But I would advise you to believe it, because it's your chance to change before it's too late.''

"Lucky me," he drawled.

"And just to clarify things, Carl, Miss Hathaway and I not only showed you the way things were and are, but we've given you opportunities along the way. Opportunities to enjoy Christmas again, and opportunities to be with Marley.''

"Like squishing me in the back seat with her? That worked well.''

"Maybe she knew your intentions weren't exactly honorable?''

"I suppose you mean I didn't have a diamond ring ready to slip on her finger? Hell, I only wanted to kiss her.''

"What you do with the opportunities you're given is up to you, Carl. At this point you still determine your destiny. But don't wait till it's too late.''

"You're giving me the creeps, Ralph. Let me out, will ya? It's no wonder I quit coming to the family get-togethers. Now, instead of drinking cocoa and singing carols around the fire, you probably exchange UFO stories and read tea leaves. Has the whole world gone nuts?''

"Sometimes it seems that way. I'm sure that's the way you felt seven years ago when Andrea stood you up at the altar to run off with her old boyfriend from New York. Especially after she made you believe she was—''

''I don't want to talk about that, Uncle Ralph.'' Carl felt his usual reaction to mention of Andrea and that horrible night. He felt sick and ashamed and betrayed.

''Maybe you should. Maybe if you'd talked about it a long time ago, you wouldn't have wasted so much time.''

''If you call turning a modest business into a hugely successful enterprise, I guess I *have* been wasting my time for the past several years,'' Carl said tiredly. ''But I don't think so. Now, if you don't mind, Uncle Ralph, Marley and Tim are probably wondering what's become of me.'' He smirked. ''Or do they even realize how much time has passed since they went inside? I suppose you fixed things so they wouldn't notice.''

Ralph just stared at him, his eyes gentle and sad and forgiving. ''I won't end this meeting between us on a sour note, Carl.'' He reached over and squeezed Carl's shoulder with his big hand and smiled. ''I love ya, son. So does your dad and your mom and all the rest of the Merrick clan. And so does Marley. You remember that...you consider that...and then you decide what you want to do with the rest of your life. G'night, Carl. See ya around.''

And before Carl knew it, he was outside on the sidewalk and Ralph's '55 Chevy was nothing but a couple of tiny red taillights in the snowy distance. He couldn't even remember getting out of the car. Blinking confusedly, he turned and walked slowly up the sidewalk toward the open front door. About halfway there, Christmas lights suddenly turned on and the whole front of the small house burst into multicolored brilliance.

At the door, Tim greeted him with a smile, holding a large black cat with tuxedolike patches of white on its chest and paws. "I turned on the lights! And this is Felix," Tim announced grandly...and Carl couldn't help but smile back.

Maybe his uncle was nuts. Maybe *he* was nuts. Maybe the whole world was nuts. But whether he was dreaming or not, this night was the only reality he knew at the moment and he had to quit assuming his actions had no consequences. He would be far more careful of Marley's feelings, and he would make sure Timmy had a great Christmas Eve. After all, he may not like Christmas, but he had nothing against little boys who still believed, or beautiful, naive women who still believed, either. And, speaking of beautiful women, his first order of business was to apologize to Marley.

Carl closed the door and followed Timmy into the living room. It was a small, homey room, very tidy, and sparsely furnished with one small slip-covered couch and two worn chairs. Bright pillows were scattered all around and photos, mostly of Tim and a dark-haired young man in a uniform—Tim's dad, no doubt—covered a long table behind the couch. In the corner was a small Christmas tree decorated with popcorn and cranberry strings and gingerbread cookies. Timmy had apparently already turned the lights on and watered it. Carl could see a trail of water drops from one end of the room to the tree.

Marley was just taking off her parka, which led him to believe that neither she nor Tim had noticed that he'd sat in the car with Ralph for ten minutes talking about miracles. She glanced at him, then looked away quickly, unsmiling and intent on removing the rest of her winter gear.

"You wanna help me feed Felix?" Tim asked Carl.

"I certainly do," Carl answered, smiling down at the child as he shrugged out of his coat, unwound his scarf from around his neck and peeled off his gloves. "But first don't you think you'd better take off your coat?"

"Yeah. I might get cat food on it, and then it'd stink. B'sides, I gotta go to the bathroom."

Perfect. "Okay. Don't forget to wash your hands. I'll meet you here in five minutes."

Tim set down the cat and ran off down the hall, and Carl turned to Marley. She was laying their coats across the back of one of the chairs and neatly placing the gloves and scarves on the seat. She seemed very absorbed in what she was doing.

"Marley?"

"Hmm?" She didn't look up—which was not very encouraging—but he decided to make a stab at an apology, anyway.

"I'm glad we've got a moment alone."

Marley sat on the couch, ran a hand through her wispy hair and finally looked up at him. Her expression was as flat as her tone of voice as she asked, "Why, Carl?"

"Because I have to tell you I'm sorry about what happened in the car. You asked me not to…well, you know…unless I really meant it. And it's not that I didn't mean it, but it wasn't probably the same as what you meant when you said I should really mean it. Know what I mean? Oh, hell. I'm not making any sense. I'm sorry. Let's just leave it at that."

There, he'd said it. But she still wasn't responding. He tried again.

"We're friends, Marley, and I value our friendship. I want us to forget any harsh words or misunderstandings between us and just have fun tonight."

"Fun? You, Carl? It must be for Tim's sake."

"And for yours."

She stared at him for a long moment. Finally the corners of her mouth turned up slightly and her eyes took on some life. "You're a piece of work, Carl Merrick. But I'm going to accept your apology because I want to have fun tonight, too. For Tim's sake, for my sake, and for your sake." She jabbed a finger at him. "Just remember, we're friends, and friends don't jerk friends around."

He nodded vigorously, glad they were on amicable footing again. He'd mind his p's and q's if it killed him. And judging by how cute she looked in that sweater and those tight jeans, it just might.

"I'm ready!" Tim called as he raced back into the living room, carrying Felix again as if the cat wouldn't come as soon as he heard the can opener whirring. Judging by the cat's size, Carl guessed Felix didn't miss many meals.

"You're pretty strong to carry that cat around, Tim," Carl said as he removed his suit jacket and tie, undid the top buttons of his white shirt and rolled the sleeves up to the elbows. He caught Marley watching him, but she quickly looked away. He couldn't help it, he liked her watching him.

"Long as I take my medicine, I'm very strong," Tim proudly informed him, flexing his right arm.

"Speaking of medicine, Tim, it's time for your evening dose," Marley said, briskly getting up from the couch. "Is this the way to the kitchen?"

They followed Marley through a small dining room and through a swinging half door to the kitchen, Carl admiring the view of Marley from behind. She had a darn cute wiggle in her jeans.

In the kitchen Carl located the cat food, allowed Tim to run the can opener with supervision, then together they watched Felix hunker down and, with eyes squeezed nearly shut, devour the entire can in record time. Meanwhile, Marley found Tim's medicine on a high shelf, read Bev's instructions carefully, then gave Tim his dosage.

Watching Tim down his pills, Carl was reminded again that Tim was really sick. It was easy to forget, because he behaved so normally. Just looking at him, no one would ever know.

Carl felt a pang of guilt. He couldn't believe he didn't even know that Bev was a widow and that Tim had a heart defect that would need surgery to correct. He spent fifty hours a week with Bev at work and he never knew about the most important things in her life. He didn't even know she lived only three blocks away!

The thing was, he never wanted to know about her or any other of his employees. He was afraid of getting involved. Now, at least with Bev, it was too late. Somehow, though, he didn't regret it. He was glad he'd met Tim. He was happy to be helping by getting the insurance coverage they needed, and which many of his other employees might need just as desperately.

"Are you ready to see my dinosaur collection?" Tim asked as soon as Felix had finished his meal and had gone off to lie in the corner and lick his paws.

"Did you ever have dinner, Tim?" Marley interrupted.

"I ate at the hospital."

"Did you get enough? Are you still hungry?"

"Mommy made some cookies shaped like stars and Christmas trees. I'd like one of those with some cocoa after my bath."

Marley laughed. "You're got it all figured out, haven't you? After you show Mr. Merrick your dinosaur collection, you'll have a bath, then some cookies, then bed...okay?"

"A story, too?"

"Sure. Which story is your favorite?"

"On Christmas Eve Mommy always reads me *The Night Before Christmas*."

"I love that story," Marley said. "Where's the book?"

"It's in my room by my bed." Timmy hesitated, then blurted out, "But would it be okay if he read it to me?"

Carl wasn't surprised that Tim was pointing at him. But *The Night Before Christmas?* Why couldn't it be *The Three Bears* or even *Beauty and the Beast?* He would have a hard time reading the Christmas story without showing his cynicism.

"I think it would be very nice if Mr. Merrick read that story to you," Marley said, giving Carl a measured look. "But maybe you should ask him yourself."

Tim looked up at Carl. "Will ya, mister?"

Apparently Carl couldn't refuse Tim anything, no matter how painful it might be for himself. "Sure, Tim." He ruffled Tim's spiky hair. "Now let's go see the dinosaur collection."

Over the next hour, Marley played second fiddle to Carl as Tim claimed his undivided attention. She watched from the bedroom door as Tim showed Carl the dinosaur collection, which was comprised of several plastic creatures ranging from two to approximately twelve inches in height. Along with a couple of plastic trees, which were supposed to represent the prehistoric jungle, they took up the entire top of Tim's chest of drawers.

After making a roaring sound for each dinosaur, Tim also illustrated how the brontosaurus enjoyed eating the plastic trees. Carl was duly impressed and—with a self-conscious look in Marley's direction—even made a couple of dinosaur sounds himself. Tim was delighted.

After enjoying the dinosaur exhibition, Carl helped Tim undress for a bath while Marley ran the water, dumping in a generous dollop of bubble bath from a plastic bottle shaped like Batman. Tim expected company for his bath, too, and showed Carl his various seafaring vehicles, then paddled his feet "like a frogman" till the front of Carl's white shirt, his bare forearms, his hair and his face were spotted with clumps of bubbles. Marley half expected him to be angry, but he just laughed and pulled Tim out of the tub, wrapping him in a huge white towel.

Marley was mesmerized. Watching this "picture" moment between Carl and Tim was almost unbearably painful. Her heart pounded with bittersweet joy to see Carl behaving so humanly, and actually seeming to enjoy it.

He looked so handsome with his sleeves rolled up and his hair mussed with a few strands falling forward onto his forehead. Marley had always found a man's forearms very sexy, and Carl's had to be the sexiest on earth.

And he was so good with Tim: patient and gentle, but good at that big-guy kidding around that little boys thrived on. Carl teased and tickled and joked Tim right through getting his pajamas on, then, in no time at all, they were back in the kitchen looking for cookies and cocoa.

Marley was glad that, at least in this regard, she could be useful. She had the cookies already laid out on a plate and the cocoa poured. She didn't resent Tim's preference for Carl; in fact, she thought it was good for both of them. She just wished that someday she would see Carl acting the same way with *their* son.

Marley banished this thought from her mind as she carried her own cup of cocoa into the living room, while Carl carried his and Tim's and Tim carried the cookie plate. There was no way she was going to get her hopes up again. No-sirree-bob.

Before Tim's bath, Carl had built a fire and now it was briskly burning and filling the living room with warmth. Felix was lying on the braided rug in front of the fire, flexing his front paws and purring ecstatically.

Carl sat on the sofa with Tim nestled against him, and Marley curled up on one of the chairs with her stocking feet tucked under her. They munched on cookies and stared into the fire. It was very peaceful, very...well...familyish. The only difference Marley wished she could make to this affecting scene would be to put her on the couch, too, snuggled up against the other side of Carl. Marley found herself daydreaming again, wishing that she and Carl could really be a family with a little boy—or boys and girls—of their own.

Suddenly Carl asked, "Tim, what did you ask Santa to bring you for Christmas this year?"

Marley was glad he'd asked. Maybe Carl was just making conversation, but she was curious for a specific reason. She remembered Bev saying that she hadn't had to do much "preparing" for Christmas that year. The costs of Timmy's prescriptions had probably taken a big bite out of their Christmas budget. Maybe she could help Bev make Tim's wishes come true.

"I never asked for nothin'," Timmy revealed, surprising Marley.

"Didn't you write Santa a letter?" she asked. All kids wrote letters to Santa, didn't they?

"Yeah. Mommy wrote it for me. But she said Santa could only bring me a few small things this year, so I never tol' Mommy 'bout the big thing I wanted and she never put it in the letter."

Marley took another sip of cocoa before casually inquiring, "So what was the big thing you wanted?"

Tim's eyes got a faraway gleam in them. "I wanted a fire truck, just like Matt's, with a siren and everythin'."

"You should have mentioned it to Santa when you saw him tonight," Carl suggested teasingly.

Tim shook his head again. "Nope."

"Why not?"

"'Cause Mommy already tol' me Santa couldn't bring me a big thing, and, b'sides, that wasn't Santa."

Marley and Carl exchanged shocked glances that quickly became amused. "It wasn't?" Carl said.

Tim screwed up his face in a comical expression. "Santa's got a real beard. He doesn't need rubber bands 'round his ears t' hold it up. That man was a nice man, but he wasn't Santa. B'sides, he looked an awful lot like that man I met in Mommy's room...that Ralph guy.''

Enjoying Tim's calm, worldly-wise demeanor, by now Marley and Carl were having a very difficult time keeping their laughter in check. ''If you knew he wasn't Santa, Tim, why did you play along?'' Marley asked him.

Tim shrugged. '''Cause I thought you might think he was Santa and I didn't want t' spoil it for ya. But then I figured you were as smart as me and you'd know he wasn't Santa, neither.''

Marley and Carl laughed. Tim watched them for a moment with a puzzled expression, then laughed, too.

''It was very considerate of you to think of our feelings, Tim,'' Carl told him, setting down his empty cocoa cup. ''And now I think it's time we read that story and you went to bed.''

''Can we read it in here?''

''I don't see why not.'' Carl looked at Marley. ''Is that okay with you?''

''Hey, you're pretty much running the show here,'' Marley said good-naturedly. ''Whatever you want to do is fine with me.''

Carl nodded. ''Okay, we'll read it in here, then. Go get the book, will you, Tim?''

Tim instantly scooted off the couch and ran to the bedroom, and Carl turned to Marley with an expression almost of pride on his face. ''What a bright kid! Can you believe he knew all along it was Ralph under those fake whiskers? But you'd never have known it by the way he acted on the way over here. Pretty cool character, isn't he?''

"He's wise beyond his years," Marley agreed. She hesitated, then couldn't resist adding, "And the thing that struck me most was that even though he knew this Santa was a fake, it didn't turn him off to all Santas."

Carl looked sharply at Marley. "You're not trying to moralize again by comparing me unfavorably to a four-year-old, are you?"

Marley made an innocent face. "If you're finding double meanings in everything I say, Carl, maybe you're the one comparing yourself unfavorably to a four-year-old."

Carl's mouth clamped shut. He apparently didn't want to argue with her, which was just fine with Marley. While she couldn't resist making the analogy, she didn't want to argue, either. What was the use? Since they'd called a hands-off and a truce, the evening had been going very pleasantly and she wanted it to stay that way for Timmy's sake.

Timmy came in with the book and climbed up on the sofa beside Carl, snuggling against his chest and putting his hand on Carl's leg. Carl put his arm around him and settled down to read. Once again Marley got a lump in her throat at the sight of the two of them together, Carl's dark head bent close to Timmy's blond, spiky one. Gathering up the dishes, she hurriedly left the room.

Marley stayed in the kitchen while Carl read the story, but his deep voice carried and she heard, if not the words, the melodic tone and rhythm of his reading. She could tell he wasn't hurrying through the text, and there was plenty of expression in his voice, which children always loved.

She washed the dishes and straightened things and

forced herself to stay away till the very end of the story, only allowing herself the pleasure of witnessing Carl read the very last line, "'Merry Christmas to all, and to all a good night.'"

With his head resting on Carl's chest, Timmy was fast asleep. He looked adorable. They both looked adorable. Before Carl knew Marley was watching, she actually caught him stroking Tim's hair. Of course as soon as he noticed her, he stopped.

"I'll carry him to bed," Carl whispered gruffly.

Marley nodded, then followed him into Tim's bedroom. Carl laid him down and Marley covered him up. Gazing at him from the door, they turned and made the mistake of gazing at each other, too.

Chapter Ten

Marley had always found Carl incredibly appealing, but at that moment he was irresistible. He leaned one broad shoulder against the doorjamb, his usually crisp white shirt creased where Timmy had laid his head, and a strong column of throat showing above the unbuttoned collar. He had a sexy five-o'clock shadow and mussed hair, and he smelled of Batman bubble bath, cocoa and a hint of spicy aftershave. His shirt was tucked loosely in his trousers, the leather belt cinched around his narrow waist. And those sinewy forearms of his...whew!

"He's...he's a sweet kid, isn't he?" Marley said, just managing to get the words out. She was standing too close to Carl to be able to breathe correctly.

Carl nodded slowly, his blue eyes shuttered with thick black lashes as he gazed down at her. "Yeah, he's a good kid. I really enjoyed spending time with him tonight."

Carl couldn't have said anything that would have pleased Marley more. It proved again that he still had a heart, that it hadn't withered away to the size of a pea over the past seven years.

"You were great with him. You made up for his

mom not being here and sent him to bed feeling safe and happy.'' She lifted her right hand and laid it gently against his chest where she could feel his heartbeat through the pads of her fingers. Playfully she whispered, ''I knew there was a heart in there.''

Carl looked down at her hand where it remained on his chest. Then he looked up and into her eyes, his lips tilted in a half smile. He reached up and cradled her jaw in the cup of his warm palm. With his thumb he gently stroked her cheek and teased the corner of her mouth lingeringly.

Marley's eyes fluttered shut. Exquisite feelings surged through her, making her knees weak and her heartbeat as uneven as a thrown rock skipping over a pond. She remembered telling him not to touch her or kiss her, but her whole body screamed for the feel of his hands, his lips, every inch of him against every inch of her.

Then, suddenly, the pressure of his hand went away and Marley's eyes flew open. Carl shook his head. ''I told you I wouldn't,'' he said hoarsely. ''And I won't.'' He turned and walked toward the living room.

Watching him retreat down the hall, Marley wanted to cry from disappointment. She followed him, her arms crossed over her chest as if to hold in the pain.

He stood by the chair that held their coats and other winter gear, his back to her, rolling down his shirtsleeves. Marley couldn't resist. She went to him and wrapped her arms around him, resting her cheek against his back.

''Marley, I have to go,'' he said, sounding as miserable as she felt.

''What if I asked you not to?''

''I'd say you'd regret it tomorrow.''

"Why?"

"Because I can't give you everything you want."

She asked again in a much smaller voice, "But...why?"

Carl turned around and clasped her hands in his. His expression was grim. "I have to go, Marley, and I have to go now or I won't be able to."

"Just tell me why, Carl," she persisted. "Is it because of Andrea? Or is there something else?"

Carl looked down at Marley and knew that he owed her an explanation, that he'd owed her an explanation for a long time. But he'd opted for avoidance tactics up till now, staying away from anything and anyone that could touch his heart and make him as vulnerable as he'd been seven years ago.

"Sit down, Marley."

She sat on the couch and he sat down beside her, but he leaned forward, resting his elbows on his knees and looking at the floor. He might be ready to talk, but he wasn't sure he could look Marley in the eye while he was doing it.

"Uncle Ralph said I should have talked about this a long time ago."

"Uncle Ralph is a very wise man," Marley answered encouragingly.

Carl pinched the bridge of his nose and sighed. "I never thought it was anybody's business but mine. But since it's probably affected you more than anyone else in my life, I'm going to tell you what really happened with Andrea."

There was a pause, then, "What do you mean 'what really happened'?"

Carl chuckled humorlessly. He looked over his shoulder at Marley where she sat in the corner of the sofa, one leg tucked under her, watching him with her most serious, most tender expression. "You know most of it already. Everyone knows most of it. Just about the whole town was at the wedding."

"That must have been so painful for you."

Carl was grateful that her tone was kind but matter-of-fact. He would have hated it if her voice had been dripping with sympathy...or worse, pity.

"Your mother and I wanted to urge you to talk about it, but your dad said to give you time and you'd come around," she continued. "He said you'd talk when you were ready. But that never happened, and you grew so distant nobody dared bring up the subject again."

"Well, I guess I'm not the first person who's been stood up at the altar, and I won't be the last. But that wasn't the main reason I felt like such a fool."

"It wasn't?"

"And, now that I look back on it, I'm not even sure I really loved her."

"You aren't?"

"No, although believing I was in love with her certainly made it easier to go through with the wedding."

"Go through with the—? Carl, why did you propose to Andrea in the first place?"

Carl took his time answering this one. He stared at the floor for several minutes. As far as he knew, he and Andrea and her husband were the only people who knew this part of the story. "She was pregnant."

Not a single sound came from Marley's end of the couch. Finally he looked up and saw that she was stunned. "With...with your baby, Carl?" she said faintly.

"She told me the baby was mine and I believed her.

But she was lying. I thought we had an exclusive relationship, but I was wrong. She'd been seeing her former fiancé even while she and I were dating. When she found out she was pregnant she told him the baby was his, but he refused to marry her. She decided to use me to make him jealous, which is what she'd been doing all along, anyway. She threatened to raise his baby as mine.''

"I can't believe she did that!"

"It took him till right up to the hour of the ceremony to decide what he wanted to do, but her plan worked. As I'm sure you recall, he swooped into the bride's room at St. Mary's and carried her away just as the wedding march began.''

"How did you find out the baby wasn't yours, and...and are you quite sure it isn't?''

"She left a note, the writing barely legible, but clear enough to get her point across. She told me she'd lied about the due date and that the child was conceived during a three-week period when I was out of town.''

"Oh, Carl.''

"They settled in New York, but I kept track of her, and when the baby was born I demanded a paternity test because I wasn't going to be made a fool of twice. Besides, if the kid was mine I wanted parental rights.'' He grabbed the back of his neck and started kneading. "Turned out she was right. The child wasn't mine.'' He smiled grimly. "But it wasn't her husband's, either. They've since divorced.''

"Good heavens, I had no idea Andrea was so dishonest! And no one knows any of this, not even your parents?''

"I didn't want them involved. Besides, I was so

damned embarrassed. Andrea fed me a line and I swallowed it, hook, line and sinker.''

"Well, I never liked her, but I figured I was just jealous. I never would have guessed she was so deceitful and selfish.''

"She didn't just jilt me, Marley, she tricked me into the whole sham in the first place. She never had any intention of going through with the wedding. And ever since then—''

Carl made a vague and ineffectual gesture with his hands.

"And ever since then, you haven't been able to trust anyone. You figure you're not a very good judge of women and you don't want to get taken advantage of again and made to look like a fool.''

Carl shrugged. "You've summed it up pretty well, but I don't consciously think all those things. All I know is that after two or three dates with a woman, something inside me just shuts down. There doesn't seem to be any other option but to break it off.''

He turned and looked earnestly at Marley. "I do this to nice women, women whose company I've really enjoyed. I don't want that to happen with you, Marley. I want to be your friend, now more than ever. I don't ever want to hurt you and I can't predict what would happen if you and I got involved. With every other woman—''

"Carl, I'm not every other woman.''

Carl was silenced. He stared at her, sitting there so patient and loving and beautiful. She was right. She wasn't like any other woman he'd ever met. He'd known her and cared about her for twenty years. And it had become patently clear in the past few hours that he would enjoy taking their friendship to the next level, to be intimate with her, maybe fall in love with her. But was that possible? Would it be different with Marley, or would he, as he feared, end up hurting her?

"You're right, Marley," he conceded. "You're not like every other woman. I care about you. But I'm not ready to explore how much I care about you, and that's why I have to go." He stood up.

There was silence for a moment, then she stood up, too. "All right," she said, looking resigned and disappointed, yet somehow decisive as she watched him put on his suit jacket, then his overcoat. "I understand, Carl. You've had a traumatic experience and you're dealing with it the best way you know how, I suppose. But I think you ought to know that by the time you're ready to explore our relationship, as you put it, I might have moved on."

In the process of pulling on his gloves, Carl froze and turned to her with a frown. "Is that a threat?"

She smiled pensively and shook her head. "Just a fact. I've waited my entire life for you, Carl, but I'm twenty-eight years old. I want a family. I want to spend a Christmas Eve like this with my husband and my children before I'm fifty. And if someone comes along who wants what I want and truly cares about me—and isn't afraid to tell me so—I might just decide that it's time to get on with my life. Time doesn't stand still, you know." Her smile curved into a rueful grin. "Except for Santa Claus every Christmas Eve."

Carl stared at Marley, an uneasy feeling building inside him. She seemed so calm, so resolved. And even though she denied having threatened him, what she'd done was issue an ultimatum. And it dawned on him that no one, not even Marley, could wait forever for him to get his act together. It was a sobering, frightening thought, but Carl wasn't ready to deal with it.

Doing what he'd been doing so well for the past seven years, Carl decided to deal with it later. Much later. He stuffed his necktie in his coat pocket and wrapped his scarf around his neck.

"Too bad you don't have boots," Marley said, sounding her usual self again. "Your house is only three blocks away, but the sidewalks will be several inches deep in snow."

He avoided her eyes. "I'll be fine."

"Change your socks when you get home."

"Yes, Mother."

She laughed and grabbed his coat lapels, forcing him to look at her. "I'm not your mother, Carl."

She was damn right about that. He stared into her green eyes and down at her lush, full lips, still tilted in a smile left over from laughing. His hands lifted to her shoulders, kneading them once, twice, then into her hair, his fingers sifting the fine blond tresses with worshipful delicacy.

Her face was tilted to his, her eyes burning with a deep light of tenderness. He wanted to throw caution to the wind. He wanted to kiss her. Hell, he wanted to—

But what he wanted was interrupted by the doorbell.

"Who the hell could that be at this hour?"

Marley, seeming a bit dazed, glanced at the mantel clock and said, "It's not that late, Carl. It's only eight o'clock. It's probably a neighbor bringing over Christmas goodies or something. I'm sure whoever it is won't be staying."

Carl didn't care who it was. Although initially irritated by the interruption, now he was glad this mystery person had shown up just in time to stop something he should never have started.

He followed Marley, intending to make his escape while the door was still open. But that was before he saw who was standing on the porch with a large, colorfully wrapped present tucked under each arm.

"Cosgrove," Carl growled. "Just passing by... again?"

Stewart laughed. "Not this time. I came by specifically to drop off these presents."

"How sweet of you," Marley enthused, grabbing Stewart's arm and pulling him inside, or at least trying to. Carl stood stubbornly in the way until the last possible minute, then stepped aside only far enough to allow Stewart to squeeze past. Marley gave Carl a reproachful look, then turned her smiling attention back to Stewart. "Tim and Bev will be so pleased."

"Well, to tell you the truth, the presents aren't for Tim and Bev," Stewart confessed.

Marley looked surprised.

"They're for Tim and you," he clarified. "I've already dropped off a gift for Bev at the hospital."

Carl watched Marley blush. "Oh, how very—"

"I suppose that's how you found out where we were," Carl interrupted, not eager to hear Marley's effusions.

"But you're leaving," Stewart observed, scanning Carl's attire. "Is that wise?"

Prickles of suspicion crawled up Carl's spine. "What do you mean?"

Stewart shrugged innocently. "Marley's here without a car. What if something should happen and she needed transportation?"

"What could happen?"

"I don't know—"

"She can call me if she needs me," Carl said gruffly.

Stewart turned to Marley. "But wouldn't you feel better if someone stayed with you? I could stay. I don't mind sleeping on the couch."

"Well, I—"

Instead of flatly refusing, Marley was considering. Incredulous, Carl looked from her blushing, beautiful face to Stewart's handsome, eager one, and knew a feeling of real dread. He tried to catch her eye, but Marley refused to look at him. What the hell was going on?

"I don't know, Stewart," Marley finally said in a weak-willed sort of way. "You must be freezing. Why don't you come in and set those presents down, then I'll fix you some warm cocoa? We'll talk."

"Don't mind if I do," Stewart said. He started for the living room, then stopped and juggled his presents so he could pull a small rectangular box out of his coat pocket. "Oh. I almost forgot. This is for you, Carl."

Carl frowned. "For me?"

"Don't worry. It's not a present. I know you don't do presents."

"Who says I don't do presents?"

"Well, since you don't do Christmas, I just thought—"

Carl flicked a glance at Stewart's packages, crossed his arms over his chest and lifted his chin. "It's true I don't usually do presents, but this year I might make an exception."

Undaunted, Stewart's smile broadened. "Well, great! But I hope you've got your shopping done, because the downtown stores are closing at nine to-night.''

He pushed the rectangular box at him and Carl finally took it. ''Now I'm wishing that really was a present, but it's only a tape of the Little Angel commercial. I thought it was about time you saw it. See you, Carl. And, don't forget—'' he walked away, smiling over his shoulder ''—if you wait till after nine o'clock, it will be too late.''

Carl slipped the tape in his coat pocket, wondering why Stewart's parting words sounded so ominous. *If you wait till after nine o'clock, it will be too late.* Then he pushed aside the superstitious feeling and got down to more practical matters, like what he was going to do next.

He was in a hell of a quandary. He was standing at the open door with Marley watching him. He was bundled up and ready to go and had been on the verge of leaving till Stewart showed up. Now he didn't want to go. But if he stayed, if he took off his coat and scarf and gloves and planted himself on the sofa to play chaperon, he'd look like a fool. Worse still, he'd be sending mixed messages to Marley.

Speaking of Marley, she'd crossed her arms and was shivering in the cold air that streamed in from outside. She looked both defiant and exasperated. He knew he had only one choice. Because he wasn't ready to say and do what she needed him to say and do, he had to leave her alone with Stewart and let her make her own decision about whether or not that creep slept on the couch.

''Goodbye, Marley.''

She sighed. ''Goodbye, Carl.''

Carl stepped out onto the porch and she immediately closed the door behind him as if relieved to get rid of him. He stood there for a minute, agonizing over his decision, but when he heard Stewart and Marley sharing a laugh, he determinedly stepped away from the shelter of the porch eaves and started his walk home.

No doubt about it, Carl was in a foul mood. The snow didn't bother him; he hardly noticed it. He was too busy thinking about Stewart and Marley, wondering what he'd given her for a present.

He pictured the scene vividly. He saw Stewart urging Marley to open the present and Marley laughing and finally giving in. She'd rip off the ribbons and wrappings, root through a bunch of tissue paper and squeal with delight as she held up to her chest...a sexy black teddy.

Get a grip, Merrick, Carl scolded himself. Marley wasn't the type of girl you'd give a black teddy to after just a couple of dates. Black teddies belonged within the bounds of intimate, committed relationships. But how did he know they'd only dated once or twice?

Carl's imagination took over again. He saw Marley batting her lashes as she coyly suggested, "Should I try it on to see if it fits?" And Stewart's wolfish leer as he replied, "As long as you model it for me."

Carl turned around and took several steps back toward Bev's house, then, with a herculean effort, changed direction again and forged homeward. He was being a fool. That's what caring about a woman did to you, and he didn't like it one bit.

He consoled himself by remembering that Timmy was at the house and his presence should curtail any amorous ideas Stewart might have. Not that Timmy's

presence had done much to stop Carl himself from
forming amorous ideas just a few minutes ago.

He couldn't stand it anymore. He had to quit thinking. He blinked through the snow and looked around
at the houses he was passing, most of which had some
kind of Christmas decor, and many of which were so
heavily hung with lights and wreaths and every other
sort of Christmas regalia, they resembled department
store displays. But for some reason, the profusion of
Christmas decorations didn't disgust him. Strangely
enough, they actually cheered him up a bit.

At one such lavishly decorated house, a station
wagon pulled into the driveway and promptly dis-
gorged a large family with lots of noisy children scrab-
bling to the front door where an elderly couple awaited
them. Hugs and kisses were given and received.

Carl turned away from the happy scene, his own
words to Marley coming back to haunt him. *What's
the matter, Marley? Afraid I'll die alone? Afraid there
won't be a grieving widow and two or three generations of posterity standing by my deathbed, weeping
softly?*

Carl trudged on, the snow seeping into his shoes
and building up on his shoulders and hair like a hor-
rific case of dandruff such as one might read about in
a Steven King novel. The cold and the wet were starting to penetrate and he was more miserable than ever.
He was really looking forward to getting home.

Home. He was there, but Carl wasn't as happy as
he thought he'd be. He stood at the end of the sidewalk
and looked up at the two-story brick house he inhab-
ited during the few hours a day he wasn't working.
Mostly he just slept there. It was a big house, too big

for a bachelor. But he'd bought it because of its lo-
cation so very close to work.

The outer facade of the house looked as miserable
as he felt. Not that it was run-down or anything. It just
looked cold and dark and uninviting. There was no
wreath on the door, no candy canes bordering the sidewalk leading up to the porch, no garlands or bows or
twinkling lights. Nothing.

But at least he could get in out of the weather. With
this bracing thought, Carl sloughed his way up the
unshoveled sidewalk and climbed the several steps to
the porch. Digging into his trouser pocket for his keys,
he wondered why he hadn't at least left the porch light
on so he wouldn't have to grope in the dark to unlock
the door. But it seemed so wasteful to leave the porch
light on all day just so he'd have an easier time of it
when he got home hours and hours later. The price of
lightbulbs these days was ridiculous.

Carl had to laugh at himself. Maybe he was getting
a bit miserly. Marley thought so.

Marley. Carl had found his keys and was about to
insert them in the lock when his gaze fell on the door
knocker. Now why this should happen was beyond
him. The door knocker, which was a run-of-the-mill
lion's head with a ring in its mouth, was an unre-
markable object he never took the time to notice. But
tonight there was something about it.

Despite the fact that there was no porch light, the
door knocker was faintly glowing, as if it had inter-
nally generated luminescence. Or as if someone had
coated it with fluorescent paint. This strange phenomenon drew Carl's attention, then, as he stared, the
lion's head gradually changed in shape and features
till it looked just like…Marley! Marley smiling…her

face pale and lovely, her hair stirred by an undetectable breeze, her eyes fixed on him in tender and amused contemplation. Marley...just as she'd appeared to him in that dream within a dream.

Carl's jaw dropped. He blinked several times and rubbed his eyes, and suddenly the door knocker was just a door knocker again. Marley was gone.

Carl wasn't sure if he was happy or sad. But he was quite sure he was in a fragile state of mind. He was hallucinating, for crying out loud! When would this terrible nightmare be over?

His hand visibly shaking, Carl fumbled with the key, finally got it in the lock, then opened the door and hurriedly closed it behind him. At least he was home now and in familiar surroundings. He'd do what he routinely did when he got home from work at night and maybe his life would return to normalcy.

Carl flipped on the hall light and snatched a look at the door, making sure the back of Marley's head wasn't sticking out into the entry hall. He was relieved to see nothing but the gold plate and the screws and nuts that held the knocker on.

Then he took off his scarf, coat and gloves and put them in the closet, immediately registering how icy cold the house was. Rubbing his hands together, he moved to the thermostat and cranked it up from fifty to seventy. Really, he saw no reason to be cold just to save a few pennies on the gas bill.

Next Carl went upstairs to his bedroom, changed into warm flannel pajamas, wool socks and a heavy robe, then returned to the kitchen, intent on his usual bedtime snack...a bowl of frosted flakes.

When he opened the fridge, it struck him that it was incredibly empty. It contained approximately a cup of milk, a half-empty bottle of A.1. sauce, a withered apple and two limp carrots. Opening the pantry, he found even less. He didn't know why this paltry supply of food struck him as so depressing, because he never kept much food in the house.

He never cooked. He always ate out, or skipped eating altogether. The only thing he made sure he had plenty of was frosted flakes, his one indulgence. But even that, like the milk he needed to go with it, was in short supply tonight.

As Carl poured his bowl of cereal and dumped the last of the milk over it, then went into the living room and sat down in an easy chair in front of the TV to eat it, he tried to feel self-righteous. After all, most of the world were gorging themselves on fudge and cookies and cheese balls and fruitcake and eggnog. He, at least, was not clogging his arteries.

But as Carl ate his frosted flakes, all he could think about was the fact that the house was so quiet he could hear himself crunching. He was sitting in front of the TV, but it wasn't on. Except for the news, he never watched TV during the holiday season. There was just too much sugary sentimentality on the airwaves this time of year, and his cereal was sweet enough, thank you very much.

Suddenly Carl wasn't hungry anymore. At least not for cereal. He'd rather have a sugar cookie shaped like a tree or a star or an angel.

He set down his bowl on a table by the chair and heaved a deep sigh. He looked around at his empty house and wished he at least had a cat to keep him company. Then he remembered Tim's words. *Gosh, it sounds like you don't have nothin' at your house.*

"You're right, Tim," Carl said out loud. "That's

exactly what I've got. Nothin'.'' But it had never bothered him before. Now he was wishing he was back at Bev's with Marley, curled up by the fire, drinking cocoa and eating cookies. But Stewart Cosgrove was there instead of him.

Carl stood up and paced the floor. What was happening to him? The strange events of the day had knocked him out of his comfortable orbit and now he felt as though he were spinning through uncharted space. He was restless and dissatisfied with life as he'd known it for the past seven years. He wanted more.

Meeting up with Miss Hathaway had made him remember his childhood and the innocent pleasures he'd shared growing up with Marley as his best friend, and the memories had reminded him how much he truly cared for her. Uncle Ralph had made him recognize that his present feelings for Marley were stronger than ever and definitely of a romantic nature. And both of them had indicated that they were part of a Christmas miracle ordered by The Powers That Be. They were his self-described ''redeemers.''

Carl sat down and rubbed his temples. Maybe it was time he accepted the possibility that he wasn't dreaming, that all this was really happening, that he really was in the midst of a Christmas miracle. But Marley had told him he'd encounter three people before nine o'clock who would remind him of who he was, who he is, and who he's destined to be. If Miss Hathaway was the first and Uncle Ralph the second, who was the third person sent by T.P.T.B.?

Carl glanced at his watch. It was eight-thirty. Time no longer seemed to be moving at a miracle-making snail's space. There were only thirty minutes left till zero hour. So where was the third part of this miracle?

Carl wondered if it was possible that he had proved to be so difficult and appeared so hopeless that The Powers That Be had decided to give the third redeemer the night off?

Carl stood up again and resumed pacing. He was driving himself crazy thinking about all this stuff. He had to think about something else. If only he dared watch TV.

Then it hit him. He'd watch a tape! In fact, maybe he'd watch the Little Angel commercial. It didn't seem like the best diversion for not thinking about Stewart and Marley and Christmas and The Powers That Be, since at least three of these components of his present misery and confusion were in the commercial. But suddenly Carl couldn't wait to check that puppy out.

Striding into the hall, he opened the hall closet, took the tape out of his coat pocket, returned to the living room and popped the tape into the VCR. Resettling himself in the easy chair, he clicked the appropriate button and the television screen flared to life.

Chapter Eleven

The commercial opened on an idyllic winter scene, probably taped right there in Mount Joy, of pine trees and rolling hills covered with snow, the sunshine sparkling on every frosty surface. Festive music overlaid with jingle bells played in the background.

Then the camera zoomed in to a white clapboard two-story house, and a large picture window framed by lacy curtains with a bushy pine wreath hung dead center.

First, as the viewer, you observed the family through the picture window—a mom and a dad, a small girl wearing an ankle-length pink nightgown, and a toddler boy in red footed pajamas—then you were instantly inside the house watching close-ups of the four actors as they joyously opened Christmas presents.

Carl had no idea who the children were, although, knowing Marley, they were probably relatives of an employee or employees of Little Angel with movie-star ambitions. Whoever they were, they were convincing little actors, just as convincing as Stewart and Marley were as the mom and dad.

The first shots showed the cute, engaging children

opening presents, then the mom and dad opened presents from each other. The music changed, becoming more sentimental, more romantic.

Dad—Stewart in plaid pajamas, his hair mussed attractively—beamed over the plush robe his wife gave him, and Mom—Marley in a white nightgown, her hair perfectly arranged—was moved nearly to tears by the dainty angel locket on a gold chain. He put the necklace on her, then turned her gently around and kissed her tenderly.

While watching this sweet scene, Carl clenched his jaw and felt his fingers ball into fists. But it wasn't over.

Suddenly Stewart pulled a card out from behind the sofa cushion and, with an adoring look, handed it to Marley. "Sweetheart, you do so much for the whole family. I can never find the words to tell you how much I appreciate you...how much I love you."

Flustered, Marley opened the card and read it, her eyes really welling with tears this time.

"Oh, darling," she gushed, "this card says it all. Thank you. *Thank you!*" As the music swelled to a poignant crescendo, she threw her arms around his neck and they kissed again, this time passionately.

The children interrupted their parents and clambered up on the sofa for a group hug, then the camera backed up and away, out through the picture window as a mellifluous male voice suggested, *"Let Little Angel say it for you. Available wherever you purchase fine greeting cards."*

The screen went blank, but Carl didn't move. He just glared at the TV as if it were somehow responsible for the terrible feelings coursing through him.

They were just acting, he told himself. It was just a

commercial, a staged vignette designed to help sell Christmas cards. But Carl couldn't get over how convincing Stewart and Marley were in their roles.

He grabbed the remote control and rewound the commercial, then pressed the play button. He figured that watching the commercial again would reassure him that the whole thing was just an illusion of television magic, not reality. But watching it again only made him more tense, more angry, more jealous.

Stewart didn't have to kiss Marley so thoroughly, did he? Wasn't this commercial broadcast during prime time when children were up and watching? He'd bet his bottom dollar that Stewart had slipped in a little tongue during that staged smooch!

Carl rewound the tape and watched it again...and again...and again, every viewing making him more frustrated, more frightened. They looked so domestic together, so happy, so perfect. So *in love.*

During the eighth viewing of the tape, Carl's imagination started working overtime again. Instead of a locket, he saw Marley pulling a black teddy out of a box and holding it up to her. Then they kissed like daytime soap stars instead of first-time actors in a Christmas card commercial, and the children did not climb onto the sofa for a group hug but seemed to have disappeared. By the time the tape was done, Carl was nearly frothing at the mouth.

Carl pressed the off button, then sprang out of the chair and started pacing again, dragging his hands through his hair till it stood on end. He felt there was a point to the commercial he was missing, a terrible truth just out of his mind's grasp. Then it hit him like a bolt out of the blue.

Stewart! Stewart was the third player in the plan put

together by The Powers That Be! But while Carl could believe that Miss Hathaway and Uncle Ralph were rooting for *him,* he had the sneaky suspicion that Stewart was in this scam for himself. Why else would he sense a certain sinister enjoyment in Stewart's parting words, *If you wait till after nine o'clock, it will be too late?*

What exactly did Stewart mean? Carl knew he was supposed to be visited by three different people before nine o'clock, but was he supposed to make some decisive move to prove he was a changed man by that hour, too? What were the consequences if he didn't make that move? Would he lose Marley forever? Suddenly that was a totally unacceptable possibility.

Carl sat down and held his head in his hands, trying to make sense of it all. The third messenger was supposed to show him the man he was destined to be, but what had Stewart shown him of himself? All Stewart had done was horn in everywhere they went, being cheerful and charming and a general nuisance, doing everything that Marley wished Carl would do.

Carl's head reared up. Was it possible to be hit twice by lightning? Suddenly he knew exactly what Stewart's role was in this whole wacky scenario. He was Carl's replacement! If Carl continued the way he was going, he wouldn't figure in Marley's future at all! Marley would marry the man in the commercial…the loving partner, the husband, the father. Stewart Cosgrove!

And Carl would be home alone. Tim's words came to him once more. *Gosh, mister, it sounds like you don't have nothin' at your house.*

Carl looked at his watch. It was eight forty-five. He had exactly fifteen minutes to do something to stop that stupid commercial from coming true. If Marley had to have domestic bliss, by hell he was going to be the one supplying the bliss!

He didn't take the time to ask himself if he was really the changed man Marley wanted and deserved, or if he was just acting out of jealous spite, all he knew was that he had to do something before nine o'clock.

There was no time to change clothes, so Carl simply threw his long overcoat on over his pajamas. He decided his slippers wouldn't do in the snow, though, so he kicked them off—violently stubbing his toe against the doorjamb in the process—and yanked on a pair of sturdy boots. He was nearly out the front door when he remembered his keys were on the dresser in his bedroom, so he limped upstairs to fetch them.

His plan was to go directly to Bev's house, but, halfway down the stairs, he realized that he couldn't go empty-handed...not after that slickster, Stewart, had shown up with presents for everyone! He'd go shopping first, then he'd break up Stewart's cozy little cocoa party with Marley.

Carl finally slammed the front door shut behind him, but nearly pulled his arm out of its socket when he gripped the porch rail to keep from falling as he barreled down the snow-covered steps, his feet slipping and sliding beneath him. Now his arm *and* his toe hurt.

Since his car was parked in the garage, he figured there'd be no need to scrape ice and snow off the windows. But when he walked around to the back of the house, he discovered that he hadn't closed the garage door that morning and the snow had blown in and covered the car, anyway! Like a madman, he hastily scraped, then climbed in to turn on the engine.

Despite the fact that it was a new model, for some reason the car ignition cranked and cranked before finally turning over.

Carl was beginning to feel as though there were a conspiracy against him getting back to Marley before nine. A conspiracy of one...Stewart Cosgrove!

He backed out of the driveway at breakneck speed, then zoomed toward town, the rear end of his car doing fishtails. On the way, the car stalled twice.

The only good luck he had was that he didn't encounter much traffic till he reached the tiny downtown district of Mount Joy, then he was forced to slow down. Fortunately the snowplow drivers had been busy and the road conditions were much improved, but he couldn't find a place to park! He glanced at his watch; it was eight-fifty! Desperate, he parked in a loading zone in front of Laceys' Department Store.

Carl hurried into the store, then stood stock-still just inside the revolving doors. It suddenly dawned on him that he didn't have a clue what to buy Marley! Tim was easy, of course. He'd buy him a fire truck. But the only thing Carl could think of to buy Marley—the thing that filled his head to the exclusion of all else—was lingerie! But somehow he didn't think that ought to be his first gift to her in over seven years.

Intending to give the matter further thought as he took care of Tim's gift, he searched the directory and discovered that the toy department was on the third floor. He took the escalator, but tried to hurry things along by running up the moving steps two at a time. However, his extra effort was wasted because an elderly woman who was also riding the escalator was blocking the way, and even though he whispered, "Excuse me," directly into her ear several times, she didn't appear to hear him and didn't budge till she got off, very slowly, at the top.

Despite the fact that the store was closing in a matter of minutes, there were several other wild-eyed customers besides himself rushing around the toy department doing their last-minute shopping, and the lines at the checkout counters were incredibly long. Carl didn't have any idea where to look for a fire truck, so he grabbed the arm of a harried-looking salesclerk as he walked by.

"Er...yes, sir, can I help you?" the college-age kid asked distractedly.

Carl got right to the point. "I need a fire truck."

"I'm afraid we're completely out of fire trucks," the young man answered, his gaze sliding down to Carl's plaid pajama legs then up to his face again with a slightly perplexed expression.

Carl blinked. "What do you mean you're 'out'?"

"We sold them all, sir. But, if you can wait till I'm finished with another customer, I'll try to help you find something else."

"It has to be a fire truck! That's what he wants!"

The salesclerk looked bored and beleaguered, as if he'd heard this story many times before. "Then you should have come sooner, sir." He started to walk away, but Carl grabbed his arm again.

"Are there other toy stores in town that might have fire trucks?"

The salesclerk glanced at his watch. "Two or three, but they'll be closing up at this hour. They've probably already locked their doors." He walked away, mumbling, "Which is what we should have done."

Carl didn't know what to do. His watch showed exactly three minutes to nine! Instead of going unnaturally slow, now time seemed to be flying by, and not because he was having fun! He thought about grabbing some other toy for Tim, but it hardly seemed worthwhile to buy him something he didn't want, so he decided instead to think about what he could buy for Marley.

The answer came quickly. Of course! An angel! He headed for the fine china department where he knew they also sold elegant figurines and porcelain dolls. He arrived just as a motherly looking salesclerk flicked off the last light in the display cases. Another younger woman was locking them up.

"You can't close yet!" Carl shouted, leaning on the glass surface with his hands splayed in front of him. "I need an angel!"

Both women were startled by his outburst. The older woman said, "I'm sorry, young man, but the angels are sold. In fact, they were all gone by yesterday afternoon. We only get a limited stock for the holidays."

Carl closed his eyes and slumped against the case. "Oh, great, what am I going to do now?"

The woman seemed concerned. "Oh, dear, I'm very sorry you're distressed." Suddenly she seemed to have an idea and said, "There was an order for a Nuremberg angel that came in, and no one's picked it up yet. I could check the holding date on it."

"A Nuremberg angel?" Carl repeated wonderingly. "You can order those?"

She smiled. "Yes, of course."

Carl reached for his wallet. "How much is it?"

"The order was picked up, Mavis," the younger woman informed her co-worker.

Carl was immediately deflated. He should have known it was too good to be true.

"Are you sure, Sally?"

"You were at break. It was that tall, handsome man in the dove-gray coat who spent so much time looking at the angel displays over the holidays. You remember, don't you? He was so friendly and charming. And he had a smile like a—"

"Neon sign," Carl bleakly finished for her. *Stewart Cosgrove strikes again.* "I think I know him."

"Well, you should take a lesson from him," the older salesclerk lectured like a schoolmarm. "Plan ahead and you won't be disappointed at the last moment like this. I do hope you've got something else in mind for the person who was supposed to receive an angel."

Carl sighed heavily. "Sure. Sure I do." He cleared his throat, then tried to smile even half as brightly as Stewart, but he had the feeling he was probably only generating enough wattage for a small, dim lightbulb. "Will you ladies do me a favor? Will you open up your cash register just long enough to sell me a couple of gift certificates? Please?"

FIVE MINUTES LATER, Carl was standing on the pavement outside Laceys'. He stashed away the gift certificates in his jacket pocket, along with the parking ticket he'd found on the windshield of his car, then got behind the wheel and drove toward Bev's house.

Things were not going well for him, and it was after nine o'clock, but something inside him refused to believe it was too late. He wasn't about to concede defeat to Stewart Cosgrove. The stakes were too high.

Carl pressed the pedal to the metal and fishtailed his way to Bev's house, trying not to let his imagination get the best of him again. But it was impossible to picture Marley anything but touched, ecstatic and deeply grateful when she opened Stewart's present and discovered it to be a Nuremberg angel. The present *he* should have bought for her.

At nine-fifteen, he pulled into the driveway, nearly skidding into the garage. He jumped out and ran to the door. He was about to pound on the weathered wood but remembered just in time that Timmy was sleeping and rang the doorbell instead.

Up until the moment the door opened and he saw Stewart standing there, smiling smugly, Carl hadn't been sure what he was going to do. Now he knew exactly what to do. He was going to have it out with Stewart.

Pressing his forefinger into Stewart's chest, he advanced. "Listen, buster, it's about time you and I had a little talk."

Walking backward to accommodate Carl's forward march, Stewart willingly preceded him into the living room. "I'm perfectly happy to talk to you, Carl," he said serenely. "But I think I would prefer it if you removed your finger from my rib cage."

Stewart sounded so calm and sensible, Carl became embarrassed and dropped his arm to his side. He looked around the room. "Where's Marley?"

"She's down the hall."

Carl pictured her trying on lingerie to model for Stewart. "What for?" he growled.

There was that maddening smile again. "Tim woke up and asked for a drink of water. I don't know what's keeping her. Maybe she's reading him a story."

Carl nodded sharply. "I hope so. It's better she doesn't hear this. She wouldn't believe it. I'm not sure *I* believe it."

Stewart got an enlightened look on his face and crossed his arms. "Ah, so you've finally caught on?"

"To the fact that you're trying to screw up my miracle? Hell, yes! What I want to know is why they—"

"They?"

"The Powers That Be. Why they trusted you in the first place."

Stewart shrugged. "I'm very good at my job."

"Too good, damn you. This time you've gone too far. I think you're in this for yourself. You caused all those problems and accidents to happen on my way over here. You aren't giving me the chance I deserve."

"The chance to do what, Carl?"

"To be what Marley wants me to be, what else?"

Stewart clicked his tongue. "Carl, you still don't get it, do you? If you're only changing to compete with me, there's no guarantee the changes will be permanent." He poked Carl's chest. "They have to be from the heart, Carl, because Marley deserves no less than the best. Besides, I'm not so sure you've really changed at all—" Stewart's amused gaze skimmed Carl's attire—except into your jammies."

Carl ignored Stewart's jab. He had other things to think about...like whether or not he'd really changed.

He remembered his loneliness at the house.

He remembered the wistfulness he felt when he saw the station wagon pull up to that neighboring house and all the kids piling out to run to their waiting grandparents.

He remembered how the Christmas decorations had actually cheered him up.

He remembered how good it felt to spend time with Tim.

He remembered skating with Marley, eating fudge with her, kissing her.

And, yes, he remembered how jealous he felt when he saw Stewart kissing Marley in the commercial.

"I've changed," he said firmly. "I know I have."

Stewart looked dubious. "Have you? Or have I just pressed certain buttons and this is a knee-jerk reaction? Are you trying to elbow me out of the picture because of some kind of macho pride thing, or do you have certain feelings for Marley that can no longer be denied?"

"Why do I have to explain myself to you?" Carl blurted, agitatedly pacing the floor. "You've done your bit, now isn't it time you disappeared?"

"Why do you think I'm going to disappear? Your uncle and Miss Hathaway won't be disappearing."

Carl pointed his finger at Stewart. "I have a sneaking suspicion that you came to Mount Joy specifically to be part of this!"

He smiled. "Carl, you may be a grinch, but you're not stupid. You're right. Mildred Hathaway and Ralph Merrick are mortals and were recruited for the job. But I do this sort of thing all the time. In fact, I work full-time for T.P.T.B. I'm an—"

"Shh!" Carl glanced down the hall. "What are you, nuts? Marley will hear."

"An emissary, Carl. I'm an emissary. Besides, Marley won't hear. The door's closed, and she doesn't even know you're here."

"She's been in there a long time." Carl felt a niggling of worry. "Are you sure Tim's all right?"

Stewart nodded. "Perfectly. But I'm glad you asked. It does appear that you may have changed, Carl."

"You've slowed down time again, haven't you?" he accused. "She doesn't even realize how long she's been in there. Why couldn't you have slowed down time while I was shopping?"

"It's always a mistake to leave things to the last minute. And it's after nine o'clock, Carl," he reminded him.

"I don't care what time it is," Carl argued. "It's never too late when you love someone. And I love—"

Both men looked startled, but while Carl was shocked and slightly appalled by what he'd almost said, Stewart looked pleased as punch. "We're finally getting somewhere! Who do you love, Carl?"

Carl was speechless. He was still absorbing the incredible thing that had just occurred. Had he really almost announced that he was in love with Marley? And was he? But how else could he explain the raging jealousy he felt toward Stewart? He was not the type to be piqued by the attention other guys got. He couldn't care less who Stewart kissed on a commercial as long as it wasn't his Marley.

His Marley. Had it always been Marley? Had he always loved her and just didn't know it? Had he been wasting all these years agonizing over Andrea's deceitfulness when he could have been enjoying the sweet, honest love of his life?

"Who do you love, Carl?" Stewart repeated.

Carl looked Stewart in the eye, stunned by the revelation. "I love Marley. I've always loved Marley."

"And she loves you, you lucky dog," Stewart drawled. "She made that pretty clear in the office this afternoon. But you didn't give her much hope of her feelings being returned. What are you going to do about that, Carl?"

Carl answered promptly. "I'm going to tell her that I do return her feelings. Then I hope to God she gives me a second chance. Maybe we can spend Christmas together, celebrating it like it should be celebrated."

Stewart nodded with satisfaction. "My work here is done."

Carl was thrilled. "Does that mean you're leaving?"

"Yes. But before I go, there's something I have to do."

"What's that?" Whatever it was, Carl was willing to help.

"I have to knock you senseless."

"What?"

"Don't worry, Carl," Stewart said as he pushed up his sweater sleeves. "Although you might not believe me, I'm not allowed to enjoy this and I wouldn't dream of going against the rules. Besides, I'm sure it'll hurt me more than it hurts you."

"But—"

But before Carl knew what was happening, before he had the slightest idea of defending himself, Stewart's fist had connected with his jaw and he was sprawled on the floor.

He blinked through circling stars at this so-called emissary from The Powers That Be, then, just before passing out entirely, heard Stewart say, "I went against the rules, Carl. I have to admit, I quite enjoyed that. But it was worth it." And he must have been telling the truth, because the smile on his angelic face was totally unrepentant.

CARL WOKE UP TO the rather disconcerting sight of Miss Hathaway at close proximity, sniffing his breath.

Involuntarily he flinched.

"He's coming to!" she barked.

"Oh, thank goodness!"

Carl's heart leaped. That was Marley's voice! Now he was treated to a close-up view of her beautiful face. She was leaning over him, her soft hands pressed against either side of his face. Her eyes were misty with emotion.

"Carl, are you all right? Does anything hurt? What happened to you?"

"No booze on his breath, so he's not drunk," Miss Hathaway announced over Marley's shoulder.

"Of course I'm not drunk," Carl mumbled indignantly. "He hit me." He reached up to rub his jaw, which felt amazingly unbruised considering the punch Stewart had delivered.

Marley looked confused. "Who hit you, Carl? When I came out of Timmy's bedroom, I just found you lying here on the floor."

"He must have tripped over the cat," Miss Hathaway theorized, "and hit his head on the sofa."

Carl pushed to his elbows and was assailed by dizziness. "No, that's not what happened. I told you Stewart socked me in the jaw."

Marley and Miss Hathaway exchanged glances.

"I know it's hard to believe that wonderful, angelic Stewart could do such a thing, but he did." Carl waited till the dizziness passed, then peered around the room. "Where is he, anyway?"

Marley and Miss Hathaway exchanged another glance, this one rather anxious.

"Don't look that way. I'm not going to hit him back. I wouldn't start a brawl on Christmas Eve."

"I think he's still a bit out of it," Miss Hathaway said from the side of her mouth, her Safari Red lips twisted comically.

"Do you think we should take him to the hospital?" Marley whispered back.

"Don't talk about me like I'm not here," Carl complained. "I feel fine." And the amazing thing was, suddenly he did feel fine. He worked his jaw and found that it felt perfectly normal. He stood up and he didn't feel the least bit dizzy. However, he was a bit confused about one thing. "Where's Stewart?"

"Carl, we don't know who you're talking about," Marley informed him a bit helplessly. "Have you been dreaming? After all, you are in your pajamas."

Carl considered this. Had he been dreaming? Had he, as he'd first suspected, dreamed up this whole night? But, if that was true, what was he doing at Bev's house? It *was* Bev's house, wasn't it?

"Where are we?" he asked.

"We're at Bev's," Marley told him, looking anxious again. "Don't you remember? Bev asked me to come and stay with Timmy, then he said he wouldn't come without you. Then—"

"Yes, I remember," Carl assured her, and she seemed relieved.

"Do you also remember going to Sheila's and Miss Hathaway's and skating at Reindeer Pond?" she further quizzed him.

"Yes, I remember all those things," Carl answered carefully. "But Stewart was there, too. At Reindeer Pond and at the Putnam Road Inn. He came to tell us about Bev. We *did* go to the inn, didn't we, Marley?"

Marley laughed nervously. "This Stewart person, whoever he is, seems to pop up everywhere. Yes, we were at the inn, but it wasn't somebody called Stewart who told us about Bev. It was Miss Hathaway.''

Miss Hathaway nodded decisively. "Yes, indeed. It was I who saw her in the ER as I came down from the children's ward.''

"How did you know we were at the inn?''

"After our little visit, I saw you two from my front window as you were getting in the car with Ralph. After calling your houses and getting no answers, I figured you might be at the inn. Ralph always stays at the Putnam Road Inn when he comes to town.''

Carl sat down on the sofa. He was beginning to feel overwhelmed. "But isn't Stewart in the volunteers group with you, Miss Hathaway?''

"There's no Stewart in my volunteers group, Carl.''

He turned to Marley. "But who's in the commercial with you? Who's the good-looking blond guy with the neon smile?''

Marley's brows knitted. "To tell you the truth, I don't remember, Carl. That's surprising, because I'm usually pretty good at remembering names. He's just some actor the agency sent over. I would have cast him from the employee pool, but no one seemed suited for the role and you wouldn't do it, remember?''

Carl struggled to figure out what the hell was going on. Was it possible that everything could have happened just the way he remembered it, but with the exclusion of Stewart? Was this Stewart's way of disappearing yet still leaving the miracle intact? And, if so, did Miss Hathaway remember her part in the miracle? How about Uncle Ralph?

"Marley, would you get me a drink of water?'' Carl asked. "Suddenly I'm parched.''

"Of course,'' she answered, hurrying away.

As soon as Marley had disappeared around the corner of the dining area, Carl turned to Miss Hathaway. "Miss Hathaway, why are you here?"

She looked surprised and a little offended by the question. "I called the hospital to check on Bev and she told me you and Marley were here with Tim. I just dropped by with some divinity I made. I thought you three might enjoy it."

Carl nodded soberly, not yet satisfied. "Okay, but let me ask you one more question, if I may. Do the words 'The Powers That Be' mean anything special to you?"

She shrugged, looking baffled. "No. Should they?"

He smiled, relaxing a little. "I guess not."

She stared at him a minute longer, as if trying to decide if he was nuts or not. Finally she said, "You're still a bit woozy, Carl. I'd take it slow the rest of the night if I were you. And you shouldn't be driving. I'll stay here with Tim while Marley drives you home. In fact, I think I'll spend the night, sleep on the couch, keep her company. You can pick up your car tomorrow."

Carl was about to tell her that *he* intended to keep Marley company that night, but he knew how immovable Miss Hathaway was once she'd made a decision. Besides, considering how he and Marley had left things between them earlier that night, she would undoubtedly prefer Miss Hathaway's company and side with her.

So, actually, Miss Hathaway's idea of Marley driving him home was the perfect opportunity to get some private time with her. He needed time to tell her how he felt, time to convince her that he'd really changed. And he'd definitely have to do some convincing, because she'd already given him several chances that night and he'd blown them all.

"Here's your water, Carl."

Marley handed Carl the water and he took it with a grateful smile. He watched her over the rim of the glass as he drank it down, but she never bothered to smile back. Although she'd obviously been worried about him after finding him passed out on the floor, she was still feeling hurt and playing it cool after his last "I'm not ready for a relationship" speech. He didn't blame her, but he wasn't about to get discouraged and give up.

"What are you doing here, anyway, Carl?" she asked him. "I thought I locked the front door. How'd you get in? And why are you wearing pajamas?"

Carl set down his empty glass. "I'll answer all those questions in the car." Hopefully he'd have some answers by then.

Marley looked wary. "In the car?"

"Miss Hathaway says you'd better drive me home."

He could see her lips starting to form the word *no*.

"She says I'm not fit to drive."

He could see the indecision in her eyes. "But you seem fine."

Carl shrugged. "Suit yourself. But Miss Hathaway said I might have an accident and freeze to death while waiting for someone to rescue me."

"I never said all that, Carl," Miss Hathaway scolded. She pursed her lips consideringly. "Although I suppose it could happen that way."

That settled it. "Oh, all right," Marley said irritably as she grabbed her coat off the chair and shrugged into it. "Let's go, Carl. But hurry up, because I don't intend to ruin my Christmas Eve by spending the whole night with you!''

Satisfied, Carl stood up. His coat was already on, so they headed for the door. As they passed the Christmas tree, however, Marley stopped and looked down. ''Where did those presents come from?''

Carl followed her gaze and was horrified to discover that Stewart's gifts to Marley and Tim were still under the tree!

Chapter Twelve

Carl couldn't believe an emissary from T.P.T.B. could be so sloppy about details! When Stewart disappeared, he should have taken his presents with him! How was Carl supposed to explain Stewart's name on those gifts, especially since he'd just been raving about someone by the same name?

While Carl racked his brain, Marley stooped and inspected the gift tags, then looked up at him with an expression of patent disbelief.

"I can explain," he began. But how? Should he tell her that Stewart was his middle name and take credit for the presents? But she knew his middle name was Ebeneezer, and no one forgot a middle name like that.

Slowly she stood up and moved to stand in front of him. "Carl, I don't understand."

"I know you don't." He stretched his neck and scratched under his chin in a nervous gesture. "Fact is, I don't understand, either."

By now, Miss Hathaway was curious and had gone to inspect the gifts, too. This was unfortunate because Carl knew she wouldn't rest till she'd got a satisfactory explanation out of him.

She stood up and turned around. "Why are you

making such a big deal out of this, Carl? So you finally broke down and bought presents. I'd say it's about time!''

"What do you mean?" he asked carefully.

"Is this your name on these gift tags or not?" She brought over one of the boxes and showed it to him.

Carl looked at the tag and saw his own name, in his own handwriting. It read, "To Marley, Love from Carl," as plain as the nose on his face.

Filled with wonder, Carl thought, *This really is a miracle! And now even Stewart is helping me!*

Carl controlled his urge to jump for joy and tried to look sheepish. "I guess I *am* making too big a deal out of it." He took the present from Miss Hathaway and handed it to Marley. "Merry Christmas, Marley."

Marley's jaw dropped. "Carl, that's the first time I've heard you say that in seven years!"

She was right, it was the first time in seven years. And it felt damned good. "Merry Christmas to you, too, Miss Hathaway," he said, getting the hang of it now and enjoying it more and more. "Sorry I don't have a present for you, but I didn't know you'd be here."

Miss Hathaway smiled. "That's okay, Carl. Just hearing you say 'Merry Christmas' is a good enough present for me. I'm sure it's a present your parents will enjoy, too. Don't you agree, Marley?"

But Marley seemed incapable of speech. She just gaped at the present, then at Carl, then at the present again.

Carl winked at her. "Got something for *me,* Marley?"

She finally managed to collect herself and blushed a lovely shade of pink. "As a matter of fact, I do."

"You do?" Carl was surprised. He'd only been kidding. They hadn't exchanged presents for years!

"It's something I bought for you seven years ago, but, as you know—"

As he knew, that's when he'd quit celebrating Christmas. "Maybe on the way to my house we could go by your house and pick it up," he suggested. It seemed a perfect way to stretch out their time together.

She hesitated, staring at him as if he'd suddenly sprouted extra appendages. He'd been Jekyll and Hyde all night and it was obvious she was afraid to believe what seemed to be happening. He smiled reassuringly. "Trust me."

MARLEY KNEW THAT TRUSTING Carl was possibly the stupidest thing she could do. But now she was curious. And, as long as she didn't allow her feelings to run away with her again, it was probably safe enough to accept his present and to take him by her house to give him his present.

Marley tore his eyes away from Carl, who was looking especially appealing with his ruffled hair and that rare, devastating smile, and turned to Miss Hathaway. "You really don't mind staying with Timmy?"

"Not a bit," she replied. "Take your time. I'll be here all night."

Marley wanted to assure Miss Hathaway that she wouldn't be needing a baby-sitter for Timmy all night, that she'd only be gone a few minutes, but she might reveal where her mind had been straying, and that just wouldn't do. So she simply said, "Thank you, Miss Hathaway. See you soon." Then she turned to Carl and said nonchalantly, "Okay, let's go. Got your keys?"

Carl produced his keys and Marley took them, waved to Miss Hathaway, and was soon outside and headed for the car.

"It quit snowing," Carl commented.

Marley looked up at a clear black sky studded with stars. "You're right. It's beautiful."

She opened the driver's door and placed Carl's present on the seat between them. She started the car and, eager to make some sort of safe chitchat, asked him, "What did you get Tim? After we found out tonight that he wanted a fire truck, I was planning to buy him one during the after-Christmas sales. I wanted to get away tonight and find one for him, but I didn't have a car and, anyway, I couldn't very well have left him alone to go shopping." She suddenly realized she was babbling and told herself to shut up.

"And you didn't dare ask me to shop for you, or to stay and watch Tim," Carl said ruefully.

"No, I didn't dare," she agreed quietly. She marveled that he actually sounded apologetic. "But I had no idea you intended to go shopping."

"Neither did I," Carl admitted, still in that rueful tone.

Marley wanted to ask a million questions, but she was afraid to. Carl had seemed to make a turnabout in attitude earlier that night at the inn, but then he'd changed back to his old self and nearly snapped her head off.

Then, later, he'd seemed to be really getting into all the Christmas stuff with Tim, but she figured he'd only done it for the child's sake.

And after her conversation with him about Andrea, while she'd understood better why he'd been running so scared all these years, she'd also ended up with even less hope that he'd eventually get over his hang-ups and fall madly in love with her.

She'd told herself to be mature, to be realistic, to be open to other men in her life. After all, she couldn't wait forever for Carl. And just when she thought she'd got a handle on such a novel idea, he was suddenly there again, acting so...strange. So human. So wonderful. Did she dare open up her heart one more time and see what might happen?

She was so deep in her own thoughts, Marley was surprised when Carl said, "I'd rather his present was a surprise. You don't mind waiting till tomorrow to find out what he got, do you?"

"No, but I confess I'd rather not wait till tomorrow to see what you got for *me*," she blurted.

She looked over at him, his smile evident even though the only light in the car came from the street lamps outside and the thin eyelash of a moon that hung in the night sky. "I want you to open my present, Marley," he assured her. "As long as I get to open yours."

"Okay." She smiled, feeling herself getting excited...more excited over a Christmas present than she'd been in years. "It's a deal."

Marley's cottage-style house was only a few miles away, and they were soon there. Carl hadn't been to her house in ages, and since she hadn't been home since that morning, all was dark except for the back porch light. She wondered how Carl would respond when he saw the inside of her house and all the decorations. Perhaps this would be the definitive test to see whether or not he'd really changed his attitude about Christmas.

As for whether or not he'd changed his attitude

about *her,* she wasn't sure what could convince her of that except maybe a mad, passionate declaration of love and a marriage proposal. She smiled wryly to herself. That'd be the day.

Carrying her present under one arm, Marley led the way up the back porch steps. As she lifted the key to insert it in the lock she became very aware of how close Carl was standing behind her. She could actually feel his body heat, feel his breath, warm and gentle, against her temple. Her hand began to tremble and, to her utter embarrassment, she found she couldn't line up the key with the keyhole.

"You must be cold," he murmured.

On the contrary, she thought. *I'm way too hot.*

His hand settled over hers. "Let me do that."

She relinquished the key and he quickly unlocked the door. They went inside and Marley just as quickly flicked on the overhead light, flooding the kitchen with a safe brightness.

"Hey, you've remodeled," he commented, looking around, his hands shoved deep in his coat pockets. "I like it."

"Even the decorations?" she teased.

He continued to look around with a considering expression on his face. She saw his gaze fall on the poinsettia centerpiece on the breakfast bar and winced when she remembered that they'd decked the church with poinsettias for his "almost" wedding, but he said nothing.

Then he turned slowly in the middle of the room, taking everything in from the gingerbread dish towels, pot holders, tablecloth and curtains, to the jars of peppermints and gumdrops and sugar cookies that lined the counter. She'd even bought Mr. and Mrs. Santa

Claus salt and pepper shakers, and a Santa Claus tea-pot with matching elf mugs. Christmas was in evidence everywhere.

"You ought to bring Tim over here," he said at last. "He'd love it."

"But you hate it," Marley supplied for him.

His smile started slowly, then curved into a sexy grin. "Actually I like it, but—"

"But?"

"It makes me hungry. I was wondering if I could talk you into making some cocoa and we could drink it out of those elf mugs and have some cookies with it?"

Marley laughed. "Really?"

"Really."

Her heart skipped a beat, then started again with a hard thump she felt clear to her toes. "Well, okay, I'll make some cocoa. In the meantime, why don't you go ahead into the living room and wait for me there."

"Okay. Give me the present and I'll put it under the tree." He looked sly. "You do have a tree?"

She arched a brow. "Does Dolly Parton have wigs?"

He laughed and went through the kitchen door into the living room and formal dining area. After he'd gone, Marley stood in the middle of the room for some time, feeling stunned. This was all too good to be true! When was she going to wake up from this wonderful dream? But whether she was dreaming or not, she was going to take full advantage of every delectable moment of time with this new "old" Carl.

She slipped out of her coat, made the cocoa, then ran up the back stairs to her bedroom to touch up her makeup, comb her hair, brush her teeth and splash on a little perfume. Moments later, when she entered the living room carrying a tray with the teapot, mugs and a plate of sugar cookies on it, she was so shocked by what she saw, she nearly dropped the whole kit and caboodle.

Carl had plugged in the Christmas tree lights, as well as the lights to the little Dickens village she had spread out in picturesque style on a long table behind the couch. He'd turned on the outdoor lights, too, and made a fire in the fireplace. None of the overhead lights or lamps were turned on, so the room had a wonderful festive, and—dare she think it?—romantic atmosphere.

Carl had taken off his coat and his boots, too, and was sitting on the couch in his pajamas, his chiseled jaw stubbled with five-o'clock shadow, looking very relaxed and very sexy.

"Sorry about the casual attire," came his deep voice out of the semidarkness. "I was in a hurry when I left the house. The stores were about to close."

She giggled. "You went shopping in your pajamas?"

"Like I said, I was in a hurry. I didn't make up my mind about going shopping till eight forty-five. With only fifteen minutes to shop, I didn't dare take the time to change."

"And you came to Bev's house directly from the store to drop off the presents?"

"Exactly."

She shook her head wonderingly. "That doesn't sound like you, Carl."

He shrugged and smiled, so she didn't pursue it.

She walked toward the couch. "Well, you look very comfortable. I'm jealous."

"Then why don't you put on something more comfortable, too?" he teased. "Got any pink baby-dolls, red silk pajamas, or...er...a black teddy?"

Marley laughed nervously. He was teasing, wasn't he?

Her legs were quivering, but she made it to the couch and set the tray on the coffee table. Hoping her voice wouldn't betray her, she said in a pitch just a tad higher than normal, "You've made everything very cozy in here."

"I probably should have shoveled your front walk, too, but that would just encourage visitors, and, frankly, I'd rather we weren't disturbed for a while."

She slid him a sideways look as she poured a cup of cocoa. "Oh? Why's that?"

"I hate to be disturbed when opening presents."

She grinned. "I should think you'd scarcely remember."

"Well, I don't remember, but why take chances?"

She handed him the mug of cocoa, which he immediately lifted to his lips, then poured herself a cup and left it on the tray.

"Will you open my present first?" she asked him, suddenly feeling shy and wanting the whole thing over with as soon as possible.

"I thought you'd never ask." He looked speculatively toward the tree. "But where do you keep a Christmas present you've had around for seven years?"

She stood up and went to an antique side-by-side in the corner of the room, pulled out a drawer and picked up the small, square box. She carried it to the couch and sat down again.

"The wrapping paper is a little faded," she apologized.

"That's not your fault," Carl admitted ruefully. "If I hadn't been such a grinch, you'd have given it to me ages ago."

"That's okay. I'm giving it to you now." And she did.

"Do you realize that this is the first Christmas present I've opened in seven years?" he told her, holding it and examining it as if it were a precious object. Suddenly Marley felt the gift was woefully inadequate for the occasion.

"It's not much."

Carl only smiled and tore off the paper. She was glad he wasn't the type who tried to save wrapping paper for future use, which proved again that maybe he wasn't a total tightwad.

He opened the box and lifted one of the two objects inside. "Cuff links! Angel cuff links. How perfect."

Marley blushed with pleasure. He really seemed to like them. "I bought them before we ever considered taking over Little Angel. Maybe it was prophetic."

"If not prophetic, at least inspired," he suggested, turning them so the gold caught and winked brightly in the Christmas lights. "I'll wear them my first day back at the office. Thank you, Marley."

His smile was warm and she almost expected him to bend forward and kiss her, but, even though it would be perfectly innocent, after her warning to him in the back of Ralph's Chevy, he was probably afraid to come anywhere near her!

"Now my present to you," he announced as he got up and fetched it from under the tree.

Marley took another sip of cocoa, but it didn't help

calm her jittery stomach. She was incredibly excited
to open the present, but she was even more excited
just being where she was. It was like a dream come
true, the way she'd always pictured spending Christmas Eve with Carl. Only in her dream they were married and ended the evening going upstairs together and
making a little Christmas magic of their own.

"Marley?"

Marley looked up and he handed her the present.
She placed it on the sofa between them and began to
undo the ribbons. Her heart was knocking against her
ribs and she could feel the blood rush to her head. She
was so excited she just hoped she could stop herself
from thanking him with a kiss! But banish that
thought! There was no way she could keep her emotions in check if they kissed again. Just remembering
the kiss under the mistletoe at the inn made her lips
tingle.

The wrapping paper off, Marley lifted the lid of a
glossy gift box, pushed aside some glittery tissue paper
and stared down at what had to be the most wonderful
Christmas present anyone had ever given her! She
blinked through tears as she lifted the Nuremberg angel out of the box and held it high. The wax face and
golden halo, the shimmery dress and fragile wings
were just like her great-grandmother's, only brand-
new!

"Oh, Carl," she whispered reverently. "Oh, it's so
beautiful. How did you ever find one at such short
notice?"

Carl breathed a sigh of relief. Although he had de-
pended on the gift being the Nuremberg angel, it was
a comfort to see it with his own eyes. But, as far as

he could without bringing Stewart's name up again, he had to tell Marley the truth.

"Someone else ordered the angel, but they didn't...er...end up needing it after all, so I got it instead. As I told you, I didn't go gift shopping till almost nine o'clock tonight, so this was a real stroke of luck."

"That doesn't matter," she assured him, her beautiful eyes looking back and forth between him and the angel. "I'm just so glad you remembered that I wanted one. It was very thoughtful of you."

He was touched by her gratitude and elated by her delight in the gift. *This is what Christmas is all about*, he told himself. *Making others happy, and being with family*. That must have been what his dad had been trying to tell him that very afternoon when he was going on about crass commercialism and cholesterol.

"Carl?"

"Hmm?"

Marley was a vision, her eyes a soft, deep green, misted over like a Scottish lake in the morning. She replaced the angel in the tissue paper, carefully transferred the box to the coffee table next to the tray and scooted close to him. She lifted her hand and rested it lightly along his jaw. "Thank you," she whispered, then she kissed his stubbled cheek.

After the kiss, which was as light as the touch of a butterfly's wing, she pulled back and looked at him, her hand still resting on his jaw. Her lips were moist and parted invitingly. Did she want him to kiss her?

He hesitated. He didn't want to go too fast. He took her hand and drew it to his mouth, kissing the tender palm. He watched her as she shivered and made a little gasp. That, he decided, was invitation enough.

He found her slim waist under the bulky sweater and pulled her close. His other hand slid up her arm to her neck and curled around the nape. She responded by slipping both arms around his shoulders. Finally they were kissing-close.

Simultaneously their eyes drifted shut and their lips met. The initial touch sent waves of electric awareness throughout Carl's body, along every nerve, exploding in every cell. He drew her closer, shaping her body to his. She was so soft, so curvy, so warm.

Marley was lost from the instant their lips made contact. Her arms tightened around him instinctively. She was immediately dizzy with desire. Then, when he nudged her lips open and slipped his tongue inside to explore, she thought she was going to faint. Her heart beat wildly against her rib cage.

She knew she shouldn't have kissed him in the first place, but after giving her such a touching gift, he deserved no less. Now she was trying to hold back, to temper her reaction, but it was useless. She told herself it was only a kiss, that she shouldn't be allowing herself to be swept away by it, but her body had a mind of its own.

The kiss deepened and Carl's hands began to roam her back. Her hands moved along the smooth muscled contours of his back, too, and then his hard, wonderful chest. She couldn't help it; she slipped her hands under his pajama top, seeking the warmth of his skin. Ah…the tactile paradise of silky chest hair and turgid male nipples. She trembled with desire.

Carl shuddered, consumed by so many exquisite sensations and emotions. Marley was initiating more than he'd anticipated and moving much faster than he'd ever dared hope. But was it too fast? It wasn't that he wasn't sure of *his* feelings, but he wanted her to be sure of hers. His emotions were completely engaged now. He was in love and as vulnerable—hell, a hundred times more vulnerable—than he had been seven years ago.

"Marley, do you think we're moving too fast here?" Carl murmured against her neck, then dipped lower to kiss the pulse at the base of her throat. She tasted delicious, like fruity spices and leafy ferns.

"I don't think waiting twenty years is too fast," she answered, her voice husky yet utterly feminine, her tone tempting yet timid. "I've wanted you...like this...for a long time."

Her eagerness was tantalizing, intoxicating... damned arousing. His hands roamed more freely now, over the curves of her hips, along her thighs, then under her sweater and up to cup a breast. He felt her nipple tighten to a hard bud. She moaned into his mouth and arched into his palm.

Marley was awash with sensual sensations the likes of which she'd never experienced before. She'd known instinctively that physical pleasure would be extraordinary with Carl, but she hadn't expected such earthshaking, all-consuming need. She wanted him. She wanted him right then and there in the living room in front of her Dickens village! She began to unbutton his pajama top with inexpert, trembling fingers.

Carl's laugh was low and shaky. "Slow down, Marley. Darling, we have the whole night."

Carl's soothing voice, his lightened tone, settled her down a bit. She took deep breaths and averted her eyes, embarrassed. But he would not allow her to be embarrassed. He touched her chin with his forefinger and made her look at him.

Was she dreaming, or did she see love there? If she was dreaming, she hoped she'd never wake up. He hadn't made a mad, passionate declaration of love or proposed marriage, but she didn't need that. Well, at least not for the moment. For the moment, she'd settle for the man she'd loved her entire lifetime to make love to her, to make her his…finally and completely.

He smiled at her, his beautiful blue eyes crinkled in the corners, then he drew her into his arms gently, wonderingly. "I'm so glad you didn't drown twenty years ago at Reindeer Pond, Marley Jacobs," he whispered, his breath soft and warm against the sensitive areas of her skin. "You're my best friend in the whole world." He dropped light, lingering kisses over her face, her neck, as though she were a precious gift. She felt treasured, adored.

But their intense passion could not be denied; it flared again, hotter than ever, and soon they were both working on buttons and zippers, eager to feel bare skin against bare skin. In the golden glow of Christmas lights, they finally stretched out on the sofa, their naked limbs entwined, just as Marley had always known they were meant to be.

His hands caressed her shoulders and gently explored the curves of her hips as his mouth sought the softness of her breasts. Her fingers caught and clutched rhythmically in his thick hair as his tongue sent flames of fire along her nerve endings, from her nipples to the quivering core of her stomach.

Her own hands moved restlessly over his sleek, muscled body, from his broad shoulders and back to his firm buttocks. Finally his strong thighs separated hers and she drew him into her.

The moment of their joining was a miracle. Two

bodies and two souls came together. It felt so natural, so easy, so right. They were in perfect sync, as tuned to the other's needs as to their own. But the feelings went far beyond the physical into spiritual realms Marley had never imagined.

She loved him. She loved him more than she ever thought possible. She wanted to say it out loud, to whisper it in his ear, to scream it from the rooftops. But she didn't dare, because he hadn't told her his feelings.

When they climaxed, the experience was so intense, so tender, so affirming, Marley felt tears gather in her eyes. But when the spasms of pleasure subsided and their breathing and heartbeats settled to something nearer normal, she tried to hide her high emotional state by drawing him close and tucking her head against his chest. She was afraid to look at him. She was afraid he'd see how much he meant to her and be scared away for good.

You're my best friend in the whole world. Those had been his words, and while they were precious, they weren't enough. Was a friend all she was to him, all she'd ever be?

Marley realized then how even profound joy could sometimes be bittersweet. Oh, if only he loved her as she loved him. Closing her eyes, she pretended to sleep.

CARL FELT A WONDERFULLY satisfying physical exhaustion, but at the same time experienced a spiritual elation he'd never imagined possible. He wanted to share this joy with Marley, tell her how much he loved her, but she was fast asleep!

He laughed softly to himself and pulled a thick afghan from the back of the couch to cover them. It would be hard to wait, but it was no use making a mad, passionate declaration of love and issuing a marriage proposal to an unconscious woman.

He lay there with her head propped against his chest, rubbing her arms and threading his fingers through her tousled hair, smiling sleepily.

Tomorrow is Christmas, he thought just before he drifted off. *How perfect.*

Chapter Thirteen

"Carl," Marley whispered. "Carl, time to get up."

It was five-thirty in the morning and still pitch-black outside, but Marley was fully dressed and staring down at Carl, who was sleeping like a baby. With the fire going and with a warm afghan to cuddle under—not to mention their shared body heat—she and Carl had been snug as bugs together on the couch, not stirring till this late hour of the morning.

Well, it was late for Christmas morning, especially when you were responsible for getting a child's presents under the tree and a couple of pills down his throat!

Tim, like any other normal kid, would be out of bed at the crack of dawn and looking under the tree for his presents from Santa. He knew he wouldn't be opening his Christmas presents at the house, that they'd transport them up to the hospital to be shared with his mother, but he'd still be looking for them. And, as far as Marley knew, they were still in the basement of Bev's house where she'd hidden them weeks ago.

Marley stared a moment longer at Carl, so heart stoppingly handsome in the glow of the Christmas tree lights, resisting the urge to strip off her clothes and crawl under the afghan with him again. Not only did they have responsibilities to Tim and Bev, but it probably wouldn't be such a good idea, anyway. Marley didn't know what mood Carl would be in when he woke up. He'd seemed transformed into another person last night, but that was last night.

Marley was afraid he might regret their lovemaking. She even considered the possibility that last night had been a desperate attempt on his part to wipe away the memories of that horrible Christmas Eve seven years ago. She'd already told him she loved him, and she'd tried to show him how much by giving herself to him heart, body and soul, but now it was up to him.

He hadn't said he loved her. Not once. But she wouldn't push. She wouldn't even let on that last night had been all that special to her. She'd even be just a little bit cool, thereby protecting herself from hurt and giving Carl all the space he needed.

"Carl."

Finally he stirred, stretching his arms above his head and blinking his eyes open. Slowly a smile spread across his face. "Morning," he drawled, his voice early-morning husky and sexy as all get-out.

Marley's guard went up immediately. "Morning, Carl," she said briskly. "Rise and shine. I have to get to Bev's house right away. I've got to get Tim's Christmas presents under the tree and give him his medicine the minute he gets up. And since I've got to use your car to get over there, and I didn't want to leave you stranded here, you'd better get up, too, get dressed, and I'll drop you off at your house on the way to Bev's, then return your car later when—"

"Whoa! Slow down." Carl chuckled as he sat up

on the couch, rubbing his eyes with the heel of his hand, then smoothing his hair back from his brow by raking his fingers through it. The afghan slipped to his waist, exposing his sleek torso.

Marley swallowed hard and averted her eyes.

"Don't we have time for coffee...or a shower?" He grinned up at her. "Have you had a shower yet? Maybe we could—"

"No time for coffee," she interrupted him. "No time for anything." She tossed his pajamas at him. "Sorry, Carl. Don't mean to give you the bum's rush, but I don't want to disappoint that little boy. I've already been very irresponsible by staying away all night like this. Please get dressed and I'll go warm up the car. Lock the back door and pull it shut behind you when you leave the house."

Carl watched Marley fly out of the room as if she were being chased by a ghost. He winced when he heard the back door slam shut and decided that such a rude awakening wasn't at all what he'd expected this morning. He sat there stunned for a moment, quickly put on his pajamas, socks and boots, then shrugged into his overcoat, turned off the Christmas lights and went outside, locking and shutting the back door behind him as he'd been instructed.

Marley had a point: they did need to get back to Bev's house to get Tim's presents under the tree and to administer his medication. However, the tension Carl felt in the air as he slipped into the passenger seat of his car had less to do with responsibilities connected with Tim than it had to do with them, but he wasn't sure how aggressive he should be in pointing this out.

"I could have driven," he said in a friendly manner

as Marley backed out of the driveway. "I'm fully recovered from last night."

She glanced at him. He could have sworn she looked sad, as if he'd just given her bad news. "Are you?" she inquired cryptically.

He shrugged, smiled. "Of course. Now, instead of driving me home first, why don't we both go to Bev's and I can help you with Tim's presents."

Marley shook her head firmly. "No, that won't be necessary. Miss Hathaway can help me. You probably want to go back to bed. It's awful early."

"But—"

"I'll have her follow me to your house to drop off your car, then she can drive me and Tim up to the hospital. I'll only stay long enough to deliver Tim and the presents to Bev's room, then Miss Hathaway can take me home."

She flashed him a tight smile. "By the time you're up and showered—even before then—your car will be back in your driveway where it belongs. You won't even miss it."

"But I wanted to see Tim open my present."

"I'll tell him not to open it till you get there. From what Bev told me last night, she won't be released from the hospital till after lunch when her mother arrives from Kentucky. You'll have plenty of time to sleep, clean up and eat before you have to go back to the hospital."

Carl clamped his mouth shut. It was pointless to voice any more objections or make any more offers of help. She had the day worked out, right down to the last detail.

He was beginning to get the picture. Marley was either scared or embarrassed, or both, about what had happened last night. She didn't trust him not to hurt her, and she was putting up barricades like crazy, making it easy for him to bow out of the picture gracefully...or rather, slither away like a snake in the grass.

It suddenly occurred to Carl that although he knew he loved Marley, he hadn't yet taken the opportunity to tell her so. She was feeling vulnerable and he knew how awful that could feel. She needed a hefty dose of reassurance.

Carl rubbed his stubbly jaw consideringly. He, on the other hand, needed a shave and a shower and a shot of mouthwash. There was no way he was going to profess his love to Marley looking like a bum. Not the romantic scene he'd visualized, or one that he wanted Marley to remember forever.

He'd go to her house after she got back from the hospital and open his heart to her then. He'd only be delaying things by a couple of hours. By the time she was expected at his folks' house for Christmas dinner—which grand occasion always took place at one in the afternoon and lasted for hours—everything would hopefully be settled between them and they could go to his parents' house as a couple.

Carl smiled to himself. It was a perfect plan. "Fine, Marley," he said cheerfully, settling down in the seat and facing resolutely forward. "Take me home."

Marley said nothing in return and she maintained a tense silence for the remainder of the drive to Carl's house, which was, thankfully, very short. After he got out of the car, he turned and smiled at her. "See ya."

Her expression was contained, reserved. "Yeah, see ya, Carl." Then she quickly drove off.

As he watched his car disappear into the morning gloom, Carl felt a niggling of unease. Maybe he should have at least told her he'd see her later that day for sure, but it was too late now. To be honest, he wasn't exactly sure how to deal with her in this strange mood. But he'd make it up to her later. After all, it was Christmas Day, he was filled with optimism, and nothing could go wrong.

With this happy thought in his head, Carl hurried up the walk to his house. As he unlocked the front door he gazed fondly at the door knocker, then gave it an affectionate pat just before going inside.

As Marley had promised, and even without him going back to bed for another hour or two, Carl's car was in the driveway by the time he'd shaved and showered. There was nothing to eat in the house, so breakfast wasn't an issue, but that meant he had nothing to do to while away the next hour till he could reasonably show up at Marley's house and beg her to make him the happiest man on earth.

It was the slowest hour of Carl's life. But once he told Marley he loved her—and if she said the magic word *yes*—he wouldn't waste another moment of what had become so precious to him...his life, *their* life together. Staring out his front window at the stunning blue sky and glistening snow, he felt a contentment, a euphoria he'd never experienced before.

Last night had been a miracle, a kick in the head to straighten out the thinking of a stubborn jackass named Carl Ebeneezer Merrick. He'd never understand exactly what happened, but he'd bless The Powers That Be for the rest of his life.

And while today wasn't a miracle in the strict sense of the word, it was a miracle to Carl just as every day would be a miracle from then on.

Carl glanced at his watch, decided he'd waited long

enough, and headed for the door. He glanced in the mirror over the hall table to make sure his hair was still neatly combed, then checked out his forest green sweater and charcoal gray slacks once more to make sure they were still exactly what he wanted to wear to propose in. Satisfied, he strode purposefully out the door.

Ten minutes later he was at Marley's house. After ten more minutes of ringing the doorbell, knocking and waiting impatiently on the front, then the back, porches, Carl came to the maddening conclusion that Marley wasn't home!

Carl stared up at the unresponsive house, wondering what could have gone wrong with his plan! After their conversation that morning, he figured he had a pretty good idea about where she'd be at any given hour that day. But he supposed there was always the possibility of a change of plans.

He thought hard. Instead of having Miss Hathaway drive her home, maybe she'd stayed at the hospital, expecting Carl to show up later—as he fully intended to do—and was planning to catch a ride home with him. She could be waiting for him that very moment!

Carl got in his car, sped to the hospital and hurried to Bev's room. But as he entered, he saw only Bev and Tim and a lot of wrapping paper strewn about. There was no Marley.

Hiding his disappointment, Carl walked in with a smile. "Merry Christmas!" he called.

Bev turned with a responding smile, and Tim was so thrilled to see him he actually scrambled off his mother's hospital bed and threw his arms around Carl's knees. Carl was touched and lifted the boy in his arms. "Have a good Christmas, Tim?"

Tim nodded, his eyes shining. "Wanna see?"

"Sure, sport," Carl told him, then set him down on the floor again and turned to Bev. "Feeling better today?"

"Much better. I'm more than ready to go home and only have to wait for my mom to show up." Bev looked at him with a quizzical expression. "You seem different. And it just occurred to me...for as long as I've known you, I've never heard you say 'Merry Christmas.'"

Carl smiled sheepishly. "I *am* different."

She smiled warmly. "I'm glad. Would you care to elucidate?"

"I would if I had time, Bev, but I'm looking for Marley. She's not in the hospital somewhere, is she?"

Bev shook her head. "No, she left some time ago with Miss Hathaway." She frowned. "She didn't look like she quite had the Christmas spirit, though, which is odd for Marley."

Carl agreed. "Did she say she was going straight home?"

"She didn't say." Bev observed him, her gaze keen. "You really want to see her, don't you?"

"Yes, I really do," Carl admitted soberly.

"I'm sure you'll run into each other before the day's over," Bev offered, sounding determinedly cheerful.

Carl wasn't so sure. He was beginning to fear his Christmas Eve miracle hadn't quite taken. He was wondering if he was mistaken about Marley's feelings for him, if he'd taken too much for granted. He was even beginning to worry that Stewart might have something to do with it and had materialized again, "spiriting" Marley away for his own pleasure and enjoyment! After last night, he wasn't discounting anything as impossible.

Carl stayed long enough for Tim to show him all his presents, and to open his own package to the boy...or, at least, the package with his name on it that Stewart had left behind. He saw, with some relief, that the box did contain a fire truck and was very pleased with Tim's reaction: he went into deliriums over it!

Half an hour later Carl left, buoyed up by the happiness he'd left behind in the hospital room. Now he was more determined than ever to find Marley. He ached to hold her and kiss her and tell her he loved her.

Carl went back to her house and still found no one at home. Acting on a hunch—or desperation, he wasn't sure which—he drove to the office. Sure enough, Marley's car was gone! Somehow she'd figured a way to get her tire inflated and changed, but the process had probably taken up most of the morning.

It was now a quarter to one and time to go to his folks' house for Christmas dinner. He was sure to find Marley there, and, although a house packed full of relatives wasn't exactly conducive to privacy, if he wanted to see her at all that day it might be his only opportunity.

Carl pulled next to the curb across from his parents' house about half a block down the street. The driveway and most of the curb on their side of the street was already lined with cars.

The house itself, a brick rambler that sprawled over nearly half of the huge, beautifully landscaped lawn, was as elaborately decorated as it was every year, the twinkle lights that adorned the bushes turned on despite the fact that it was the middle of the day.

As Carl walked to the house, he looked for Marley's car and was profoundly relieved when he saw it parked by Uncle Ralph's candy-apple red Chevy. His pace quickened.

He rang the doorbell and waited perhaps three seconds before the door swung open and his father stood there, looking poleaxed. The smile he'd been wearing slid off his face like wax off a hot candle. Carl nearly laughed at his father's expression but politely smiled instead and said, "Merry Christmas, Dad." He spread his hands wide in a teasing, theatrical fashion, and announced, "I'm *heee-ere.*"

John Merrick didn't move, didn't speak. As his stunned silence stretched on and the cold winter air streamed into the house, other relatives wandered to the door, peering over John's shoulder to see what their host was staring at.

The silence and the stunned expressions spread through the group. Aunts and uncles and cousins, pint-size second cousins, close family friends, all stared at him, still as statues, their faces frozen into comical masks of astonishment.

Carl was beginning to think this moment was going to continue endlessly when his mother wended her way through the crowd to his father's side. She looked astonished, too, but not for long. As only a mother could, she had remained steadfastly optimistic and hopeful all through the long years of Carl's estrangement from family gatherings.

"Carl," she said, her face lighting up as she stood on her tiptoes to wrap her arms around his neck. "I knew you'd come!"

That broke the spell. Suddenly Carl was being hugged, kissed and clapped on the back. Everyone was talking at once. He was dragged inside and made the center of about twenty different conversations, everyone beaming, his mom and dad all misty-eyed. He felt like the Prodigal Son!

Then, when he could finally be heard above the din, he asked, "Is Marley here? Have you seen Marley?"

"Sure, Marley's here," his dad said, turning to scan the room, peering over and around the heads of all the Merricks that had crowded around them. "There she is!"

The crowd parted and Carl saw Marley standing in the doorway between the dining room and the kitchen, holding a plate of steaming artichokes. Uncle Ralph and Miss Hathaway stood just behind her, his smile nearly as broad as his belly, her smile as garishly red as ever. Carl wondered just how much those two remembered.

But he had no time for idle speculation. He had something far more important to think about. Marley...

She wore a white angora sweater and red slacks, and had a colorful Christmas apron tied around her narrow waist. Her eyes were wide, her expression questioning...and maybe hopeful? For a minute, neither of them said anything and the crowd of onlookers, made curious by this interesting development, stared from Carl to Marley and back to Carl as if they were watching a tennis match.

"Y-you came," she stuttered at last. "You r-really came."

"Yes, of course I did. I've changed. Everything's changed, Marley," he assured her, hardly aware of their audience, only caring that Marley knew and believed that he was a redeemed man, that that darn thorn was gone from his paw forever! "Everything. If you'd given me a chance, I would have told you so this morning."

"But...but I couldn't be sure. I mean, I...I hoped, but I didn't know...." Her voice trailed off.

He took a tentative step forward. "Marley, you're my best friend. Even if you agree to marry me, we'll always be best friends. I love you, Marley. I always have. Will you marry me?" It wasn't the private proposal Carl had had in mind, but he wasn't going to take the chance of postponing again!

Marley's eyes filled with tears. Her mouth trembled, then turned up at the corners in a faint smile. "Oh, Carl...."

Anticipating involuntary muscle spasms and clumsiness along with the other apparent symptoms of lovesickness, Great-aunt Bessie tottered forward and relieved Marley of the tray of hot artichokes.

"There you go, honey," she said, nodding her white head and clacking her false teeth together. "Now you can go and hug 'im and kiss 'im. That's what I'd do if I were you! But first say yes."

Marley laughed and a couple of happy tears escaped from under her lashes. "Yes, Carl. I'll marry you. You know I love you. I want to be your wife more than anything in the world."

Then, to Carl's delight, Marley took Great-aunt Bessie's advice and flew across the room and into his arms. Everyone cheered and laughed and a toast was immediately proposed by Carl's father.

Bottles of champagne that were meant for later were

quickly fetched and opened, each cheerful pop and fizz followed by shouts and laughter.

"To the happy couple," Carl's father proposed.

"To my son and his return to the bosom of the family," his mother put forth, teary eyed.

"To family," said Uncle Ralph, his blue eyes twinkling merrily.

"And to Christmas," Miss Hathaway announced briskly.

Now it was Carl's turn. He lifted his glass to the assembled group. "But most of all, to my best friend in the whole world, my bride-to-be, Marley Jacobs." He smiled down at her, his arm snugly entwined around her waist. She beamed up at him. "Because of her, Christmas will always be a beautiful memory for me."

"How soon will the bride-to-be be a bride?" Uncle Ralph demanded to know.

"As soon as she'll have me," Carl immediately replied.

"How does Valentine's Day sound, Carl?" she suggested coyly. "Might as well plan all our momentous events around the holidays."

"Sounds perfect."

"Does that mean we can expect a grandchild by next Christmas?" Carl's father inquired in his most booming voice, followed by a lot of laughter and elbow ribbing.

Marley blushed and Carl grinned. "Maybe," he replied, then bent to Marley's ear and whispered, "I think we ought to start practicing right away, don't you? Wouldn't want to disappoint the old man."

She nodded and whispered back, "I have this black

teddy I think you'll really like. Or would you rather I wore pink baby-dolls or red silk pajamas tonight?''

Carl stared down at his soon-to-be wife, visions of her in his office dream coming back to haunt him with a vengeance. Suddenly he knew Christmas would never be the same.

"Darling...why not all three?"

Epilogue

One year later, Christmas Eve

"Merry Christmas, Carl."

"Merry Christmas, George," Carl answered with a smile, waving but not stopping to talk with one of the senior salesmen as he strode quickly past him down the hall toward the staff lounge.

"Merry Christmas, Mr. Merrick," called another employee, one of the new secretaries in the orders department. She'd been halfway through the door to the supply room, but she'd stopped when she saw him coming and leaned out to extend a greeting. Carl slowed his pace a bit and racked his brain. The company had grown so much in the past year, sometimes it was a challenge to remember the names of all the new employees.

Ah, that was it. Marge Stratton, married, mother of three teenagers. He smiled and nodded congenially. "Hello, Marge. Merry Christmas. Don't forget the party at four."

She beamed. "Oh, I won't forget. I hear it's a blast."

"That's what I've heard, too," Carl answered,

chuckling at Marge's mystified expression. Apparently no one had clued her in on what a party pooper he used to be. But then, like he himself, maybe they hardly remembered the old Carl.

Carl exchanged several more greetings with employees on his way to the staff lounge, but continually kept his feet in motion. It was tempting to stop and chitchat, and it was obvious that's what his employees wanted him to do, but Carl wasn't about to leave Marley with all the work of setting up the party alone. Not in her condition.

Carl entered the large, gaily decorated room and stopped just inside the door. His gaze zeroed in on the shapely backside of his wife as she bent at the waist to take something out of the refrigerator. As she straightened up, one hand held a plate of cookies and the other hand was pressed against the small of her back in the classic, weary pose of advanced pregnancy. In her blousy white top, jingle-bell earrings and green slacks, she was adorable.

Carl grinned. "Hello, darling."

She turned, revealing her beachball-shaped profile, and smiled back. Carl's heart swelled with love. "Hello, handsome. Thought you'd show up this year, did you?"

Carl sauntered over, took the plate of cookies out of her hand and set it on a nearby table. He turned and pulled her into his arms, her firm tummy pressed against his ribs. "I wouldn't miss this party for the world." He leaned close and whispered confidentially, "I hear there's a cute blonde that shows up every year in a tight little elf costume."

She chuckled. "Not this year." Marley glanced ruefully at her large stomach. "Spandex can only stretch so far, you know. It's big tops and maternity pants for me till D-Day, I'm afraid.''

"I think you look delicious," Carl murmured, nuzzling her ear. "Like a ripe fruit ready to be plucked from the tree and devoured.''

Marley's bottom lip stuck out in a slight pout. "Well, I think I look large enough to exert my own gravitational force and have a small moon orbiting around my midsection.''

Carl threw back his head and laughed, then immediately grew tender. "Well, okay—if I can be the moon," he murmured, nudging the underside of her chin with a curved forefinger so she'd look him in the eye. "Wasn't my conduct last night proof enough that you're still a very desirable woman, Marley Merrick?"

He'd finally coaxed a smile out of her, in fact, it was a flirtatious smile that made him wish they were alone. They kissed lingeringly, then she drew back with a contented sigh, her arms locked around his neck.

"I can't wait till the baby comes.''

"It won't be long now. Your due date's just a week away.''

Marley nodded thoughtfully and ran her hand down the lapel of his navy blue suit jacket. "Yes, maybe it'll be a New Year's baby. But sometimes I think it's destined to come sooner. After all, we did tell your dad we'd try to make him a grandfather by Christmas.''

Carl grinned again. "And no one tried harder than us.''

Marley laughed. "You're right. Besides, anticipation is half the fun. If I can put up with not seeing my feet for another week, I suppose your dad can be patient, too.''

Just then the baby kicked energetically. They both felt the movement and smiled wonderingly into each other's eyes.

''I think our baby's the impatient one,'' Carl suggested.

Marley gave a lopsided smile of agreement, then caught a glimpse of the wall clock over Carl's shoulder. She reluctantly untwined her arms from around his neck and became businesslike. ''It's almost four, Carl. We'd better get the cookies and punch on the table before the onslaught.''

''One more kiss,'' he insisted, pulling her against him again. She laughed and went willingly, her lips as eager as his.

''What's going on in here? Maybe I should tell my boss a couple of the employees are necking on company time!''

Carl and Marley looked up as Bev strolled into the room carrying a large, colorfully wrapped package. Her smile was full of mischief.

''It won't do any good to tell your boss,'' Marley retorted playfully as she slipped out of Carl's embrace and picked up the plate of cookies again. ''He's a soft touch if I ever saw one, a real sucker for an office romance.''

Carl grinned and swatted her lightly on the fanny.

''Well, that's good news,'' Bev said, stooping to place the white elephant gift under the Christmas tree in the corner of the room.

Carl dragged his gaze away from his wife and turned to Bev, standing with his hands lightly resting on his hips. ''What's good news?''

Bev straightened up and turned to face them, but kept her eyes trained on the table, her fingernail tracing a snowman shape on the holiday-printed paper tablecloth. "That you're a real sucker for an office romance."

Carl exchanged a surprised look with his wife. "Well, you know we've never disapproved of you and Mike dating," he said. "In fact, we were the ones who got you two together in the first place. Remember?"

Bev nodded, looking wistful for a minute as if she were reliving her first date with Mike. It had been Marley's idea to invite the new ad man to the small barbecue at their house last August and to pair him with Bev at the table. They'd taken it from there and had been a couple ever since. Or should he say, "triple"? Tim had instantly bonded with Mike, and even though Carl had been a little jealous at first of Tim's new best buddy, he was thrilled to see the three of them so happy together.

"I know you like Mike and approve of our dating," Bev finally said. "I mean, how could anyone not like Mike? He was great during Tim's surgery and recovery...great for both of us. He spent as much time at the hospital as I did."

Carl and Marley both nodded in agreement. "He was there every time we showed up," Marley affirmed, "and we were there—"

"Almost constantly," Bev finished for her with a grateful smile. "You guys have been so good to us. And now that Tim's going to be just fine, there's only one thing that could make me even happier."

Carl and Marley waited patiently while Bev bit her lip, then smiled shyly and showed them her hand. They looked down and came face-to-face with a sizable diamond flashing on her left ring finger. "How do you feel about married couples working together?"

Marley squealed and grabbed Bev around the neck, hugging her as closely as she could manage with her stomach in the way, then snatched Bev's hand to admire the ring. "How did you manage to hide this rock all day?"

Bev shrugged sheepishly. "We just picked it up during my lunch hour."

"Congratulations, Bev," Carl told her, smiling broadly as he gave her a hug, too.

"Then it's okay if we're married? Some employers don't like married couples working together." She looked a little anxiously at Carl.

Carl crossed his arms, put on a stern face and said nothing.

Marley glanced questioningly at her husband, then finally broke the silence. "I don't see any problem with it. Besides, Mike works in a totally different department." When Carl still said nothing, Marley squeezed his arm and smiled into his face. "Anyway, how could we possibly disapprove? We work together and it's great...isn't it, honey?"

Carl decided he'd teased Bev enough and allowed a smile to steal over his features. "As long as you don't sneak away to the lounge to neck. That, of course, would be grounds for dismissal."

The three of them were still laughing when the Christmas music that heralded the beginning of the party blasted through the intercom system. They hurriedly finished setting out the refreshments and the paper dishes and greeted the employees as they arrived.

Mike was one of the first to enter the room—a tall redhead with an easygoing demeanor and an affable smile—and Carl immediately went over to congratulate him. As Mike and Bev stood arm in arm, a toast was raised to the newly engaged couple and the party was off to a rousing start.

Later that evening as they drove to Carl's parents' house, where sitting around the fire to eat, sing and snuggle was the main objective of a small gathering of friends and family, Marley felt her first twinge. Actually, it was more than a twinge; it was nothing less than a contraction.

She glanced over at Carl and almost said something, then decided against it. It was probably just a false alarm and she didn't want to get his hopes up over nothing. She shifted in her seat and looked out the window at the fast-falling snow.

The night was much like the night just a year ago when she and Carl had finally admitted their love for each other. She smiled contentedly at the memory. It had been a magical night she'd never forget. More like a dream, actually. Somehow, in a matter of just a few hours, Carl had changed back into the man she'd loved since they were both in elementary school. And now she had everything she'd always dreamed of: a wonderful, loving husband and a baby on the way.

She felt another pain, felt her stomach muscles tighten quite hard and couldn't help a small gasp. Perhaps sooner than she thought...?

Carl caught her hand and looked across the semi-darkness at her. "You okay, sweetheart?"

By the light of the street lamps they passed, Marley could see just enough of Carl to make her heart flutter. Even after many months of marriage, the man still gave her goose bumps. Tonight, dressed in a cream-colored sweater and dark slacks, he looked so handsome, so masculine.

And he was such a good man, too. Since that magic Christmas Eve a year ago, Marley was convinced that you'd have to search the planet to find a better employer, a better son, a better husband, lover and friend. To Tim, he'd become like a father, yet he'd graciously and tactfully stepped aside to allow Mike to fill that role as his relationship with Bev and Tim developed into one of committed love.

Now Carl would be a father to their child...and Marley knew he'd be great at that, too.

As for Christmas, he'd thrown himself into the festivities with such enthusiasm this year, Marley could hardly keep up with him!

"I'm okay," she said with a smile, still not ready to sound the alarm. "I think I'm just hungry."

"Well, there'll be plenty to eat," Carl assured her, turning his attention back to the snow-packed roads. "Everyone's bringing their favorite Christmas goodie."

"So...just Uncle Ralph, Great-aunt Bessie, Miss Hathaway, Bev, Mike and Tim will be there besides your parents?" Marley asked, suddenly worried that she might have to break up the party with the announcement that her water had just broken.

"That's it." Carl chuckled. "Isn't it enough? The rest of the Merrick clan won't converge on the house till tomorrow."

Marley nodded, satisfied. Everyone who would be there was as dear to her as her own flesh and blood. Which reminded her...if she were in labor, her mother and father wanted to be called pronto. They were packed and ready to jump on a plane from Florida at the first sign of an impending birth. Sun worshipers, they were nonetheless quite willing to brave the rigors of a Vermont winter to get a glimpse of their first grandchild.

By the time they'd pulled into the driveway of the Merrick home, Marley was sure she'd simply had a false alarm. She'd felt perfectly normal for the past several minutes. Well…normal for a pregnant woman in her final month!

They were the last ones to arrive and, once they got inside, were waylaid by everyone with kisses and hugs, manly handshakes and claps on the back. Tim joined the throng, grabbing hold of Carl's leg till he got his attention, then giving him a "high five." Marley gazed at the little boy with satisfaction. Since the surgery, his complexion was pinker and his body more robust. And his energy was endless! Marley was sure Bev was going to have her hands full with that one.

They hadn't seen Uncle Ralph in several months and he smiled down at Marley's stomach and patted his own, saying, "You're almost as big as me, Marley m'girl. That's one good-sized bun in the oven you've got there. Look's like it's about done to me!"

"The baby's father is tall, Ralph," Miss Hathaway informed him, her Safari Red lips pursed primly. "Marley's bound to have a good-sized baby in keeping with the gene pool." She eyed Ralph. "And, after all, you're the child's great-uncle."

Ralph laughed heartily, nodding his agreement, and Carl's father stepped up, puffed out his broad chest and proudly proclaimed *his* contribution to the baby's gene pool, too. All the men were sure the baby was going to be a boy.

The women merely rolled their eyes at each other

and clicked their tongues with affectionate forbearance. Great-aunt Bessie sucked on her false teeth and shook her head. "Men don't know squat," she whispered in an aside to Marley.

Marley fell into a daydream, wondering if the men were right or wrong. She'd asked not to be told the baby's sex when they did the ultrasound, wanting to keep it a mystery till the moment of birth. She was rudely awakened from that daydream when she felt another pain, this one much harder than the others.

"Oh!" Marley said, instinctively clutching her stomach.

"What is it, Marley?" Miss Hathaway demanded, hovering over her. "Are you in labor?"

"Labor? Did someone say labor?" Carl was instantly at Marley's side. "Darling, are you...?"

Marley nodded, a tentative smile quivering on her lips. "Yes, I think so, Carl. It's just started, though, so I'm sure we've got plenty of time, but—"

She bit her lip as another contraction grabbed her like a tight band around her middle. "Oh...there's another one."

Mrs. Merrick raised her brows. "Already? Well, my dear, your labor may have just begun, but it might already be well under way. Impatient babies are the norm in the Merrick family. I was only in labor three hours with Carl! Maybe you'd better sit down."

Carl took Marley's arm and led her gently toward the couch. But halfway there, Marley had to stop as a hard contraction gripped her and left her breathless. As soon as she was able, and with a look of chagrin, she turned to Carl and said, "Honey, I think you'd better take me to the hospital now."

Carl looked stunned for a minute, then swallowed hard and said, "Whatever you say, Marley."

As Carl helped Marley with her coat and slowly led her out the door, a flurry of excitement was going on all around them. Everyone was looking for their coats and car keys.

"It looks like you're going to have your own personal motorcade to the hospital," Carl whispered in her ear.

Marley chuckled. She was the one having the baby, but she felt like the calm eye in the middle of a hurricane! Inside, though, she was anything but calm. *This is it!* she told herself. *This is really it!*

Carl had just settled Marley in the front seat and slipped behind the wheel when, as Tim and Mike and Bev walked hand in hand past the car, they overheard Tim ask, "Is Marley goin' t' have the baby tonight, Mike?"

"Looks that way, Tim."

And Bev added dreamily, "A Christmas Eve baby. How perfect! It's the best gift ever."

The key was in the ignition and Carl was about to start the car, but he paused and looked across the seat at his wife. At the moment between contractions, Marley gazed back at him, her eyes reflecting all the wonder and hope and nervous excitement of a woman on the brink of a miracle...a miracle they shared.

"Bev's right," Carl said. "A baby born on Christmas Eve, a year to the day after we first made love, is the best gift ever."

Marley's smile was teasing. "And you used to be such a humbug about Christmas."

Carl grinned. "Not anymore." Then he started the car and drove his wife to the hospital, convinced he was the happiest, most blessed man on the planet.

HARLEQUIN®

AMERICAN ◆ ROMANCE®

A HOLIDAY RECIPE FROM THE KITCHEN OF
Emily Dalton

Here's a sweet and crunchy treat I make every year. It's a great gift for neighbors, and the kids love it, too!

OVEN CARAMEL CORN

6-10 qts popped popcorn, kernels removed
1 cup butter or margarine
½ cup light Karo syrup
2 cups light brown sugar
1 to 2 tsp salt
½ tsp soda
1 tbsp vanilla
1 or 2 cups peanuts

Place popcorn in a large roaster in oven to keep warm (200°F). In a large pan, melt butter, stir in syrup, sugar and salt. Boil for five minutes on lowest heat possible, without stirring. Remove from heat, stir in soda and vanilla. Stir fast! The soda will expand when added to hot syrup. Pour over popcorn and nuts. Coat well. Put in 250°F oven for one hour, stirring occasionally. Cool on wax paper.

REC706

Take 4 bestselling love stories FREE

Plus get a FREE surprise gift!

Special Limited-time Offer

Mail to Harlequin Reader Service®

3010 Walden Avenue
P.O. Box 1867
Buffalo, N.Y. 14240-1867

YES! Please send me 4 free Harlequin American Romance® novels and my free surprise gift. Then send me 4 brand-new novels every month, which I will receive months before they appear in bookstores. Bill me at the low price of $3.12 each plus 25¢ delivery and applicable sales tax, if any.* That's the complete price and a savings of over 10% off the cover prices—quite a bargain! I understand that accepting the books and gift places me under no obligation ever to buy any books. I can always return a shipment and cancel at any time. Even if I never buy another book from Harlequin, the 4 free books and the surprise gift are mine to keep forever.

154 BPA A3UM

Name   (PLEASE PRINT)

Address   Apt. No.

City   State   Zip

This offer is limited to one order per household and not valid to present Harlequin American Romance® subscribers. *Terms and prices are subject to change without notice. Sales tax applicable in N.Y.

UAM-696   ©1990 Harlequin Enterprises Limited

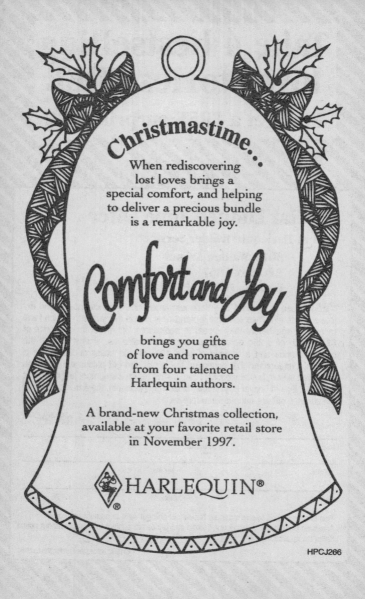

Christmastime...

When rediscovering
lost loves brings a
special comfort, and helping
to deliver a precious bundle
is a remarkable joy.

Comfort and Joy

brings you gifts
of love and romance
from four talented
Harlequin authors.

A brand-new Christmas collection,
available at your favorite retail store
in November 1997.

HARLEQUIN®

HPCJ266

He's every woman's fantasy, but only one woman's dream come true.

For the first time Harlequin American Romance brings you THE ULTIMATE...in romance, pursuit and seduction—our most sumptuous series ever. Because wealth, looks and a bod are nothing without that one special woman.

THE ULTIMATE...

Pursuit

They're

#711 ~~SHE'S~~ THE ONE! by Mindy Neff
January 1998

Stud

#715 HOUSE HUSBAND by Linda Cajio
February 1998

Seduction

#723 HER PRINCE CHARMING by Nikki Rivers
April 1998

Catch

#729 MASQUERADE by Mary Anne Wilson
June 1998

Look us up on-line at: http://www.romance.net   HULTMAT

Free Gift Offer

With a Free Gift proof-of-purchase
from any Harlequin® book, you can receive
a beautiful cubic zirconia pendant.

This stunning marquise-shaped stone is a genuine cubic
zirconia—accented by an 18" gold tone necklace.
(Approximate retail value $19.95)

Send for yours today...
compliments of HARLEQUIN®

To receive your free gift, a cubic zirconia pendant, send us one original proof-of-purchase, photocopies not accepted, from the back of any Harlequin Romance®, Harlequin Presents®, Harlequin Temptation®, Harlequin Superromance®, Harlequin Intrigue®, Harlequin American Romance®, or Harlequin Historicals® title available at your favorite retail outlet, together with the Free Gift Certificate, plus a check or money order for $1.65 U.S./$2.15 CAN. (do not send cash) to cover postage and handling, payable to Harlequin Free Gift Offer. We will send you the specified gift. Allow 6 to 8 weeks for delivery. Offer good until December 31, 1997, or while quantities last. Offer valid in the U.S. and Canada only.

Free Gift Certificate

Name: _____

Address: _____

City: _____ State/Province: _____ Zip/Postal Code: _____

Mail this certificate, one proof-of-purchase and a check or money order for postage and handling to: HARLEQUIN FREE GIFT OFFER 1997. In the U.S.: 3010 Walden Avenue, P.O. Box 9071, Buffalo NY 14269-9057. In Canada: P.O. Box 604, Fort Erie, Ontario L2Z 5X3.

FREE GIFT OFFER   084-KEZ

ONE PROOF-OF-PURCHASE

To collect your fabulous FREE GIFT, a cubic zirconia pendant, you must include this original proof-of-purchase for each gift with the properly completed Free Gift Certificate.

084-KEZR